The Tower Hill Terror

Leipfold Mysteries • Book 2

The Tower Hill Terror

Leipfold Mysteries • Book 2

Dane Cobain

Encircle Publications, LLC
Farmington, Maine U.S.A.

Paperback ISBN 13: 978-1-64599-052-9
E-book ISBN 13: 978-1-64599-053-6
Kindle ISBN 13: 978-1-64599-054-3

Editor: Cynthia Brackett-Vincent
Book design: Eddie Vincent
Cover design by Christoper Wait
Cover images © Getty Images

Published by: Encircle Publications, LLC
PO Box 187
Farmington, ME 04938

Visit: http://encirclepub.com

Sign up for Encircle Publications newsletter and specials
http://eepurl.com/cs8taP

Printed in U.S.A.

A Note on the Text

MAILE AND LEIPFOLD live in a London that's similar to, but not identical to, our own. It's a London where the villains are straight from the pages of a comic book, where the heroes are unusual (but normal) people, struggling to do the best they can in the knowledge that life doesn't always turn out like it does in the storybooks.

Because of that, not all of the city's geography is one hundred percent accurate. If you walk along Balcombe Street, you won't be able to follow it down an alleyway, up the stairs and into Leipfold's office. You won't be able to visit Cholmondeley at the Old Vic, either.

Likewise, all of the characters are creatures of the imagination. Any similarities with real people—living or dead, fictional or otherwise—are purely coincidental.

The Tower Hill Terror originally had a different name, which we can't actually print here because it includes a registered trademark. Still, kudos if you've been reading my books and following my journey for long enough to know what that other title was!

If you ever find yourself falling through a rabbit hole and resurfacing in Leipfold's London, be sure to buy him a lemonade from me. And if he's riding Camilla, give her a pat on the handlebars.

Chapter One:
Murder at the
Grosvenor House Hotel

MAILE O'HARA'S first official task at Leipfold Investigations was to carry out surveillance on Jayne Lipton, a suspect in the case she'd helped to crack as an unpaid intern. At first, when Leipfold told her what he wanted her to do, she was confused.

"I don't get it," she said. "Why? I thought we were finished with the case."

"We are," Leipfold replied. "But I like to cover all the bases. Besides, I have a bad feeling about her."

As the owner, founder and one-half of the brains behind Leipfold Investigations, James Leipfold had a bad feeling about a lot of things, but Maile was used to it by now. It was his job to have bad feelings and to figure out what was causing them.

"About who, boss?" Maile asked. "Jayne Lipton?"

Leipfold nodded and scribbled down the answer to another one of the clues in *The Tribune*'s daily crossword. He barely even noticed he was doing it.

"Last time we saw her, I thought she wanted to tell me something," Leipfold said. He shrugged. "It might be nothing, but then again it might not. I'd like to find out."

Maile stared woodenly across the gap between their desks at the top of his ginger head while his eyes roamed across the newspaper. She waited for a moment, expecting him to say something more, but all she could hear was the scratching of his pencil as he answered the clues.

"Can I help?" Maile asked.

"That depends," Leipfold replied. "Can you find out where she's staying?"

"She's staying at the Grosvenor House Hotel," Maile said. "Remember it?"

"How could I forget? We went there for the Thompson case. But how do you know where she is?"

Maile smiled at him and held up her smartphone. "GPS," she said. "Well, that and geolocation. I got it from her Twitter feed. I already checked it out."

Leipfold laughed and scribbled down the final answer, then tossed his pencil onto the desk and turned to look at her.

"Have you got the room number?" he asked.

"No dice," Maile said. "Soz."

"All right."

Leipfold stood up suddenly and grabbed his phone before patting his pockets for his keys. Maile watched him as he rushed across to the coat stand beside the door and pulled his leather jacket on. Then he grabbed his helmet and tucked it under his arm.

"Man the phones while I'm gone," he said. "I won't be long."

"Where are you going?" Maile asked. But she thought she already knew the answer and Leipfold didn't bother to tell her. He stalked silently out of the office and left her alone with her thoughts.

* * *

The hotel lobby was huge, intimidating. The closest Leipfold had come to the opulence of the place was when he stayed in a Newport Travelodge on one of his rare spells away from the city. It had been nice enough, but it had nothing on Grosvenor House with its wide-open spaces, marble busts and mahogany furniture.

Leipfold felt keenly out of place as he walked up to the reception desk, but he'd felt out of place for most of his life. He looked shiftily around and then rang the little bell on the reception desk. It was answered by a long-legged Italian man in an expensive suit with a thinning thatch of hair and a well-groomed beard. When Leipfold introduced himself as a private investigator, the receptionist looked sceptical, but he asked politely how he could help.

"I need to speak to one of your guests," Leipfold replied. "A pretty girl in her early twenties with long brown hair. Mid-twenties. About five-six, maybe five-seven. Brown eyes and decent clothes. Her name's Jayne Lipton, but I have reason to believe she booked under a pseudonym."

The receptionist frowned. "I don't believe you," he said. "A man like you doesn't have friends who stay in a place like this. Besides, I can't give a guest's details to just anyone."

"I could slip you a tenner."

"I could call security."

"Please," Leipfold said. "Just do me a favour. I'm worried. Just send someone to see if she's okay."

The receptionist sighed and mumbled something into a walkie-talkie. Leipfold watched him apprehensively, trying to figure out what was happening. It seemed like a whole heap of nothing until the Italian man was joined by one of his colleagues, a woman whose badge identified her as the shift manager. She shot Leipfold a withering look and sent the Italian to check on the room.

Then she led Leipfold outside and told him to stay there. The two of them were still arguing about it when the walkie-talkie crackled and the Italian's voice filtered through. It sounded different, distressed. The calm authority had disappeared and been replaced by an awestruck terror.

"Karen!" he shouted, as Leipfold's eye wandered towards the woman's right breast where a high-end badge confirmed her name. "Karen! Call the police, okay? Call the police!"

The shift manager blanched and tightened her grip on the walkie-talkie, holding it more like the handle of a hammer than a thick chunk of plastic and computer chips.

"Carlo?" she asked. "What's going on?"

"There's a body up here," he replied. "A body and blood. *Merda! Non puo' essere vero!*"

The shift manager dropped the walkie talkie to the floor, thinking only of her phone and the triple digits of the emergency services. She panicked, like the people in plane crashes who burn to death after forgetting how to undo their seatbelts. She patted her pockets in desperation and then lowered her head and started rooting through her designer handbag.

Leipfold saw his chance, and he took it.

* * *

Leipfold heard Karen calling after him, but if anything, it made him run a little faster. Adrenaline was coursing through him, his legs and his arms were pumping, and for the first time in as long as he could remember, he felt ready to take on the world. A suited security guard made a grab at him, but Leipfold, unencumbered in jeans, a leather jacket and a pair of trainers, dodged aside and skidded across the glossy tiles towards the elevator. He veered right at the last second and then raced up a short flight of stairs.

Leipfold had the advantage of surprise, but neither of them knew where he was going. He hit corners at random and went in out and out of Personnel Only doors in a mixed attempt to find the Italian and to lose the flat-footed klutz who was trying to stop him. It didn't take long to accomplish the latter, and he found the Italian shortly afterwards. He just had to follow the man's panic-stricken voice. As Leipfold slowed to a stop on a third-floor corridor, he heard the man still swearing softly on the other side of a half-open door.

Leipfold approached it slowly and looked inside.

His first impression was of blood and viscera, the sort of scene that played across his mind on the darkest nights but that he hadn't actually *seen* since he last saw action. This was worse. It was more unexpected, out of place in a high-class hotel. A quick visual on the corpse's face told Leipfold that it *was* Jayne Lipton, but he couldn't be sure without a closer look and that was the last thing he wanted to do. But it was a woman all right. That much was clear, even though the face had been battered so badly it was almost unrecognisable.

At a glance, Leipfold thought that if the trauma to the face hadn't killed the girl, it must have happened after her death. No one could survive that. She also showed signs of sexual assault, at least if her clothes were anything to go by. Her bare skin shone a pallid, deathly grey under the hotel lighting, and there was more of it on show than Leipfold cared to look at. At that moment, he was focusing on something else.

Carlo, the Italian receptionist, was on his hands and knees at the foot of the bed, breathing heavily and dribbling saliva onto the carpet. Leipfold sympathised with him. It was one of several common reactions to seeing a body for the first time, and this one was in particularly bad shape. Leipfold himself felt a little queasy, but his mind was working on autopilot.

"You bloody fool!" he shouted, launching himself into the room towards the receptionist. "You're contaminating the crime scene."

Leipfold was gagging on the coppery smell of congealing blood and dragging the insensible Italian out of the room when the security guy with the bad hat caught up with him.

He'd brought reinforcements.

Chapter Two:
The Old Vic

GARY MOGFORD was about to knock off when the call came in. It was a Friday evening and he was ready for the weekend. He was on call, but he knew from experience that the crime rate would drop because it was cold, wet and rainy. But someone—*some bastard*—had screwed it all up by reporting a corpse in a hotel room.

And then a helpful young lady called Karen had led him up to the third floor of the Grosvenor House Hotel, where a guilty-looking James Leipfold was dragging a concierge, spitting, cursing and still spewing, out into the hallway.

"James Leipfold," Mogford said, as Constable Jenny Groves grimaced and fingered her handcuffs beside him. "Fancy seeing you here. We're going to need you to make a statement."

* * *

Back at the Old Vic, the nineteenth century police station that still housed two-fifths of the city's woefully underfunded coppers, Mogford checked in with his boss. He found Cholmondeley in the empty canteen. The guvnor was hiding out with a stack of paperwork, trying to make a dent in it without being disturbed every ten minutes by a knock on the door.

"Ah," Cholmondeley said, marking his place with a finger at the end of a paragraph. "Mogford. How can I help you?"

"Bad news, boss," Mogford replied. "A body's been found at the

Grosvenor House Hotel. Your old pal James Leipfold was at the scene. I thought you might want to have a word with him."

"What happened?" he asked. "Who was killed?"

"Looks like Jayne Lipton, guv. Remember her? We've got men on the ground to secure the scene, and the body's on its way to the coroner. Leipfold was there when I arrived, boss. Dragging their receptionist away from the crime scene."

"Is there any chance that the receptionist was behind it?"

"Doesn't look like it," Mogford said. "He needed a change of underwear, if you catch my drift. Doesn't seem the type to kill a fly."

"Nevertheless, it's a possibility."

Mogford said nothing, and Cholmondeley sighed and looked shrewdly across at his second-in-command.

"Okay," Cholmondeley said. "You speak to the hotel staff and see what you can figure out. I'll have a chat with James Leipfold. But you know what he's like. He's always in the wrong place at the wrong time."

* * *

It was the following day, a Saturday afternoon, and Leipfold had just escaped a stressful meeting with a new client. He unlocked his mobile phone and dialled the office.

"Are you busy?" Leipfold asked when Maile answered the call.

Maile laughed. "The phone hasn't stopped ringing. You'd better be paying me time and a half."

"Can you meet me at the Rose & Crown?"

"Sure thing. Just give me a couple of minutes to power down. What's up?"

"I'm not convinced that the Thompson case is over," Leipfold replied. "And besides, I could murder a lemonade."

Leipfold arrived first, and he went up to the bar and ordered a lemonade, a gin and tonic and a pint of lager before selecting a discreet booth in the corner. Leipfold sat with his back to the wall, an old habit that allowed him to keep an eye on the doors. It was a useful surveillance trick, but it also came in handy if he had to make a quick getaway.

Maile arrived ten minutes later, dressed all in black but still showing a slight lick of colour that Leipfold struggled to place until he realised she'd had her fringe done. He wondered how she'd found the time. She spotted Leipfold at his table and made a beeline for the booth.

"Hey," she said, pulling out a chair and sitting down beside him. "What's new?"

"This is for you," Leipfold said, sliding the G&T across to her. He kept the other two drinks for himself. Maile stared at him as he took a slow sip from the lemonade before picking up the lager, sniffing it, swirling it delicately and putting it back down on the table.

"And that one's for you?" she asked.

"I don't drink," Leipfold reminded her. "Not anymore. But sometimes, when I feel like I've earned one, I buy something to remind me what I'm missing."

"Uh-huh," Maile said. "Because that's totally sane. You're not missing much."

"Perhaps not," Leipfold murmured, staring moodily at the drink. He took another sip of his lemonade and said, "It looks like we've got another murder on our hands."

"Yuh-huh," Maile said. "Jayne Lipton. Who do you think killed her? Is it connected to the Thompson case?"

"I don't know," Leipfold admitted. "It could be. But something tells me it's unrelated. The ferocity of the attack, for one thing. The *modus operandi* for another."

Leipfold took another sip from his lemonade while Maile slurped away at her G&T. Then he stared morosoley into the pint of lager.

"So what's next?" Maile asked, breaking the moody silence with an upbeat smile.

"The same as always," Leipfold replied. "We investigate, and if we can make some money while we're at it, even better."

"Doesn't look like we'll be short of work for a while."

Leipfold nodded and said nothing.

Maile grinned again and leaned towards him. "I wouldn't miss it for the world," she said.

She sat back and downed the rest of her G&T. Then she pointed at the pint of lager that Leipfold was still brooding over. "You going to drink that?" she asked.

Chapter Three:
Operation Aftershock

MAILE O'HARA LOVED HER JOB. After all, where else would she get paid for poking her nose into other people's business? But she had to admit that it had its downsides. Right now, she was worried about her workload. She needed an afternoon off and she wasn't sure how Leipfold would take it. Luckily, she'd grown used to his moods and knew when to talk and when not to.

At twenty-four-years-old, unattached and covered with more tattoos than a Maori tribesman, she cut an imposing figure, despite her diminutive height and her refusal to wear high heels. But she was also a humanoid chameleon, a gifted amateur at the subtle art of fancy dress and deception. That, combined with her ability to shift code and study data, multiplied by her skills at digital research and her analytical mind and driven personality, made her a valuable employee.

Not that her boss, private detective James Leipfold, had hired anyone else. When Maile had joined him six weeks earlier, she'd signed on as an unpaid intern because Leipfold had no money in the bank and Maile had nothing better to do with herself. The two of them had taken on the case of a young woman called Donna Thompson who'd been killed in a hit and run. Leipfold had solved it with Maile's help, and the ensuing publicity meant that business was on the up. Leipfold and Maile had taken on half a dozen new clients in the weeks that had passed.

It was a Monday. The weather was cold and miserable, and an overcast sky hung over the capital and cast bleak, grey shadows over Wandsworth, Hammersmith, Fulham and Putney, threatening to roam further north towards the Houses of Parliament, where the Conservative government was in session to discuss the pressing matters of the week ahead. The newspapers were full of the usual trash: celebrity deaths, international espionage, tension between the Russians, the Chinese and the Americans, and a second-rate singer who'd caused a furore by dressing as a Nazi at a swanky costume party. There was no mention of the murder that Leipfold had discovered a couple of weeks ago. After an initial splash across the papers, the case had gone quiet. As far as Maile or Leipfold knew, no one had been formally charged.

But that was in the past and today was a new day. Maile had been the first to arrive at 19a Balcombe Street. She put the kettle on, dropped the day's newspapers on the boss's desk, sorted through her emails and made a start on a little research for their latest case. Alan Phelps, a journalist at the local rag *The Tribune*, had commissioned them to follow the money at a nearby non-profit. Phelps thought it was a scam, and that the board was squandering the money on annual retreats, bonuses and parties, and Maile was inclined to agree with him. But so far they'd been unable to prove it.

There was a faint tinkle as the office door opened, and Maile looked up briefly as James Leipfold entered his domain. At barely five feet six inches, with a hard, lined face and a thin crop of ginger hair that he spiked with a little gel, he looked more like a shopkeeper than a detective. He nodded wordlessly at Maile, hung his coat on the back of the door and strolled over to his desk, where a cup of lukewarm coffee was already waiting. He drained it in one gulp, made himself another one and then sat back down and started nosing through the papers.

They worked in silence. Construction noise blended with the traffic and filtered in through the window. Maile *hated* working in silence, but Leipfold never seemed to notice his surroundings. She slipped her headphones on and listened to Killswitch Engage, looking up every couple of minutes to check what the boss was doing.

Eventually, he finished the papers and beckoned her over. It was time to attack the day's crossword. Maile steeled herself to ask her question and then wandered over to join him.

* * *

"You want a *what?*"

Maile smiled nervously and chewed at her fingernails, a habit she'd picked up at university when her lecturers asked questions that she couldn't answer.

"I want an afternoon off," Maile repeated. "Tomorrow, if I can. I am *allowed* to take time off, right? I still haven't seen a contract."

"I need to write one," Leipfold replied, waving his hand impatiently. "I've never hired before. It's always been just me. What do you need an afternoon off for?"

"I have a life," Maile said. She laughed. "Ask me no questions, I'll tell you no lies. Can I take it off or not?"

Leipfold sighed. "Okay," he said, reluctantly. "It's not like you haven't earned it. Just try to give me more warning next time. Shit, Maile, you've picked the worst possible time. Look at how busy we are."

"I know. If we keep this up, we'll have to hire someone else."

"Not bloody likely." Leipfold turned his attention back to the stack of papers in front of him. "Will that be all?" he asked.

Maile paused for a moment, unsure of how to proceed. Leipfold looked up at her and asked, "What is it?"

"I just think it's weird," she said. "You know, that Jayne Lipton was killed just as we were closing in on her."

"You think her murder was connected to the previous case?"

"I don't know," Maile admitted. "Maybe. I guess it's possible. What do you think?"

"I think that's a load of crap," Leipfold said. "No, Jayne Lipton's death was something different, something new. Whoever killed her must have been planning it. It sure as hell wasn't committed on the spur of the moment. An act of passion, perhaps, but one that required a heart of stone and a sick, twisted imagination."

"Hmm…" Maile paused for a moment, examining her fingernails with exaggerated nonchalance in a movement that didn't fool either of them. "So what you're saying is that there's a psycho on the loose and nobody knows who they are or what they want?"

"That's about the size of it," Leipfold said. "But don't worry about it. That's what the police are for."

"Yeah, and they always do such a good job."

"Was that sarcasm?"

"How did you guess?" Maile asked. She didn't bother to wait for an answer. "And you're fine with that? I mean, you're going to leave the cops to investigate? You're not going to take the case on?"

"How can I?" Leipfold asked. "We've got plenty of work to go around. Besides, Jack Cholmondeley's on the case. If anyone can solve it, he can."

"Like he solved the Donna Thompson case?"

"Enough with the sarcasm," Leipfold said, but his eyes were twinkling and Maile could tell that he saw the funny side. She grinned.

"So what are we going to do?"

"The same thing we always do," Leipfold replied. "Pass me that pen. We're going to nail the crossword and get back to work."

* * *

While Leipfold and Maile were working on the crossword, Detective Inspector Jack Cholmondeley was chairing a meeting at the station. Sergeant Gary Mogford was there, looking as tired as always but wearing a fresh suit and too much aftershave. Constable Jenny Groves was there too, one of the newer recruits who had a reputation for following the rules and getting the job done, despite her low social standing as a former PCSO. Constable Ian Hyneman had joined the briefing at the last minute, a stubble-faced man with the early hint of an expanding waistline. They were joined by Constable Jessica Yates, a nondescript but attractive young copper with dreams of working undercover, and Constable Steve Cohen, who was taking a break from working reception to record the minutes.

Cholmondeley surveyed the room with grim satisfaction and called the meeting to order. The hubbub died down as the cops put on their serious faces. Most of them were new recruits. Mogford was the only other copper in the room who he really knew and trusted.

"Ladies and gentlemen," he said. "Thanks a lot for coming. As you already know, we're here to discuss Operation Aftershock. Please save any questions you might have until the end of the briefing."

Aftershock was the automatically generated code name that their computers had provided for the case. While the choice of words was random—or as random as a computer could manage—Cholmondeley thought it was a good name for a murder enquiry. Especially one like this.

"Now, as you know," Cholmondeley continued, "the initial investigation was out of our hands. We have the report back from forensics, and while I can't say it's an easy read, I'd like you to look over it. Make it a priority, please. Gary, if you could do the honours?"

Cholmondeley nodded at Mogford, who made his way around the room with a number of printed reports, stapled together and stored inside manila folders. There were only five copies, so Constables Cohen and Groves leaned in together to share one, at least for the initial briefing.

"Now," Cholmondeley continued, "I'd like you to forget about the report, at least for now. I need your full concentration while I go over the case to date."

For the next forty minutes, Cholmondeley recapped the murder of Jayne Lipton, starting with the call they'd received from the hotel staff and culminating with the discovery of a body in room 202 of the Grosvenor House Hotel.

"The victim was in a state," Cholmondeley explained. "The killer inflicted multiple lacerations and mutilated the body. We're expecting the coroner's report any minute now, which should take care of a few unanswered questions."

"Such as?" Mogford asked.

"I'm glad you asked," Cholmondeley replied. "All evidence so far suggests she was killed by a sharp object such as a knife or a machete, which was used to cut her throat like a pig in a goddamned slaughterhouse. There are photos of the scene and the body. While I hate to ask you to look at them, you're going to have to. Familiarise yourself with the scene. It might cost you a good night's sleep, but it'll give you a better idea of what we're up against."

"Anything missing from the scene?" Mogford asked.

"Not as far as we can tell," Cholmondeley replied. "All of her clothes were present, but there's a patch missing from the dress she was wearing. It doesn't look like a tear. It's more likely that the killer cut it out after her death, perhaps to take with him as a trophy."

"And what are we up against, guv?" Constable Groves asked, raising a hand half-heartedly like a kid who was too cool for school. "Are you sure that he's actually a he?"

"I don't know," Cholmondeley replied. "It's an easy assumption, given the brutality of the crime, but let's not take anything for granted. It's our job to find that out. Now, we've been brought in to offer support to the Serious Crimes Unit. This is far beyond our usual remit, and I don't want to mess this one up. There are a lot of eyes on us. I want to get results here. If we get this wrong, we'll have a major incident on our hands. We're just lucky that it hasn't been reported. A story like this sells newspapers."

"Yeah," Mogford grunted. "And puts other lives at risk. Especially if we have—"

Sergeant Mogford stopped himself before he finished his thought and Cholmondeley scowled across at him.

"We don't," Cholmondeley said. "Let's not get ahead of ourselves and start looking for the next Peter Sutcliffe. What we have here is a murder, plain and simple. A grizzly murder, perhaps, but a murder nonetheless."

Cholmondeley surveyed the room again. The atmosphere had changed, and the solemnity of the crime had started to sink in. There were no jokes, no idle chit-chat or casual banter. Even Constable Cohen was solemn-faced for once, the gum in his mouth all but forgotten.

Constable Groves raised her hand again and asked, "So what's next?"

"We put the feelers out," Cholmondeley replied. "Here's what I want you to do. Read the forensic report, keep your eyes peeled for the autopsy and speak to Sergeant Mogford to receive your list of duties. Cohen, I need you to type up and circulate the notes. Groves, pay a visit to the hotel and interview the staff. Find out who was on duty and see what you can learn from them. See who booked the room, when they booked it and whether they paid with cash or by card. Hyneman and Yates, I want you to find out everything you can about Jayne Lipton. If you check the files for the Thompson case and the Rieirson case, you'll be able to find plenty to start with. Build on it. If she so much as bought a kebab, I want to know about it. Clear?"

The coppers nodded and Gary Mogford said, "What about me, boss?"

"I want you to stay at base and coordinate," Cholmondeley said.

"Me?" Mogford asked. His face flushed and he pushed his chest out. Cholmondeley realised belatedly that the man had taken the delegation as a sign of confidence. "Sure, I can do that. But what about you?"

"I've got a meeting with some very important people," he said. "See, we're not the only team working on this. An investigation is already underway. I have superiors to schmooze with and reports to make of my own."

"Boss," Groves said, "if we're not the only team working the case, what happened to the others?"

"They're still on it, but they've hit a dead end," Cholmondeley explained. "The top brass want it solved fast. Believe it or not, we're the reinforcements."

Chapter Four:
Not An Easy Death

CHOLMONDELEY HEARD BACK from the autopsy team at quarter past four in the afternoon, and the report was in his inbox by four thirty. Unfortunately, most of his team was still out in the field, so he forwarded it on and printed off a copy of his own. By the time he'd finished reading, it was knocking off time. It was a Monday night, and Monday night was Slimming World night. Mary, his long-suffering wife—the kind of mild-mannered old woman who had a collection of plastic flamingoes, knitted blankets for charity and who'd opted for an early retirement—attended the weekly weigh-in like it was her religion, which it was. And Cholmondeley had to drive her there and back every week without fail or else there'd be hell to pay.

By the time he got back to the station, the rest of his team was off-shift.

There had been no major developments as of the following morning, and the kick-off meeting was subdued, not least because Constable Cohen was back on reception. The only good news was that the hotel had given some of its staff the day off work to talk to the police. Their PR team called it "helping the police with their enquiries," desperate to put a positive spin on the worst thing to hit the place since salmonella in the Ledbury back in the eighties.

Cholmondeley ordered Yates to join Groves for the day to help her to work through the couple dozen hotel employees who were expected to come in. Then he reported to the daily progress meeting with the heads of the other teams. After that, he had a meeting with a lawyer who was representing the Crown in the case against Eleanor Thompson, who was facing a charge of conspiracy to commit murder. The Thompson case had been the last one his team had worked on. After the meeting with the lawyer, he was off to meet the man who'd helped to solve it.

He was off to meet James Leipfold.

* * *

"Where's your assistant?" Cholmondeley asked after Leipfold answered the door and welcomed his old friend into the office.

Leipfold shrugged and dunked a ginger snap into his coffee. He wheeled his chair over to the reception area and sat down opposite Cholmondeley, who was perched uncomfortably on one of the plastic seats.

"No idea," he said. "She's got the afternoon off."

"Shame," Cholmondeley replied. "She adds a bit of colour to the place."

"Colour?" Leipfold laughed. "She wears more black than a widow."

"True," Cholmondeley murmured, rubbing his chin thoughtfully and staring at his own reflection in the pallid brew that Leipfold had offered him. "Well, it's probably for the best. Truth is, I've got a favour to ask."

Leipfold sighed. "You've always got a favour to ask," he said. "What is it this time?"

"Jayne Lipton."

"Oh no," Leipfold said, jumping abruptly to his feet. "No, not her. Don't talk to me about Jayne Lipton."

Cholmondeley took another sip of his milky tea. "Sit down, old boy," he said. "At least let me finish. Just hear me out. If you still say no by the time that I'm done, I'll leave you in peace. I'm not asking for much. Like I said, consider it a favour. This is unofficial and off-the-record. I could lose my job just for being here, but I trust you, James. I always said you'd make a good copper. Prove me right and help me out here. What do you say?"

Leipfold shrugged and sat down again. "You've got ten minutes," he said.

"Great!" Cholmondeley exclaimed, clapping his hands together. "Okay, listen. We've got teams looking into her murder already. At least three of us in different capacities, maybe more. But we're at a dead end, and there's a lot of pressure on us to get this done. It's political. Sometimes I wonder whether they'd prefer us to get it wrong fast than to take our time and bust the guy who actually did it."

"So why do you need me?" Leipfold asked.

"You don't understand how vicious the murderer was," Cholmondeley said.

"I do," Leipfold replied. "I saw the body."

"The autopsy reads like a horror novel."

"How so?"

"She had her throat cut," he explained. "But they say she was probably dead by the time that it happened. The girl was stabbed over and over again, but most of the wounds were superficial. She probably bled out. And that's not the only thing. You sure you're ready for this?"

Leipfold frowned, reluctant to admit that his old friend had him interested. He sat down opposite Cholmondeley, nursing a fresh brew of his own, and said, "So what's the deal?"

Cholmondeley frowned. "Well," he murmured, "where do I start?" He took another sip of milky tea. "Cutting her throat might have happened last, but it was only the beginning, if you catch my drift. They beat her, to begin with. She had pre-mortem bruises all over her, and the autopsy team thinks they used a bat or some other blunt instrument. It wasn't an easy death. The killer…they…"

"What?"

Cholmondeley shook his head. "It's awful," he said. "They mutilated her while she was still alive. Cut big chunks from her breasts and took a knife to her genitals."

Leipfold inhaled sharply and asked, "Any sign of intercourse?"

Cholmondeley shook his head. "That's the strange thing about it," he said. "Whatever else it was, this crime doesn't seem to be about sex. It's about something else, and I'm not sure what. Hatred, perhaps. I'd bet money that the killer knew her somehow."

"What happened to the flesh?" Leipfold asked.

"Well, that's just it," Cholmondeley replied. "We don't know. There's no sign of it. But we *do* know that it was cut from her before she died. Forensics figured out the order of things thanks to the state of the blood. They put the cause of death down as exsanguination, meaning she bled out because of her wounds. It's hard to say anything with any certainty because of the amount of punishment she received. But she suffered. She must have done."

"That's awful," Leipfold replied.

"It is," Cholmondeley agreed. "And that's why I need your help. I'm begging you, friend. Help me to catch this deranged son-of-a-bitch. We'll all be safer when he's off the streets and behind bars."

Leipfold paused for a moment. His mind was turning over and over, like it always did at the start of a case. That was when he realised he was probably going to take it. But at this stage, he still had more questions than answers.

"That's weird," he murmured.

"What is it?" Cholmondeley asked.

"The crime scene," Leipfold said. "It wasn't right."

"In what way?"

Leipfold took a deep breath and said, "It wasn't a crime scene. At least, it wasn't *the* crime scene."

"What do you mean?"

"Can you get me a copy of the photos?" Leipfold asked. "I want to take another look at them. I think…"

Cholmondeley waited for a moment before prompting Leipfold to continue. "What?" he asked.

"It's probably nothing," Leipfold said. "But have you boys been working on the assumption that the hotel room was the crime scene?"

"You mean to say it isn't?"

"Of course not," Leipfold replied. "Sure, there was a lot of blood there. But not nearly enough to account for all of the injuries. And besides, someone would have heard something. She must have been kept somewhere else. They moved her there after they killed her."

* * *

Maile didn't get home until just after midnight, but Kat Cotteril, her housemate, was still up and about when she arrived. She was curled up on the sofa with a tartan blanket covering her from her shoulders to her feet, which still felt cold despite the fact that she'd brought a fan heater through from her bedroom. To her left, she had her mobile phone, and to her right she had a glass of wine, the TV remote and half a pack of Kettle Chips. She was watching a rerun of a reality TV show where celebrities had to work on a farm. A comedian with a familiar face was milking a cow, and Kat was absentmindedly munching her way through the crisps while he struggled to get to grips with his unusual assignment.

When Maile entered the room, she took her coat off and hung it up, then tossed her handbag down on the table and slid out of her shoes. She sank into the big, leather armchair and exhaled.

Kat glanced over, then turned around properly to get a good look at her housemate. Maile was wearing skinny jeans with a studded belt, a stylish blouse beneath a cardigan, her big, black boots and an unusual amount of makeup. Granted, she didn't exactly look like a supermodel, but she'd clearly put an effort in. Kat was pleasantly surprised by how well she scrubbed up, and she said as much.

"Thanks," Maile mumbled. "It took me half the afternoon to get ready."

"Where have you been?" Kat asked.

"Out."

"Who with?"

"Some guy," Maile said.

Kat folded her arms and grinned. "On a date?" she asked. Maile nodded. Kat clapped her hands together in excitement. She tucked her legs beneath her and swivelled round to look at Maile properly. "Anyone I know?"

"No."

"How come you didn't tell me?" Kat asked. She reached across for the remote and muted the reality TV show she'd been watching.

The comedian had finished milking the cow, and now a pale-faced weathergirl was helping to deliver a litter of lambs.

Maile sighed. "I don't have to tell you *everything*," she said. "And I figured if you found out then you wouldn't shut up about it. Besides, you know how much I hate talking about dudes. It's so boring. Why do you never want to talk about CPUs?"

"How did it go?"

"It was whatever. He seemed nice enough."

"Is that why you were out so late?"

Maile shook her head. "Nah," she said. "He just wouldn't stop talking. I tried to get away a couple times, but he just changed the subject and kept on talking about his job."

"What does he do?"

"I dunno. Something in sales, maybe? Marketing? Finance? I wasn't paying much attention."

"You're being too picky."

"You think?" Maile said. "Am I the problem? I mean, is it so unrealistic for me to hope that maybe once, just once, I'd find a decent guy who doesn't bore the shit out of me and who likes me for who I am?"

"Probably," Kat admitted. "Let's face it, you're unique. It's not going to be easy to find someone you have stuff in common with."

Maile murmured something softly and made herself more comfortable on the sofa. She pulled out her phone and started to play with it.

"You need to meet some new people," Kat said. She pointed at Maile's phone. "You know there's a new dating app, right?"

Maile scoffed. "I spend half my life online," she said. "Maybe more. So yeah, I heard."

Kat shrugged, grabbed the remote and turned the volume back up on the television.

"Maybe you should sign up to it," she said. "A couple of the girls at work swear by it. Lesley snagged herself a neuroscientist. Not bad considering she dropped out of uni."

"I dunno…"

"Come on, Maile," Kat said. "You can't stay single forever."

"Watch me."

"Look, I'll even set up your profile and help you to look through it. It'll be fun."

"You reckon?"

"Yeah!" Kat said. She grinned. "Go on, grab your phone. I'll crack open the vino."

"You fricken suck," Maile said. But she grabbed her phone and drank the wine regardless.

Chapter Five:
Only The Beginning

MAILE HAD A HANGOVER the following morning, so she was glad when Leipfold asked her to man the office while he went out and about on his errands. All the coffee in the world couldn't help her, but that didn't stop her from trying. She'd also cleared three pints of water by 10AM, but at least she hadn't had the shakes. She had her breakfast, a Subway sandwich, to thank for that.

Leipfold, meanwhile, had climbed into his leathers and grabbed his keys before hopping onto his motorbike and driving into the inner city. At first, he cruised almost at random, hitting the side streets purely to give himself some time to think. Then he paid a quick visit to a potential client, one who'd come in through the website and caught his attention by offering an unusually large sum for a simple job. But the meeting was just a formality. There were some contracts to sign, and Leipfold needed to collect a USB stick that contained a previous PI's research that he didn't even plan to use.

Back on the bike again, he'd passed the Grosvenor House Hotel before he even noticed it. On some level, his mind had been retracing Jayne Lipton's final footsteps, but it was a hopeless task. Even if she'd been alive and on the streets, she would have been difficult to track down. With Jayne dead, autopsied and scheduled for a burial, Leipfold had no hope of finding any trace of her. But that didn't stop him from trying. He wanted to see what Jayne had seen and to think what Jayne had thought, even if it didn't amount to anything.

Leipfold parked Camilla in the Grosvenor House car park and was just about to enter the building for the first time since discovering the body when his mobile phone rang. It was his secondary phone, a cheap pay-as-you-go device which he only ever used to communicate with Jack Cholmondeley. That meant that every time it rang, he knew who it was. It also helped to cover their tracks in case the cop was caught out and an inquest was formed to push its nose into things.

"Leipfold," he said as he answered the call.

There was a little interference on the other end, as well as the background hum of a conversation. It sounded like Cholmondeley was calling him from the middle of a busy meeting room.

"It's me," Cholmondeley said. "Listen, I can't talk. I just wanted to see whether you'd thought about taking on the Lipton case. I don't mean to push you, but I need a decision."

Leipfold had already made his decision, but he paused and pretended to think about it, picturing his old friend waiting red-faced on the other side of the line. Then he said, "I'm in."

"Good," Cholmondeley replied. "Then listen to this. I want you to go over to Jayne Lipton's place and take a look around. It's nothing sketchy, nothing illegal. We've got a copy of the key and written permission from her next of kin. They want the bastard who did it just as much as we do. Sergeant Mogford is going to meet you there so be on your best behaviour."

"Can't you send someone else?" Leipfold asked. "I've never liked the guy."

"He doesn't like you, either," Cholmondeley said. "But this is business, James. And besides: who do you think has the keys?"

* * *

Leipfold hopped back on to Camilla and made his way over to Jayne Lipton's place. He'd been there before, albeit briefly, but last time he'd made his way to Shelden Street, he'd had to hop on the tube to get there. While he was investigating the Thompson case, he was simultaneously trying to balance the books, and his only option had been to sell his beloved motorbike. Luckily, Greg Bateman, the balding used car salesman he'd sold it to, had kept the machine on his lot and so Leipfold was able to buy her back once a couple of cheques came in.

Sergeant Gary Mogford was already there when Leipfold arrived, and he watched him, stony-faced, as he leant the bike on its kickstand and put the padlock on. Leipfold offered Mogford his hand as he walked up to the door to meet him, but Mogford just glared at him and refused to shake it.

Gary Mogford had always struck Leipfold as the epitome of a middle-aged cop. His salt and pepper hair had lost its colour, and the man had worry lines so deep that they looked like scars. That day, he wasn't in uniform. He was wearing his other outfit, a plain pair of jeans, a blue shirt with a wide collar and a faded leather jacket. Cholmondeley had once told Leipfold that he'd never seen Mogford wear anything else. He joked that the copper's wardrobe contained multiple sets of the same two outfits, with a partition down the middle to separate them. Leipfold could believe it.

Mogford nodded at Leipfold and said, "You'd better come inside."

Leipfold grunted, and the two of them entered the house in silence. Mogford showed him around the place to give him a sense of the layout and then explained the plan.

"We'll go room to room," Mogford said. "You're to stay in my company at all times, understand? The old man might trust you, but I don't."

"Yeah, well, I don't really want to be here, either."

Mogford grunted but said nothing as he led Leipfold through from the hallway and into the living room, then from the living room into the kitchen and the small, urban back garden. There was no grass out there, just a half tonne of concrete and a dilapidated shed. Mogford found the key to the shed in one of the kitchen drawers while Leipfold was looking through the pantry, and they let themselves in just as the heavens opened and a thin, grey rain started to drizzle its way down from the clouds. Leipfold was prepared to bet, before they opened it, that Jayne Lipton had never been inside. And it looked like he was right. The air was thick with mildew, and cobwebs, slime and a fug of dead insects covered everything inside.

Leipfold let Mogford carry out the inventory, preferring to stand outside in the rain than to get his hands dirty. But there was nothing there for the men to find. Nor did they find anything in the pantry, in the lounge or in the kitchen, so they climbed the stairs with some foreboding and proceeded to check out the upstairs bathroom and bedroom.

Jayne Lipton had a surprisingly sentimental streak. Her bedroom was decorated in pinks and reds, and her double bed was covered with throw pillows. Her wardrobe seemed typical enough, but Leipfold was surprised to see so many fluffy teddy bears, old family photos and swimming and dancing certificates from her schooldays. Jayne Lipton had been twenty-four when she died, but her bedroom made her seem closer to fourteen.

But there was nothing of interest. Mogford seemed dispirited as he led Leipfold back down the stairs towards the front door, but neither man had really expected to find anything. They weren't the first team to have searched the place, and both men were well aware that there had been specialists and men with dogs, people who'd been trained to find things. They were just two regular guys doing the best they could.

"Guess that was a bust then," Mogford said, ushering Leipfold towards the front door.

Leipfold nodded and said, "Guess it was."

Out front, Leipfold offered Mogford his hand again, and Mogford refused, once more, to take it. The two men nodded at each other, then Mogford watched Leipfold walk slowly back over to his bike. He was whistling as he walked.

Leipfold patted his pockets to find his keys and to check that he hadn't dropped the scrap of paper he'd grabbed from the pantry.

* * *

Later that day, when he got back to the office, Leipfold asked Maile to put the kettle on and then settled down at his desk to investigate his prize. It didn't look like much. Just a four-inch square of plain paper with ragged edges from where Leipfold had torn it out of an old notebook.

It was just a hunch, but Leipfold's hunches had a habit of paying off. He figured that if a person wrote something down, it was something that they wanted to remember. Perhaps it was just a recipe for a Victoria sponge. But there was only one way to find out.

He remembered a book he'd had as a young boy, back when his parents were still alive and they used to take it in turns to read to him until he fell asleep. It was about a spy who was a double agent during the Second World War, outfoxing his enemies with a different improbable trick in every chapter. That guy had magically made the contents of a note reappear by rubbing a pencil over the indentations the writer had left in the paper below. It was a good idea, but Leipfold found that a mixture of blotting ink and water worked better. He'd tested and refined the method, eventually settling on the perfect formula so that the ink sank into the indentations while the water was absorbed by the paper. It was a fiddly method, but it worked.

By the time that Maile had boiled the kettle and made them both a drink, Leipfold was hard at work. Maile set his coffee down, pulled her own chair over and sat down beside him. She asked him what he was doing and he explained it to her.

"Cool!" she said. "How long will we have to wait for results?"

"It depends," Leipfold replied. "How long does it take to finish a crossword?"

It took them nine minutes, which wasn't a new record but was still a good time. Leipfold jotted it down in the little notebook that he kept in his top drawer and then turned his attention back to the investigation.

The paper was still drying, but the early signs were good. Ironically enough, it was spelled out across like a crossword clue. *Something O T something something L something V something something nine.*

"What do you make of that?" Leipfold asked.

"Looks like a username," Maile replied. "Or maybe a password."

"How did you figure that one out?"

"It's got a number in it," Maile replied. "It could be an address, I guess, but it doesn't look long enough."

Leipfold smiled. Maile made sense, and her suspicions confirmed his own first impression.

"Good call," Leipfold said. "Then we know what to do next. First up, we need to figure out the rest of that username. It'll get a little better as the paper dries, but see if you can improve the image with that computer of yours. Then find out everything you can about what it means."

"Got it," Maile said. "I'll see if I can pin it back to Jayne Lipton."

"Do some digging," Leipfold continued. "I want to know everything about her. Find out what sites she used to visit and who she used to talk to. We need to find out what her routine was so we can figure out how she broke it."

"And what about you?"

Leipfold grinned. "I'm going to take the rest of the afternoon off," he said. "Two can play at that game. But you keep on working. Let me know if you find anything."

* * *

Detective Inspector Jack Cholmondeley was exhausted. His team had spent the morning reporting to Sergeant Mogford while Cholmondeley was catching up with the other teams at the daily briefing, and then Mogford himself had taken up most of his afternoon. Worse still, Mary was in a mood with him. She said it was the anniversary of the day they'd met, and Cholmondeley didn't remember enough to contradict her.

He thought that nothing else could go wrong, but then Constable Cohen came running up to his office, not bothering to knock and bursting in to interrupt Mogford and Cholmondeley in the middle of a conversation.

"This better be good, lad," Mogford said.

Cohen was out of breath, and he had to pause for a second before replying. "It is," he panted, leaning forward to rest his hands on the desk.

Mogford glared down at his hands until the constable moved them and stood up straight again.

Cholmondeley, meanwhile, felt a little sympathy for Constable Cohen. He didn't fit in with the rest of the boys, and Constable Yates was his only real friend on the force, although he got on well with the general public. He smiled encouragingly. "Go on," he said. "What is it?"

"There's a parcel," Constable Cohen explained. "At reception. I didn't get a good look at it, but apparently it came by courier. Some guy on a bike, in full leathers with a helmet on. Nobody got a good look at him, but we got a partial on the number plate."

"And what was in the package?" Cholmondeley asked.

Constable Cohen flashed him a panicked look, the colour draining from his face as bile rose in his stomach. "I couldn't exactly say, sir," he said. "It's better if you come and take a look at it. Better glove up before you handle anything. The lads from forensics are going to want to see this one."

Intrigued, Cholmondeley sped up, and Mogford increased his pace to keep up with him. The package had been collected from reception and taken away to a safe room, and that was where Constable Cohen led them. The room had an officer at the door who inspected their badges despite knowing them all on a first name basis, and the only thing inside it was a plain, stainless steel table, two chairs and the package itself, which was partially unwrapped and lying open in the middle of the table.

Cholmondeley pulled on a pair of plastic gloves, which the man on the door provided, and moved closer to inspect the package. Sergeant Mogford was at his shoulder, a step and a half behind him, while Constable Cohen watched nervously from just inside the doorway.

Cholmondeley knew there was something wrong just by looking at it. The inside of the box looked like a butcher's bin. It was half-full of blood and gore with a couple of hunks of flesh floating around in the middle of it. Genitalia stew.

Because, Cholmondeley realised, that was exactly what he was looking at. It seemed like they'd found the rest of Jayne Lipton, just in time to bury it along with her body. Cholmondeley backed away from the box and started to retch, but he was old enough and tough enough to stop the bile from slipping past his larynx.

Gary Mogford, meanwhile, had leaned in a little closer. He held one gloved hand across his face and used the other to rifle around in what the crime scene cleaners called "murk," the word they used for any unpleasant combination of bodily fluids or human remains. His hands closed around something and he pulled it out, then laid it on the table beside the bag. He made the mistake of looking at his hands, then turned away from the blood and the gore in the knowledge that his sleep would be haunted, again, for the foreseeable future.

"Sir," he shouted, "there's something in there."

Working like a tag team, Mogford moved back towards the door to inhale the fresher air from the corridor, while Constable Cohen backed out of the room altogether. Detective Inspector Jack Cholmondeley leaned closer to the table to look at what Mogford had found.

It was a message, written in blood on what looked to be a thin piece of parchment. Looking closer, Cholmondeley thought he recognised the pattern and made a mental note to check it against the missing patch on Jayne Lipton's dress. He suspected he'd find a match.

The message was short and simple, almost as brutal is the killing itself. It said, "This is only the beginning."

Chapter Six:
Occam's Razor

IT WAS THE FOLLOWING MORNING, and Maile was the first one at the office. She'd also been the last to leave. Leipfold had left just after three o'clock, and she'd stayed behind until quarter past seven. Then Kat had called and asked her when she was coming home, and the lure of a takeaway had been too much for her. But Maile had still spent the evening carrying out a little research, propping her laptop on the arm of the sofa and simultaneously chatting to her hacker friends on IRC while watching TV with her housemate.

She was hungry, so she opened up the office microwave and removed the remains of a curry that had presumably once belonged to Leipfold. Then she nuked her leftover takeaway. She ate straight out of the container with a plastic fork while she waited for her laptop to load up.

Leipfold arrived at 9:35AM, looking scruffy and unkempt thanks to a lack of sleep and a cold shower. His mop of ginger hair was gel-free for once, and it flopped over his forehead and almost reached down to his eyes. Maile realised it was the longest she'd ever seen it and wondered whether her boss was looking after himself. She'd seen him look worse, but not by much.

Leipfold sat down at his desk and checked his emails in a tense, gloomy silence. Maile finished catching up with her own emails and then scooched across on her office chair and rolled to a stop beside Leipfold. He turned to look at her.

"How's it going?" he asked.

"Good, I guess," Maile said, sliding a sheaf of paper across the desk towards him. "I've got you some reading material, but I thought you might want me to give you the overview."

"Sure," he said. "But make it quick. Lots to do today, and not just on the Lipton case. I've got a potential new client who wants to see my portfolio. I haven't *got* a portfolio. I need you to make me one."

"Er…okay," Maile said. "Sure."

"So tell me about Jayne Lipton," Leipfold said. "What did you find?"

"Nothing," Maile replied. "At least, nothing important. I had a look at her posts on the main social networks and could only find the usual stuff. Selfies, food porn, that sort of thing. But I did find a couple of photos of her shopping trips. Looks like she loved to spend money, and she can't have had a shortage of it. Some of the gear she bought costs as much as your entire wardrobe."

Leipfold, who mentally calculated the value of his wardrobe to be around £300 for a total replacement, smiled but said nothing.

"That's not all, either," Maile continued. "She said she'd booked flights home, which didn't make sense to me at first. I mean, I thought she was born and bred here, and she was. But it turns out her grandparents are living in the south of France. I guess she was planning on going to see them."

"Or fleeing the country," Leipfold replied, remembering the suspicion she'd fallen under during his last investigation.

"Perhaps," Maile said. "Do you think it could be an international crime? With the French connection, maybe she has some enemies who tracked her over here."

"I doubt it," Leipfold said. He stared moodily into the distance, thoughts already swirling around as he started to form a theory. "Did you figure out the username?"

"Yeah," Maile replied. "It was LottyLove89. Mean anything to you?"

Leipfold shook his head.

"Looks like she'd been shopping for lingerie, too," Maile continued. "She posted a couple of raunchy photos. It's strange. She doesn't seem like the type."

"Times have changed since my day," Leipfold reflected. "My father always told me never to trust a woman who owns lingerie. Now the single girls are buying the stuff just to flaunt themselves to other people."

"Not always," Maile said. "Sometimes a woman just wants to feel sexy."

Leipfold glanced across at her, looking her up and down with his piercing, steely grey eyes. She blushed and turned away, as though she'd revealed too much, and then scuttled off into the kitchen to boil the kettle.

* * *

Mr. Taplow, Leipfold's landlord, popped round that afternoon. He was a paunchy, unhealthy-looking man, an elderly chap with no hair and a smoker's cough. He'd brought a battered yellow toolbox with him and, after a little jiggery-pokery with a screwdriver and a soldering iron, he finally fixed the building's out-of-date intercom system. Leipfold had been lobbying for him to fix it for the last eighteen months, and he'd finally relented once the rent was paid up. In just two short weeks, Leipfold had managed to claw it back, and he'd even covered the next instalment a couple of weeks early. He wasn't just up-to-date with the rent. He was ahead of it.

The guy was at least twenty years older than Leipfold, and his crow-foot eyes showed the signs of a long, hard life. He almost toppled from the fourth rung of his rickety stepladder when Maile suddenly slammed her fist against her desk and shouted, "Holy fucking—"

Leipfold glanced over at her, lowering the sheaf of paper he was working through, and asked, "What?"

"Boss," Maile said, "you need to get over here. There's been another murder."

"What?" he exclaimed. In his haste to get across to her, he almost knocked Mr. Taplow off his perch for the second time in as many minutes.

The old man spluttered and cursed and shouted, "What the hell is going on in here, Mr. Leipfold?"

"Nothing that concerns you, Mr. Taplow," Leipfold replied. "Don't you worry about it. You get on with your job, and I'll get on with mine. Have you finished with the intercom yet?"

The landlord scowled down at him and murmured something threatening and vague about "useless bloody tenants," but he turned his attention back to the intercom and started to solder the last little bit of wiring that Leipfold hoped would fix the damn thing for good.

Maile, meanwhile, was showing Leipfold a series of social media posts and news reports, explaining them all as best as she could as she flicked through them.

"It's all over the net," she said. "If you know where to look, at least. There's been another murder. Look. Reported in similar circumstances. Found with their throat cut and their body mutilated. Only this time…"

"What?" Leipfold growled.

"Only this time, the victim wasn't a woman," Maile said. "No official word from the police yet, but it looks like there's a name on the rumour mill. Hang on. Ah, here we are. Abu Adewali."

"Where was he found?" Leipfold asked.

"In a hallway at the YMCA," Maile said. "A couple of people took photos before the cops arrived. Get a look at these."

Maile edged over so that Leipfold could crouch down beside her to take a look at her screen. She moused over a couple of the pictures, and Leipfold whistled softly as she blew them up to full screen. They'd been shot on a smartphone, but the quality was still pretty good, easily good enough for them to make out the injuries. Leipfold wondered briefly what sort of sick, perverse individual would take photographs of a body like this, and then he remembered that sick and perverse individuals made up seventy percent of his business.

"So what do you reckon?" Maile asked. "Could this be another attack? Are we looking for the same person?"

"I'm not sure," Leipfold replied. "If it is the same person, they changed their MO. That's unusual, but it's not unheard of, and there are plenty of similarities. The cut throat, for example, and the mutilation to the body."

"Could be a copycat?" Maile suggested.

"No," Leipfold replied. "The police kept a lid on all the details. There's not enough out there in the public domain for them to have copied it. At least, not to this level of accuracy."

"Could be a coincidence?"

"Maybe," Leipfold said. "But it seems unlikely. No, now is the time for Occam's razor. The simplest explanation is usually the correct one."

"There's a simple explanation?" Maile exclaimed. "Why didn't you tell me?"

At the entrance to the office, Mr. Taplow had finished working on the intercom and was noisily folding away his stepladder.

"I'll be off then," he shouted, but Maile and Leipfold both ignored him.

"The simple explanation," Leipfold said, "is your first assumption. The two cases are connected because the same culprit is responsible."

* * *

Maile wanted to keep discussing the case, but Leipfold told her to stay on top of the news while he put in a call to Jack Cholmondeley. In search of a little privacy, he followed the landlord out of his office and then waited for him to climb into his little black Ford Fiesta. Then he sat on the stairs and put the call through.

Cholmondeley didn't answer on the first call, so Leipfold followed their unwritten protocol of dialling back for three rings every two minutes until he answered. This was their emergency protocol, and it meant that the call was top priority.

Cholmondeley answered after eight minutes with an exasperated, "What?"

Leipfold cut straight to the chase. "Have you heard the news?" he asked.

"What news?" Cholmondeley replied. "Look, James, I'm in the middle of a briefing at the moment and I haven't got time—"

"Abu Adewali," he said. "Heard of him?" There was a short spell of silence on the other end of the line, broken only by the sound of Cholmondeley's heavy breathing. Leipfold was hit by a dawning realisation. "My God," he whispered. "You haven't."

"What are you talking about?" Cholmondeley asked.

"Abu Adewali," Leipfold repeated. "Google him. Get your whole damn team on it if you have to. The man's dead."

"Slow down," Cholmondeley said. Leipfold could hear him moving around on the other end of the line, and he suspected that the old man was trying to find somewhere quiet so he could hear him better. He hoped he was finding a pen and paper while he was at it. "Okay, start again. From the top. Who's Abu Adewali?"

"I have no idea," Leipfold replied. "But he's connected to Jayne Lipton somehow. Abu's body has just been found, and I suspect your boys are on the way to the place if they're not there already. If it's not your team, you need to put a couple of calls in and find out who's handling it."

"And you think his death is connected to Jayne Lipton? How?"

"The killing was exactly the same," Leipfold said.

"Yeah," Cholmondeley scoffed. "Except for the fact it was a bloke and not a woman. Where did it happen? Was this at the Grosvenor House Hotel?"

"No," Leipfold admitted. "It was at the YMCA. But don't you see? The two are connected."

There was another pause on the other end of the phone line. Leipfold could picture Cholmondeley there, tucked away in one of the police force's private offices, wiping sweat from his forehead and scribbling notes with a pen and paper or quickly looking things up on a new computer. He heard the clatter of keys, which seemed to confirm the latter of the two guesses.

Then Cholmondeley asked, "How do you know all this?"

Leipfold laughed. "You can thank my assistant next time you come over," he said. "Maile found it. Looks like it got leaked online before the cops showed up. You're going to want to track down whoever posted it and have a word with them. They might know something."

Another pause. "Where did you say the body was found?" Cholmondeley asked.

Leipfold gave him directions from the station to the YMCA and Cholmondeley paused for a moment again. Then he said, "Still got your bike?"

"Yeah," Leipfold said. "She's parked outside."

"Good. Hop on and meet me there."

* * *

Leipfold arrived at the same time as Cholmondeley and Mogford, the police team's two heaviest hitters, pulled into the YMCA car park in the old man's black BMW. They parked side by side and grouped together in the car park before heading inside the building, a relic of eighteenth century London with most of the original brickwork.

"Ah," Cholmondeley said, as Leipfold rushed over to greet him. "Glad you could make it, James."

"Why's *he* here?" Mogford growled.

"Good to see you again, too," Leipfold replied. Cholmondeley, the unlucky intermediary, gestured for them both to simmer down.

"Here's the deal," Cholmondeley said. "Mogford, I want you to go in ahead and secure the scene. If you find what Leipfold says you'll find, I want you to radio for backup immediately."

"Sounds good," Mogford replied, snapping off a quick salute. "I'll see you inside."

Leipfold and Cholmondeley watched Mogford's back as he walked towards the entrance. Cholmondeley put a hand on Leipfold's arm as he started out after him. "Wait," he said. "Give him a minute. Besides, I need to talk to you."

"What about?"

"I need information," Cholmondeley said. "Assuming you're right about this, and you usually are, I'll need to know how you found this out."

"Then you'll need to talk to Maile."

"Listen, I'm putting my neck on the chopping block just by getting you involved."

"Some would say it's a risk worth taking."

"Perhaps," Cholmondeley said. "It's my balls on the line either way. Whether I involve you or not, if I don't solve this one, I'm finished."

"So what do you want me to do?" Leipfold asked.

"Call your assistant," Cholmondeley replied. "Have her figure out who posted the photos, then give me the details so I can get my men to track them down and talk to them. But keep my name out of it, and keep Mogford out of it, too. You got that?"

"Sure thing," Leipfold said. He reached for his mobile phone, but Cholmondeley reached across and stopped him.

"You can do it in a minute," Cholmondeley said. "We have more pressing concerns at the moment. Let's go take a look inside, see if we can't find that crime scene of yours."

Leipfold shrugged and put his phone back, then followed Jack Cholmondeley into the YMCA. They were looking for Gary Mogford, but they didn't have much of a problem finding him. They just followed the commotion.

Most of the building was empty, including the front desk, and Leipfold guessed that people had either flocked to the body or ran away from it as soon as Adewali was discovered.

Leipfold and Cholmondeley rounded a corner and came suddenly upon the corridor. Gary Mogford had beat them to it and was trying to radio for help while simultaneously directing the security staff to hold the crowds back. Leipfold guessed there were easily thirty people in the corridor, and the sight of them was somehow awful in its own right.

But if the crowded corridor was like hell, then the body was like the devil himself. It was the second time Leipfold had seen a scene like this, and it didn't get any easier over time. Abu Adewali was sprawled across the floor in the middle of the corridor. He was naked.

And parts of him were missing.

Chapter Seven:
The Visitor

CHOLMONDELEY AND MOGFORD offered Leipfold a lift back to the office once the scene had been secured, but he refused, not wanting to leave Camilla behind. Mogford was keen to start processing the corridor, but Cholmondeley had insisted on alerting the other teams, and it was out of their hands almost as quickly as he finished the call. Only the crime scene investigators were allowed on site, and Cholmondeley was promised an informal report within the next ninety minutes. He used the respite as an opportunity to talk to James Leipfold.

The conversation was tense and to the point. Mogford kept looking at his watch and hinting that they ought to return to the station and update the rest of the team, but both Jack Cholmondeley and James Leipfold just ignored him.

"Remember to track down the people who posted the photographs," Cholmondeley said. "I'll need some answers when I'm asked why we were first on the scene."

"I'll get right on it," Leipfold said.

"You do that," Cholmondeley replied. "And James…" He paused for a moment, laying a hand on Leipfold's arm to stop him before he walked over to Camilla. "Look after yourself," he said. "Okay? I'm worried. This isn't your average murderer. This is something different."

"A serial killer?" Leipfold suggested.

Cholmondeley shushed him and looked around nervously before wrapping an arm around his shoulders and leaning in a little closer.

"It's possible," he said. "I hope I'm wrong, but it seems like the most likely option."

"I agree," Leipfold said. "Forget about the victim being male. The attack pattern looks the same, at least at first glance. You're going to want to get your autopsy team to fast track the results on this one. If the slash patterns match, you could confirm if the same blade was used."

"Believe it or not," Cholmondeley said, "I do this for a living. I've got this. Just keep your nose clean and hold up your end of the bargain. I need those names."

"I'll do my best," Leipfold said.

"And I'm sure I don't need to tell you this," he added, "but keep your mouth shut. Officially, you're not on the case. Security's going to be tight."

"Even tighter now," Mogford supplied. "Once the press gets hold of this, and they will if it's out there on the internet, the shit will hit the fan."

"Mogford's right," Cholmondeley said. "You need to keep the details under wraps. We all do. Information is like a license to print money to those vultures at *The Tribune*. Don't feed them so much as a scrap. The last thing we want is to cause panic."

"Agreed," Leipfold said. "Although…"

"What?" Mogford asked.

"The press," Leipfold murmured. "They can be a useful tool when you need them."

Then he winked at them and walked over to Camilla.

* * *

That evening, back at the office, Leipfold was replaying the crime scenes over and over in his head. His memory was damn near eidetic, but it could always use a helping hand. Cholmondeley had sent him a couple of photos from each of the scenes and they helped to bring the blood to life. It was so real he could almost smell it.

Leipfold turned the radio on and tuned into a late-night talk show, but he wasn't paying any attention. He needed the voices for company so that he didn't lose his mind in the night. There was no question of him heading home. Leipfold lived in a little bedsit apartment that could barely contain him. He went there to sleep, and he occasionally tried to cook a meal in the communal kitchen, but it was no place to work from and even less of a place to get away from things.

He rooted through his desk until he reached the bottle of whiskey in the bottom drawer. He took it out and looked at it, then poured a generous shot from it into a grim-looking cardboard cup, which he'd been refilling with coffee for the last two days to avoid washing up. He held the cup to his mouth and inhaled deeply through his nostrils, savouring both the tang of the alcohol and the specific, smoky smell that still crept into his dreams from time to time.

But Leipfold didn't drink anymore, not since the accident. He just liked to savour the smell. Maile had asked him about it once, and he'd told her, "Eighty percent of what we taste is derived from our sense of smell. That's why vegetarians sometimes like the smell of meat and why ex-smokers struggle to keep their shit together if someone sparks one up beside them."

Leipfold sighed and poured the whiskey out of the cup and back into the bottle. He put the bottle in the drawer and locked it, then nipped out to the off-license on the corner. He was back in eight minutes—a respectable time, but still as long as it took him to finish a crossword—with a bagful of non-alcoholic lager. It was a vice, and he knew it. He set himself a reminder to take the cans out before the morning and to tidy the place up so that Maile didn't know he was sleeping there.

Then he popped one of the cans and took a long, deep chug from it. He had another and another, followed by a third and then a fourth. He'd bought six of the things from the corner shop, but he found himself nipping out to get six more before they closed for the night.

"It's psychological," he murmured as he cracked open his fifth and started to swig from it. He took an A3 sketch pad and attached it to a wooden easel, then started hunting around for his marker pens. "Purely psychological."

He'd been telling himself the same thing for the last four years. Mrs.

Bachman, the woman who ran the weekly meetings, told him that if you replaced one fix with another, you were still an addict. But then, she'd hardly touched a drop in her life, even after losing her husband to the bottle and becoming a widow nine days before her fortieth birthday. Leipfold didn't trust her. If he'd replaced a crippled life behind the bottle with the occasional binge on non-alcoholic lager, he didn't see the issue.

Besides, Leipfold had a problem to solve. He had to find a serial killer in a city of nine million people with just his wits, his markers and a computer-literate assistant who carried pepper spray and wore too much eyeliner.

He had his work cut out for him.

* * *

Leipfold worked flat out until 6:28AM, then fell asleep at his desk with a marker pen in his hand. He woke up a couple of hours later with a big, black smudge on his forehead and his saliva forming little pools in the bottom of his keyboard. He lifted up his head, warily at first but with growing confidence, then nipped to the bathroom to freshen himself up.

Maile was already at her desk when he returned.

"Put the kettle on," Leipfold said. His voice shook a little and he needed to cough a couple times, but he didn't sound like a man who'd barely slept the night before.

"Check your desk, boss," she replied, so Leipfold did. He found a plain, brown bag, propped up against his monitor. He opened it up and pulled out a breakfast bagel with ham and cheese, as well as a posh packet of crisps, two napkins, an unnecessary spork and a cup of coffee in a cardboard cup, which looked like it had started to leak. A little grease had leaked through the bag and onto the screen. Leipfold attacked it with the napkin, then removed the coffee and the bagel and threw the bag into the bin. He unwrapped the bagel, took a deep, satisfying bite from it and started chewing. He smiled.

"God, you're good," he said. He took another couple of bites and then looked up, arched an eyebrow and asked, "What are you after?"

"Nothing," Maile protested.

"A likely story," Leipfold replied. Maile worked in silence while he finished the bagel and swilled some coffee around his mouth. He sighed and sat back, letting his stomach relax. It had felt like a rubber band with a knot in it since a quarter to ten the night before. Medication hadn't worked, but the bagel did.

Leipfold stared at Maile for a couple of seconds as she bashed away at her keyboard. He drummed his fingers absentmindedly and then looked up at the gibberish he'd created. A couple of the keys were sticking together, and the jumble of words was interspersed with random characters and, for some reason, the number three. He tested it out, trying to type a Shakespeare quote he'd been forced to memorise in secondary school, but no dice. His keyboard was on the fritz, and he doubted the warranty covered accidental drooling.

"Hmm," he murmured. "Bloody technology."

Maile laughed and Leipfold turned to look at her. "Seriously," he said. "You're after something."

She smiled without looking away from her monitor, tapped out the rest of her sentence and then saved the blog post she was working on about the benefits of hiring a private detective. She turned to look at Leipfold.

"You're right, I am. I want to leave early again. Not *that* early," she continued. "Relax. Let me leave at five and make the time up tomorrow if I have to."

"Fine," he said. "Take it. But first, I want to know where you're going. What if I need to get hold of you?"

"You can use my mobile," she said. "I'm not going to flee the country, if that's what you're thinking."

"That wasn't what I was thinking," Leipfold said. "And I'm not worried that you can't look after yourself, either."

"Good. You're not my father."

"Or your mother," Leipfold said. "Truth is, it doesn't hurt to get a second point of view. Some of your contributions to the business…well, I don't know how I'd cope without you."

"You'd cope," Maile said. "You'd find a way."

"Probably," Leipfold replied. "But it wouldn't be as much fun. Look, I just want to be able to get hold of you if I need you."

"I'll have my phone," Maile said. "Just text me in case I can't answer it. I'm going on a date."

"A date?" Leipfold repeated, thoughtfully. He summoned up everything he knew about her, from her eclectic taste in music to her English inner-city tan, the makeup she wore, the books she read and the shows she watched. Underneath the freak show, she was a good-looking girl. But she was also Maile O'Hara. "Doesn't sound like you," he said, at last.

"It doesn't," Maile agreed. "And let's keep it that way. I hate talking about stuff like that. It doesn't suit me."

"Fine," Leipfold said. "Want to talk about work?"

"Sure."

"Good," he said. "Do me a favour, Maile. Nip out to the shops for me. I need a new keyboard for my computer."

* * *

Maile headed straight back to the office after grabbing Leipfold a keyboard from the closest computer shop, but she didn't stay there for long. She'd already picked up a lead on her mobile, and it was telling her to hop on the 170 bus from Victoria and to ride it all of the way south to Roehampton, a little shitheap of a suburb that looked like what Putney might have looked like if the Germans had won the second world war.

It took over an hour to get there. She fell asleep in Hammersmith and woke up in Roehampton at the end of the line when the dour-faced driver nudged her with his foot and told her he needed to leave so he could lock up and smoke a cigarette. She climbed to her feet, disoriented, then disembarked the bus and checked the maps on her phone to find out where she needed to go. She was looking for a place called Hersham Close where a swell of terraced housing overlooked a basketball court with no hoops in it. When Maile arrived, she saw five kids smoking weed outside the entrance. They heckled her as she walked past, but she flipped them the finger and walked on, her right hand gripping the pepper spray in her handbag.

@LukasWh1te, the person she wanted to speak to, lived at number ninety-three. As far as the internet was concerned, his father was a ghost, and the only information she'd been able to dig up on his mother—who sounded like a mean-spirited, evil bitch queen—had come from @LukasWh1te's alias, @SnekBoi14.

It was the mother who answered the door, a raven-haired woman who could have been anywhere between thirty-five and fifty depending upon how many cigarettes she smoked. Maile told her who she was and what she wanted, and the woman turned around and shouted "Luke!" over her shoulder. "There's someone at the door."

Maile waited for the woman to either invite her inside or to slam the door in her face, which was what she was used to after four months of working with Leipfold. But Michelle White just folded her muscular arms, glared at Maile and waited.

Then her son came to the door. After swapping a few words with his mother, he took her place and adopted her posture. Maile didn't like the look in his eye, the half-stoned lazy eye that teenage boys used to look at teenage girls or fuckable moms with their 32DDs.

Lukas White looked like a male, albino Maile. His paper-white hair was more Donald Trump than Draco Malfoy, and more Boris Johnson than either. Not bad for a fourteen-year-old.

He was a thin, scrawny kid with a cheeky smile and a debatable taste in fashion. Maile detected a hint of aftershave, probably stolen from his father or his grandfather. He grinned, nervously.

"Can I help you?" he asked.

Maile smiled right back at him, hoping the cut of her dress and a glimpse of her pearly whites would be enough to bring him on to her side. "Perhaps you can," she said. "I wanted to ask you about something that you posted online the other night."

"Oh, *that*," Lukas said, cringing a little and checking over his shoulder to see if his mother was still there. "That was a joke, that's all. I'm not actually going to kill him."

"Huh," Maile murmured. She looked him up and down again. "I

think we got our wires crossed."

Lukas White looked balefully across at her and said, "I think you'd better come in."

Mrs. White kept an immaculate house, and Maile felt a little jealous of Lukas when he led her into the living room, through the kitchen and into a small conservatory overlooking a well-kept back garden where he said they were less likely to be interrupted. Maile had grown up in a cramped council flat, and the White house, while not quite presidential, certainly had an air of comfort and cosiness. It was nicer than the place she'd grown up in, and it was also nicer than the place she shared with Kat, although admittedly with a longer commute into the centre of the city.

Lukas waited for her to sink into one of the wicker sofas, then shouted something at his mother before locking the door to the conservatory and sitting opposite her in an armchair.

"Sorry about that," he said. "I'm not always nice on the internet. I thought you were here about something else."

"Man," Maile said, "you're way too young for this shit. What did you do?"

"I got fragged," he explained. "By some rookie called Mailstrom13 who had a lucky shot and got cocky. So I tracked down her profile and told her I knew where she lived. Said I was going to find her and kill her for real."

Maile laughed. "That's it?" she asked.

"That's it."

She laughed again. "Yeah, no," she said. "That's not what I'm here for. Listen closely, kid. Did you post a photo of a body? More specifically, the body of a black guy with blood all over him? A body in the lobby of the YMCA?"

"Oh shit," Lukas said. "You mean *that*. Yeah, you got me. That was me."

"I thought so," Maile replied. "Okay, next question. Where did you get the photo? Did you take it? And why did you post it?"

"That's three questions," Lukas said. He smiled thinly and ran a pale hand through his hair. "But what the hell? I didn't take it. I've never even been to the place."

"So how did you get hold of the photo?"

"Some weirdo sent it to me," Lukas replied. "The guy stopped me on the street and gave me twenty pounds to post it."

"How did he send it to you?"

"He attached it to an email," the kid said. "But don't waste your time trying to track it down. He sent it through some proxy in the Netherlands. I already looked into it. The whole thing seemed off somehow. I got curious."

"And yet you still did as he asked," Maile said. The kid nodded his head, so slowly that it looked like he was afraid it might fall off. "Interesting. What did he look like?"

Lukas White exhaled slowly. "That's a tough one," he said. "I mean, it's hard to say. I didn't get a good look at him."

"You talked to him long enough to give him your email address," Maile reminded him.

"Yeah," Lukas replied. "And I didn't look at him. He was definitely a guy, though. Maybe in his thirties or early forties. He had a black suit on with a white shirt."

"Was he wearing a tie?"

"No," Lukas said. "Does it matter?"

"No," Maile replied. "What else can you tell me?"

"Not much," Lukas admitted. "Just that he was forgettable. Average height, average build, that sort of thing."

Maile paused for a moment and then smiled as an idea hit her like a self-driving car with a manual override. "You got a tablet?" she asked.

"Yeah," he replied. "Why?"

"Bring it here," Maile said. "We're going to need it. I've got an idea."

Chapter Eight:
The Cassette Tape

IT WAS THE FOLLOWING DAY, and Maile and Leipfold were back in the office. They'd already finished off the crossword. Leipfold swore that Alan Phelps, *The Tribune's* compiler, was losing his touch. And with nothing more pressing to keep them busy, it didn't take long for the conversation to turn towards the investigation.

"This is the first proper break we've had since we cracked the Thompson case," Maile said.

"Yeah," Leipfold agreed. "I'm not sure if that's a good thing or a bad thing. We could always use more work. More money would be even better."

Maile nodded, but she didn't smile. "Boss," she said, hesitantly. "If you're worried about money, why take on cases like the Thompson case? And why bother investigating Jayne Lipton and Abu Adewali?"

"I like the challenge," Leipfold replied.

"Yeah," Maile said. "And I bet the publicity helps, too."

Leipfold snorted into his bowl of porridge, choked a little on the mush in his mouth and sprayed oats across his brand-new keyboard. Then he pulled himself together and said, "Speaking of Adewali, what's the latest? Did you follow up the lead with the kid who took the photo of the body?"

"I did," Maile replied. "And get this. He didn't take the photo. He says a stranger paid him to post it, and I believe him."

"Did he get a good look at the stranger?"

"Not really," Maile admitted. "But he did have an iPad, which meant I could get him to make a decent composition. Check this out."

She beckoned Leipfold over as she pulled up an image on the screen. It showed a man with a slight stubble and short, cropped hair, two narrow eyes and a nose that might once have been broken. The face looked familiar and yet anonymous, like the faces of the shelf stackers at a supermarket. It left Leipfold feeling ambivalent, like he was looking at an old friend in the face of a man he'd never met.

"Ugly bloke, isn't he?" Leipfold said.

"I'm sure he has a lovely personality," Maile replied. "Do you think this guy's the killer? It'd make sense. Bribe the kid to take the heat away."

Leipfold shook his head. "Whoever is behind this, they're smarter than that," he said. "They knew that the kid would be tracked down eventually. If they were smart, which I'm pretty sure they were, they would've paid a guy to pay a guy to pay a guy to pay a guy to pay the kid. We'll never track them down."

"We could try," Maile said.

"*You* can try," Leipfold replied. "I've got other things to do. If you can fit it around the rest of your work, go ahead."

"And what are you going to do?"

"I'm going to do what I do best," Leipfold replied. "I'm going to follow my nose, dig up a little dirt and sell my soul to pay the rent. Like you said, if I'm worried about money, why bother investigating Abu Adewali?"

"That's not what I—"

"I know," Leipfold said. "Don't worry, I'm still investigating. But in the meantime, we have a business to run."

* * *

Maile and Leipfold spent the rest of the morning running the business, but their plan for the afternoon took a back seat at around 1:35PM, when Maile spotted the news and relayed it back to Leipfold.

"Boss," she said, "you need to look at this."

Leipfold was on the phone to his accountant, a man called Postlethwaite who'd somehow held the company together and was finally facing the prospect of a bonus after three or four years in the financial equivalent of Dante's second circle. Maile waited patiently for him to finish the call. He hung up and looked across at her.

"What?" he said.

"You need to go online," Maile said. "*The Tribune* pushed out an article. You need to read it."

"Why?" Leipfold asked.

"Because it's an interview with a man who claims he killed Jayne Lipton and Abu Adewali."

Leipfold swore softly under his breath and raced over to Maile's desk. She had the article up on her screen, and Leipfold leaned over her to take her mouse and to scroll slowly through it.

The piece in *The Tribune* was an "exclusive interview" with a man who claimed to have killed Jayne Lipton and Abu Adewali. Whether genuine or not, the paper seemed to have nailed most of the details, and Leipfold suspected that if their killer interview was a fake, they must have had someone on the inside of the investigation. It even mentioned the mutilated genitals and breasts.

Leipfold read through the piece for a second time, then rushed back over to his desk to grab the backup phone, his own personal hotline to Jack Cholmondeley. He didn't answer, even after Leipfold redialled and redialled, signalling that the call was an emergency. Leipfold suspected that he already knew about the coverage and that he was busy following up with it. He left the phone on the desk beside him and continued to redial periodically while pulling up the coverage on his own machine.

"Maile," he barked, "I need a favour. Work a little bit of your magic and see what you can find out. Track down the journalist and get me a meeting. Then find out everything you can about their career to date and try to find a link back to Lipton and Adewali."

"Sure thing," Maile said. "What are you going to do?"

"I'm going to reread the article," Leipfold said. "And then I'm going to think."

* * *

Leipfold was worried. The article in *The Tribune* was disturbingly accurate, and it had set his mind racing with possibilities. He remembered the strange case of Wallace Souza, the Brazilian crime show host who'd been accused of hiring hitmen to kill people so his crew could be the first on the scene. But he doubted that *The Tribune* was following in Souza's footsteps. They just didn't have the brains or the initiative.

According to the article, a parcel was delivered to the paper's offices in Clapham. It had arrived by courier, like the delivery to the police office, and the driver was wearing leathers and a visor. *The Tribune* explained how a visitor had stumbled across the parcel, which had been left on the pavement outside the entrance, and handed it in at reception.

Leipfold continued to read through the article, noting that it was three times the normal length. There was a lot for *The Tribune* to cover. According to the paper, the parcel contained a cassette tape, a small, handwritten note and some chunks of human flesh, which were described as "both unconvincingly artificial and horribly, brutally real."

But it was the tape that most interested Leipfold. The team at *The Tribune* had unearthed an old cassette player to listen to what was on it. They'd described the voice as "sounding like an ominous, computerised madman, like a cross between Stephen Hawking and Charles Manson." And they explained the killer's most shocking claim yet: that there was another victim and that the trophy he gave to *The Tribune* was the proof of that. The newspaper said that the police had been notified and had been given the gory package to take it away for analysis.

And right there, at the top of the article, was the most stunning thing of all. Just a single reference, but that was all it took. The tape had been leaked, which meant that the audio was out there somewhere in the ether. He got Maile to find him a link and less than ten minutes later, thanks to the magic of the internet and Leipfold's slow but reliable broadband connection, he was able to listen to the killer's tape from the comfort of his office.

It crossed his mind that so could the rest of the city and that there'd be panic on the streets before long unless the cops made an arrest. And whether he liked it or not, Leipfold knew he was just as involved in the investigation as Jack Cholmondeley, Gary Mogford and the others. So Leipfold asked Maile to work her magic on the audio.

"The voice is distorted," Leipfold said, "but the words are clear enough. I want you to find out what you can about the recording. When it was recorded, what it was recorded with, that sort of thing. See if you can find out what they used to modify their voice. If we can figure that out, maybe we can reverse the changes and get some cleaner audio."

Maile grinned. "Good plan," she said. "You're learning. I've got a couple of other ideas as well. But there's a bit of a problem."

"What is it?" Leipfold asked.

"I'll need the original tape for the best results. I'll do what I can with *The Tribune*'s mp3, but if you can get me the cassette, I'll be able to dig a little deeper."

"I'll do what I can," Leipfold said. "In the meantime, get cracking on the rest of the research."

Maile grinned and offered up a mock salute. Then her expression altered and morphed into something a little more serious.

"I can't work late tonight," she announced. "I would if I could, but I can't. I hope you weren't relying on me being here all night."

Leipfold, who hadn't been relying on it but who was hoping for a bit of company, looked across at her. "Why's that?" he asked.

"I'm meeting someone," Maile said.

Leipfold grinned. "Another date?" he asked. "Is this with the same guy or are you meeting up with somebody different?"

"No comment," Maile said.

"Where are you even meeting these guys?"

"Ask me no questions, I'll tell you no lies," Maile replied. "Like I said before, boss, I don't like talking about this kind of stuff."

"Fair enough," he said.

An uncomfortable silence descended upon the two of them, but Leipfold didn't notice. He was busy click-clacking away at his new computer keyboard. Maile scowled at him.

"Fine," she said. "If it's gossip you want, we'll gossip about it. But not today."

"Why not?" Leipfold asked.

"Because we've got work to do."

Chapter Nine:
The Tower Hill Terror

MAILE WAS ALREADY AT HER DESK when Leipfold walked through the door. He was carrying two heavy shopping bags full of fresh supplies for the office, and Maile rushed over to help him.

"That one's from the stationery aisle," Leipfold said by way of greeting. "I've got the fresh stuff."

"Of course," Maile replied. She stashed the stationery away in a little cupboard beneath the office's tiny printer before picking up the report she'd been working on and handing it to the boss.

"What's this?" he asked.

"It's the information you asked for about *The Tribune*," Maile explained. "Including a contact number and an email address. The journalist you're looking for is called Siobhan Dent. Looks like she's got some pedigree. She worked for a major tabloid before joining *The Tribune*. Said she wanted a job she could be proud of."

"And so she moved to *The Tribune*?" Leipfold scoffed.

"Hey, there are worse places to work," Maile said. "Do you want me to get in touch with her?"

"No," Leipfold said. "I'll do it. Go grab me a coffee while I make the call."

Maile sighed but did as he asked of her. While she was waiting for the kettle to boil, Leipfold leaned back on his chair and put his feet up on the desk. He kept his desk tidy, but it wasn't clean. The surface was stained with old tea and the grease from a decade of takeaways. He stared moodily into the distance for a moment and then put a call in to Siobhan Dent at *The Tribune*. Leipfold was in luck.

"Sure," she said. "I could meet you for a coffee or two. I've heard about you, Mr. Leipfold. I'd like to have a chat with you myself. Perhaps we could talk about some of your investigations. I'm sure our readers would like to hear some of your stories."

"There'll be time for that later," Leipfold said. "Right now, I'm hoping you might be able to help me with an active investigation."

There was a pause on the other end of the line. Then Siobhan said, "A tenner says I know what this is about. You want to speak to me about the Tower Hill Terror."

"The what?" Leipfold asked.

"The Tower Hill Terror," the journalist repeated. "Every serial killer needs a nickname. That's what we've started to call him."

"Why are you making up names for him?" Leipfold asked. "You're just going to spread more panic. Fear of a name increases the fear of a thing itself. Did you never read Harry Potter?"

"Panic sells papers," Siobhan replied. "It's sad but it's true."

"And the name? The Tower Hill Terror?"

"It's the closest tube station to the second murder scene."

"Why didn't you use the first?"

"The Euston Terror doesn't sound as good. But enough about that. Where would you like to meet?"

* * *

Siobhan Dent agreed to meet Leipfold in an East End coffee shop, explaining that she had a couple of other people to meet that afternoon and so she couldn't stick around for long.

With Maile behind at the office, catching up with some of the research on their other clients, Leipfold donned his leathers, hopped on Camilla and wound his way through the streets towards the coffee shop. He parked Camilla a couple of streets away and paid the minimum fee on the ticket machine. He had just enough change to pay for an hour.

He could see Siobhan through the wide bay windows of the coffee shop. Leipfold had never met her before, but Maile had tracked down some photographs and he'd committed her face to memory before leaving. When Leipfold met her in person, he decided that the photographs didn't do her justice. She was a striking woman.

Siobhan was a grungy blonde with long hair down to her waist, a pretty face with a light touch of makeup and two piercings on the skin above her lips. She was wearing skinny jeans and a black top with a band's logo blazing its way across the front of it and, like Maile, she had the tip of a tattoo poking out of her shirt on one shoulder.

"You must be James Leipfold," she said as he entered the cafeteria and made a beeline for her. "You look just how I'd imagined."

Leipfold shrugged. He was still in his leathers and had the bike helmet tucked under one of his arms. She stood up as he walked over to the table and put his helmet down, then grabbed a notebook and a pen from his back pocket. They shook hands and then sat down. Siobhan caught the eye of one of the waiters and ordered a drink, then took her phone from her pocket, placed it on the table and booted up one of her most-used applications.

"I hope you don't mind," she said, apologetically. "I'd like to record our conversation if that's okay with you. I probably won't use it, and it won't go online without your prior approval, but I make a habit of recording my meetings."

"I don't mind," Leipfold replied. "As long as you don't mind me doing the same." He pulled out his own phone and laid it down beside hers. The journalist had a bland, transparent cover, while Leipfold's case was decorated with camo and built for ruggedness and endurance. He smiled and supposed that they reflected their personalities.

Leipfold started recording on his phone and said, "Tell me about the tape. The one you received from the Tower Hill Terror."

"What do you want to know?"

"Anything you can tell me that you didn't mention in the paper," Leipfold said.

"You really think I would have missed a detail?" Siobhan scoffed. "We published *everything*, and I mean that. Murders help to sell papers."

Leipfold grinned and bit his tongue to stop himself from saying something that he might regret. Instead, he asked, "Do you still have the tape? I might be able to get some information from it."

"I don't," she said. "But we took a couple of copies. I could get hold of one."

"That'd be grand," Leipfold said. "How quickly can you get hold of it?"

"I'll have someone drop it off at your office tomorrow morning."

"I owe you one," Leipfold said. "One final thing. Can you remember anything about the courier who delivered the package?"

Siobhan frowned and cast her mind back. "He was dressed a little bit like you are," she said. "Wearing leathers and a helmet. There was a smiley face on his helmet and some sort of logo on the jacket. FunRunz. Or something like that."

Leipfold smiled appreciatively. "Perfect," he said. "Thanks so much, Siobhan. How can I ever repay you?"

The journalist smiled, grabbed her notebook and pen and checked that her phone was still recording.

"Well," she said, "there is one thing. How about we switch things up and you answer a couple of questions for me?"

* * *

Leipfold was in a sour mood the following morning. His meeting with Siobhan Dent had dragged on for longer than either of them had expected, and Camilla had been ticketed by the time he got back to her. For her part, the journalist had to cancel one meeting and reschedule another.

But his mood started to pick up once Maile arrived, and when a courier dropped off a package from *The Tribune* as the clock chimed eleven, it got even better. Leipfold signed for the package, then stared at the delivery man as he made his way out of the building and back across to his bike. The courier was dressed head to toe in motorcycle leathers, a forcible reminder of the case. Leipfold thought about chasing the courier down, but he managed to stop himself before he caused a scene. He reminded himself that it had been a cold February, one of the coldest that he remembered, and that it was hardly unusual for couriers to wear their leathers. There must have been at least a thousand of them working across the city, and maybe more.

Leipfold took the box over to his desk, pulled his letter opener from the drawer and slit open the flaps, then reached inside and pulled out the contents from a sea of packing peanuts. It was a single cassette tape inside a plastic case and a handwritten note that read *I hope this helps!*

"Check this out," Leipfold said, holding the cassette up in his hands so that Maile could see it. "Looks like my new friend at *The Tribune* came through for me."

"Awesome!" Maile replied. "What is it?"

"It's the tape that the press received from the killer. Not the original, of course, because the police have that, but it is a true copy, not like the rubbish they put up on the website. I want you to digitise this thing and find out what you can."

"Will do," Maile said. "It's all about quality. The more accurate the conversion, the more likely it is that I'll be able to figure out what software was used to create it."

"Then get on with it," Leipfold said.

So she did, and they worked on in silence for an hour or so, the stillness of the office broken only by the recording as Maile tinkered with it.

At last, she whistled softly and said, "Looks like whoever made the recording knew exactly what they were doing."

"How so?" Leipfold asked.

"They double encoded it," Maile said. "If I'm right—and I'm pretty sure I am—they recorded their voice onto a cassette tape, digitised the recording, applied the vocoder—"

"The what?"

"Software to change the voice," Maile explained. "I need to figure out what was used if we want to reverse engineer it and get a glimpse of the original audio. After they applied the vocoder, they converted the digital audio back into analogue by playing it back and re-recording it on the cassette. Then that cassette was duplicated by your journalist friend, which further distorted the signal."

"Sounds complicated," Leipfold said.

Maile shrugged. "It is. But that's why you hired me, right?"

Leipfold grunted.

"If it helps," Maile continued, "we're dealing with a professional. Someone's put a lot of thought into how to make decoding this audio more difficult."

"It helps," Leipfold said. "So what's next?"

Maile whistled softly and checked the file she'd been working on. "Tough one," she said. "I'll start asking around and downloading a few trials so we can get a decent comparison. It's a long shot, and I don't think we're likely to find anything. But a long shot is still a shot."

Leipfold nodded. "Then what are you waiting for?" he asked. "Get to it."

* * *

While Maile was working on the recording, Leipfold suited up and hopped onto Camilla. She was running low on fuel, so he stopped off at Sainsbury's to fill up before riding on to Dulwich, where FunRunz was based.

Leipfold did a double take when his GPS said he'd arrived. He was standing in the middle of a housing estate, a grey place with grey pavements, grey buildings and grey-faced youths skipping school to smoke cigarettes. It wasn't the kind of place where you'd expect to find a business. It wasn't even a place where you'd want to leave a motorbike, but if the courier felt safe then that would have to be good enough for Leipfold. He found a place to park Camilla and triple-checked he'd locked her securely. Then he looked up and down the street to find the right number.

He spotted a FunRunz sign outside number sixty-five, just six doors down from number fifty-three, where Camilla was parked. The company's logo, the silhouette of a motorbike inside a yellow circle, was emblazoned across a large, aluminium board beneath an arrow directing visitors down the side of what would otherwise have looked like a normal house. The FunRunz office was tucked away to the side of it, through a cast-iron gate and a side door and into a room that looked suspiciously like a conservatory but which was touted as an office.

Leipfold knocked on the door.

It was opened by a tall, broad-shouldered man with clean white teeth and a charismatic smile. He was dressed in his leathers, except for his jacket, which was draped across the back of a chair. He was wearing a vest top, and his long arms hung down beside his tight stomach. Leipfold thought he could've used a shave, but he supposed that the man spent most of his time with the visor down.

He introduced himself as Asif Shaktar and offered Leipfold a seat. "How can I help you?" he asked.

Leipfold took the seat and explained who he was and what he wanted. Shaktar, meanwhile, told Leipfold a little bit about the business.

"I run things around here," he explained. "From taking the calls to making the drop-offs. The pay is good, but the hours suck."

"Excellent," Leipfold said. "Then you might be able to help me. I'm looking for one of your customers."

"Clients," Shaktar replied. "I call them 'clients.' And I'm sorry, I can't help you. I keep a tight ship. Client confidentiality and all that."

Leipfold reached into his pocket and pulled his wallet out. He scrabbled around inside it and found a couple of notes. He took them out and held them up while he slipped his wallet back into his pocket.

"You sure?" Leipfold asked. "It'd be better to talk to me than to wait until you hear from the police."

"The police?" Shaktar's brow furrowed. He sighed and crossed his meaty arms. "What do you want to know?"

"Do you remember delivering a package to *The Tribune*?" Leipfold asked.

"Yes."

"Good," Leipfold said. "I need to know who sent it."

Shaktar frowned. Then he sidled over to his desk and sat down in front of his computer. "I don't know," he said.

"You mean you're not going to tell me?"

"No," Shaktar insisted. "I can't. The guy paid extra for my silence, cash in hand. I didn't take down his details."

"But you must have met him."

"Not really," the courier said. "I only did a couple of runs for him. He used one of those voice-changer gadgets and insisted on leaving his parcels at the end of my drive and dropping me a call when he was ready for me to collect. Only, there was one time…"

Leipfold leaned forward in his seat. "Go on," he said.

"One time he came round while I was making a sandwich. I thought I heard a noise from outside and went to check it out. There was no one there, of course, but there was a package all right."

"And?" Leipfold prompted.

Shaktar shrugged. "I thought I saw the back of his head, just turning round the corner at the end of the road. I couldn't tell you much, though. He just looked…"

"Normal?" Leipfold supplied. "Average height, average build, probably somewhere in his thirties?"

"How did you know?" Shaktar said.

* * *

Leipfold got back to the office after darkness fell, and when he opened the office door, he almost blindsided his assistant. Maile had been on the other side of it, presumably getting ready to leave the place, and Leipfold's arrival made her jump and spill the contents of her handbag. He caught her pepper spray before it had a chance to hit the floor.

"You might want this," he said, handing it back to her.

"Thanks," she said, grabbing the canister and stashing it in its usual place in the pouch at the top of her handbag. "Can't hang around tonight, I'm afraid."

Leipfold smiled. "Another date?" he asked.

"Hell no," Maile replied. "I'm meeting Kat for a drink."

"Ah," Leipfold murmured. "A lady date. Give her my regards." He took his jacket off and hung it on the back of the door, then wandered over to the kitchen to turn the kettle on. "It's a shame," he shouted, as the kettle started to heat itself up and to spout a little steam. "I thought you might want to talk about the case."

Maile had finished packing her bag up and was on her feet, pulling her coat on. But at Leipfold's remark, she sat back down again. "Go on," she said.

And so Leipfold brought her up to speed and told her about his meeting with Asif Shaktar, the man from FunRunz. When he told her what he'd said about his brief glimpse of the mysterious visitor, her eyes widened.

"Average height and average weight?" she asked. "Could be the same guy that Lukas White described."

"Yeah," Leipfold said, "or any of a million others in the city. It's a long shot."

"A shot worth taking, though." Maile paused for a moment, then stared thoughtfully at her blank computer screen. "Hmm," she said. "I've got an idea."

Leipfold grinned and scootched over to her desk, rolling across the ugly wooden floor on his computer chair. "What is it?" he asked.

Maile grabbed her tablet from its resting place in her bag, a foam pocket with a cork lining to fully protect it from the elements. Her long, slender fingers with their messed-up cuticles marched across the screen and summoned up her photos. She tapped on one of them, a screenshot, and brought it up on the screen.

"Check this out," Maile said, handing the tablet over to Leipfold. "It's the composite I made when I spoke to Lukas. Notice anything?"

"Yeah," Leipfold said. "I do. He's got short black hair and he's an average height and weight."

"You reckon this is the man we're looking for?" she asked.

"Maybe," Leipfold replied. "Whoever he is, I'd like to talk to him."

"So what are we going to do?"

Leipfold shrugged. "You're going to go and meet Kat," he said. "And I'm going to stay at the office. Send me that photo before you go."

"What are you going to do with it?"

"I'm going to send it to Siobhan Dent," Leipfold replied. "The journalist at *The Tribune*. She's going to want to see it."

Chapter Ten
Meeting Marc Allman

A LAZY SUN ROSE and cast its grey light across London, and Leipfold climbed out of bed shortly afterwards. It was a Sunday, which was theoretically his day off, but that was no excuse for a long lie in. James Leipfold was many things, but undisciplined wasn't one of them. He'd had routine and efficiency drummed into him back in the army. Even when he was hitting the bottle at his hardest, he still did the same old shit. He just did it while drunk.

Leipfold lived in a tiny box flat about a mile away from the office. The place was so cramped that every square foot was accounted for, with a well-worn path from the door to the bed, the wardrobe and the bookcase. Other than the books, there were no signs of occupation, and the place looked more like a sterile room at a small hotel than the regular haunt of a private detective. But Leipfold didn't care. The less time he spent there, the better.

He brushed his teeth in the bathroom, then returned to his room for long enough to stash his toothbrush and to grab his jacket. He checked he had his keys, his phone and his wallet, then left the tiny room behind and made his way outside. February was drawing slowly but inevitably to an end. While it was still too cold to dust off summer clothes, there was at least a hint of the impending spring.

Leipfold stopped off at the corner shop to grab a pint of milk and the day's papers, then ambled slowly towards the office, meandering up and down the side streets with no real purpose other than to burn some time while he thought things through. But he couldn't meander forever.

By the time that he made it to his desk, he'd worked up an appetite. Luckily, he had a secret stash of instant noodles for when he spent the night in the office and needed something to keep him going, so he nuked a bowl in the microwave, popped the kettle on and settled into his usual routine.

Halfway through the bowl of noodles, he paused with the spoon still in his hand and smiled appreciatively as he read Siobhan Dent's latest article. She'd included the picture he'd sent to her, the composite sketch that Maile and Lukas had made. The article included Leipfold's office number and his web address, and he'd seen the emails piling up in his inbox when he checked his phone in the morning. But better than that, it was also another piece of publicity. In practical terms, it was the next month's rent.

He finished flicking through the paper and turned his attention to his emails, moving the most promising leads into a separate folder so he could follow them up in the afternoon. Then he went back to the paper, flicking through to the crossword and loading up the timer on his phone.

He was six minutes in when he was interrupted by the buzzer. He scowled, paused the timer and raced over to the intercom, which he grabbed from its holder and held up to his ear. "Hello?" he barked.

"Mr. Leipfold." The voice on the other end of the line sounded authoritative but beaten, like a man who'd grown used to power and then lost it and was ready to go gently into that good night. Leipfold had to strain his ears to hear him, as usual. The traffic filtered down the alley from the main road and made its way through the condenser mic at a level so loud it sounded like his visitor was standing in the middle of the street. "I want to talk to you."

"I'm sure you do," Leipfold replied. "Everyone does, these days. Who are you and what do you want?"

"My name's Marc Allman," his visitor said. "Please, let me in. I need to talk to you."

"Why?"

There was a pause that accentuated the sound of the traffic. Allman said something softly that Leipfold didn't catch. He asked Allman to repeat it.

"Damn it," Allman replied. "I said, 'You put my face in the bloody newspaper.'"

Leipfold buzzed him in.

* * *

Leipfold greeted Allman at the door and offered him a seat in the reception area. He didn't offer him a drink.

Marc Allman was a nondescript white guy in his early thirties. He had short, black hair and a slight stubble, with deep blue eyes that held no life in them. He had been wearing sunglasses, despite the grey glaze of a muggy February, but he removed them when he entered the office and stashed them away in a pocket. He carried himself confidently, but one shoulder was slumped as though he'd recently suffered an injury. His shirt was white but his trousers were black, as was his jacket. Allman looked like he'd stopped by the place on his way to a major awards ceremony, and he smelled slightly of peppermint and aftershave.

Leipfold looked him over and made a couple of early deductions before sitting down beside him. Allman stared at him and said nothing, waiting for Leipfold to speak. He was using the same trick that Leipfold often used on his suspects. Silence was a powerful tool, a way to force people to talk out of sheer pig-headedness, taking advantage of their primal need to avoid embarrassment. And to Leipfold's chagrin, it worked on him.

"You know, it's funny," he said. "You really do have a bland appearance."

Marc Allman said nothing.

"Apart from the suit, that is. You don't look much like the mock-up."

"Are you kidding?" Allman scoffed. "It's the bloody spitting image of me."

"I know," Leipfold said. "I just wanted to see if I could get you to talk."

"Well done," Allman replied. "I saw the piece in the paper, Mr. Leipfold. What the hell do you think you're playing at?"

"What?" Leipfold said, innocently. "It only said you were a person of interest. It's not like I accused you of being The Tower Hill Terror. Got a guilty conscience?"

"No, I haven't." Allman frowned and ran a hand through his hair. "Listen, if you throw enough mud, it sticks. I haven't done anything. Honestly, I'm in the dark about the whole thing. I mean, I heard about the murders, of course. But I had nothing to do with any of it. For all I know, I'm next."

"With any luck, there won't be a next," Leipfold said. "Perhaps you can tell me what you know about a kid called Lukas White. And a delivery guy called Asif Shaktar."

"Who?" Allman looked genuinely confused, and Leipfold even felt a little sorry for the guy.

Leipfold sighed and led Allman over to his computer. He tapped a few keys and clicked a few buttons, pulling up photos of the two men. There was a flash of recognition in the man's eyes.

"Ah," he said. "I think I know what this is all about. I recognise both of those men. The first one was the boy I paid to post a photo. And the second was the man I paid to make a delivery."

"Aha! So you admit it!"

"Of course," Allman replied. "But I didn't kill anyone."

"Then where in the hell did the photo come from?" Leipfold asked. "And what about the parcels?"

"That's easy. A guy paid me to do it."

"Did he now?" Leipfold asked. "Don't tell me. I bet I can guess what he looked like."

* * *

It was twenty minutes later and the office was in uproar. Leipfold had paused the conversation to make a cup of coffee, then asked Allman to help himself to ginger biscuits while he paid a visit to the little boy's room. While he was there, he put in a call to Jack Cholmondeley and then activated his voice recorder before heading back to his desk.

The cops arrived shortly afterwards, while Allman was still tucking into the ginger snaps. With the intercom fixed, Leipfold had buzzed them in without taking his eyes off his visitor, and Allman first knew about it when the telltale uniforms of the Metropolitan Police appeared in the doorway. Cholmondeley was leading the pack, and he'd brought Constable Yates along for the ride.

"Mogford and Groves are on their way," he explained when Leipfold led him into the office. "We don't want Mr. Allman to get any ideas about running away from us, do we?"

Allman leapt abruptly to his feet, his face a hot mess of rage and confusion. "What the hell?" he shouted. "Mr. Leipfold, what did you *do?*"

"I called the police, Mr. Allman," Leipfold said.

"But *why?*"

"You're a suspect in two murders," Leipfold reminded him. "Like it or not, it's my duty as a citizen to make sure that the police get to speak to you. But don't worry. If you're innocent, you'll be fine. Justice is a fine thing."

"Justice," Allman spat. "Hah!"

But he didn't get a chance to say much more because Mogford and Groves arrived and crashed the party. They told Allman they wanted to ask a few questions and that he could either go along to the station of his own free will or they'd arrest him there and then. He took the first option, and Groves led him out of the building with Mogford and Yates in tow.

"You coming, boss?" Mogford asked, pausing on the threshold to look back into Leipfold's office where the two men were still standing.

Cholmondeley shook his head. "You lot go on," he said. "I'll make my own way back."

Mogford scowled at his boss, but he beat a slow retreat at the heels of the other officers. When the rest of the cops had gone, Leipfold and Cholmondeley sat down in the reception area. They exchanged small talk and Leipfold gave Cholmondeley the name of a dozen dogs in the weekend derby. The old cop wrote the names dutifully down in his notebook and then abruptly clapped his hands and sat forward in his chair.

"Now then," he said. "Let's get down to business."

"What business would that be?"

"You scratch my back and I'll scratch yours," Cholmondeley said, forcing out a slim smile and trying not to meet Leipfold's eyes. "I've got some information."

"So have I," Leipfold said. "Let's hope it's not the same information."

"It won't be." Cholmondeley folded his arms and looked sternly at Leipfold. "It's police business. Don't let this get out to the press."

"I won't," Leipfold promised. "What is it?"

"Initial blood tests are back on the package that was delivered to *The Tribune*."

Leipfold jumped up from his seat, but Cholmondeley gestured impatiently for him to sit back down.

"There's more," Cholmondeley said. "I guess you want to know whose blood it was. Well, I can't tell you that. It's still early days, and we're waiting to hear back from forensics. They're running a DNA test, and it's going to take time to get results and to run it through the database. But we do know one thing."

"What's that?" Leipfold asked.

Cholmondeley shook his head. "The blood type," he said. "AB negative. It's not a match to either of the victims."

Leipfold paused and patted his pockets, hoping that his phone was still recording. Then he said, "So it belongs to someone else."

"That's about the size of it," Cholmondeley said. "And so far, we haven't got a lead on who."

* * *

The rest of the day passed slowly, and Leipfold relented in the early afternoon and headed aimlessly back home while the sun was still shining. He spent the evening in bed rereading *The Brothers Karamazov*.

The weather broke overnight. While Leipfold swore he remembered rain against his windows, the streets were dry in the morning and the clouds had cleared, allowing a mellow sun to shine down with the first, tentative promise of spring and summer. He left his room to use the shared shower, then picked up a change of clothes and hopped on

Camilla. She was running well, and Leipfold felt the thrill that never got old and leaned into the corners as he wound through the streets towards his office. It was therapeutic, like popping spots or taking a long, hot bath.

Maile was already there when he arrived, just finishing up a quick meeting with a client. Leipfold half-listened to the end of their conversation while catching up with his emails and eating a crumpet.

Their client left at a quarter to ten, and Maile paused to hit the bathroom and brew a quick cuppa before sitting back down at her machine. She took an early coffee break so she could kill a few people on the latest MMORPG. Leipfold wandered over five minutes after she logged in and watched, bemused, as she finished kitting out and preparing for combat.

"What are you doing?" he asked.

"Taking a break," she replied without looking away from the screen. "Gaming. You should try it sometime."

Leipfold laughed and leaned in closer to the screen. "What does Mailstrom13 mean?"

"It's my username," Maile replied. "Or one of them. It's what I'm called in the game."

Leipfold sighed and rubbed his chin. "I'll never understand how these things work."

"That's why you hired me," she reminded him. "And don't worry. I'm just blowing off a little steam. I'll get back to work in a minute."

"Do what you want," Leipfold said. "You worked for free for long enough to earn a break or two, and besides, I trust you."

He paused for a moment, and Maile grunted something as she squeezed the trigger and hit someone with a headshot.

"You know," Leipfold said, "you never told me about that dating app."

Maile grinned and continued her half of the conversation while chasing a half-orc warlord.

"There's not much to know," she said. "You sign up and post a couple of pictures. Then you start matching with other people and if you both like what you see, it makes an introduction."

Leipfold nodded thoughtfully but didn't say anything.

"Why?" Maile asked. "You thinking of signing up?"

"Not a chance," he replied. "I'm just not sure you should be meeting people online when there's a killer on the loose. I mean, how much do you really know about the people you're agreeing to meet?"

She shrugged. "We chat first," she said. "If they send me a dick pic, I delete 'em. It's worked pretty well so far. Besides, you don't need to worry about me."

"Why's that?" Leipfold asked.

Maile grinned and said, "Because if all else fails, there's the pepper spray. Trust me. I can look after myself."

* * *

Cholmondeley and Mogford had left the station for the day, but Constable Cohen didn't have that luxury. He didn't have much of a family to begin with, and he had to stay late to finish off some work on the case.

Marc Allman was still in the cells, but they could only hold him for twenty-four hours before charging him or releasing him back into the wild. With most of the team at home, turning Allman over and over in their heads in preparation to vote on a decision in the morning, that left Constable Cohen to put in the extra hours to transcribe the early interviews and prepare a report for the rest of the team.

And he had to do it all whilst simultaneously working the night shift on reception, but that evening wasn't destined to be a quiet one. Cohen usually kept himself sane by people-watching, and the station's reception was one of the best places to do it. He saw all sorts, from petty criminals, drug dealers, drunks and bums to sex offenders, lawyers, worried parents and good, old-fashioned members of the public. The reception staff had started playing Bing Who?, a combination of bingo and Guess Who?, where the first person to get a full house of different demographics got to leave a half hour early. That was one reason why Cohen was keeping an eye out. The other reason was that it was his job, and because Detective Inspector Jack Cholmondeley had privately briefed him to report anything that might be relevant to Operation Aftershock.

He was pretty sure that the man in the motorcycle leathers and safety helmet counted as a person of interest, even if he didn't score any points on the bingo card.

The man had a parcel in his hands, which he held under one arm as he walked up to reception. Cohen triggered a silent alarm by hitting the button beneath his desk, then tried to stall the man as much as possible. He tried to engage him in conversation, insisted he needed his signature and even grabbed his arm when he put the package down. But the man shrugged him off and beat a quick retreat just as reinforcements arrived. Cohen pointed at the man in the leathers as he raced away from the station and watched as four constables chased after him. It was a cop thing. If a suspect ran, they were guilty. If a suspect was guilty, they needed to be brought to justice.

Cohen, meanwhile, had his hands full. He pulled a pair of plastic gloves from a drawer at his side, as Cholmondeley had ordered him to do if they received another package, and then he picked up the box. It was a small, red box, made of cardboard and with a detachable lid on top which was tied down with a black ribbon. Cohen unwrapped the bow and placed it delicately down beside him, then removed the lid from the box and looked inside.

It was not a pleasant sight. Cohen, who was familiar with the case, had been expecting to see another body part. But it contained just a plastic pouch, filled with a congealing red liquid that could only be blood, and a short note which was written in black ink on a light blue Post-it.

Cohen picked the note up and placed it on the desk in front of him beside the black ribbon that had held the package together. The note was folded, so he opened it up and looked at the message. It was short, simple and to the point.

You've got the wrong man, it said. *Marc Allman is innocent, and now another victim's blood is on your hands. There's nothing you can do to stop us.*

The note was unsigned, but Constable Cohen had a good idea of who it was from. He sighed and picked up the telephone from its cradle on the desk in front of him. He dialled a number that was burned into his memory and waited for Cholmondeley to pick up.

It's going to be a long night, he thought.

Chapter Eleven:
Something casual

TENSION WAS HIGH at the police station. Cholmondeley had cancelled all leave and increased the size of his team to follow up with the different leads.

Two of his coppers had managed to catch the man who made the delivery, and he'd been dragged back to the station in handcuffs. They'd given Cholmondeley a full update, but he'd been more eager to hear from Constable Cohen, who'd already given him an update over the phone when he was sitting in front of the TV with a glass of red.

Constable Cohen wasn't at his best that morning, but Cholmondeley had expected as much. The young man had stayed at the station until the early hours, then made his way back at 6AM so he could be there for the briefing.

He spoke in short, disjointed sentences, but it was enough for Cholmondeley to build up a picture of what had happened the night before.

"Did we get an ID on the guy who delivered the parcel?" Cholmondeley asked.

"Yes, sir," Cohen replied. "His name is Asif Shaktar, and he works for a company called FunRunz. A little indie outfit trying its luck against the big boys. We questioned him straight away, of course, but we kept it generic. Figured it'd be best to hold him overnight and to wait for you and Sergeant Mogford."

"Good," Cholmondeley murmured.

The detective inspector was so impressed with Cohen's work that he brought him onto the team, and not just as a stenographer to take the minutes. The first order of business was to vote on the fate of Marc Allman. They only had a couple more hours to decide whether to charge or release him, and they had another man in the cells that they needed to talk to.

"Realistically," Mogford argued, "there's not much more we'll get out of him. We've interviewed him again and again and again. We just don't have enough to arrest him."

"I agree," Cholmondeley said. "If we take him now, it'll never make it to court, especially with the new note that says he's innocent."

"It could be a set up," Constable Groves suggested. "He could have prepared the package in advance. After all, it was his choice to visit Mr. Leipfold."

"It's possible," Cholmondeley admitted, "but I'm not so sure. No, I've decided. We'll release him and focus our efforts on the new suspect, Asif Shaktar. We'll see what he has to say and then pick our next move from there. Mogford, Yates, I want you to interview him and report to me when I get back from my meeting with the brass."

The two officers nodded and broke off to one side so that they could leave the meeting together and start to plan out their attack. Mogford always had a few questions ready, he was renowned for it, and Yates had a reputation for encouraging their less talkative suspects to open up. They said it was because she shared her surname with a popular chain of boozers.

"Meanwhile," Cholmondeley continued, "Groves and Cohen, I want you to process the release of Marc Allman. But make sure you get his details and warn him not to leave the city. We're going to want to talk to him again."

"Yes, sir," they said.

"What about me, sir?" Constable Ian Hyneman had a hand raised. Cholmondeley had almost overlooked him, despite the fact that he was six foot one and built like a brick shithouse. Hyneman had a habit of lurking at the back during their briefings, slouching slightly or slumping in his seat on one of the station's plastic chairs.

"I've got a special job for you," Cholmondeley said. "And it's an important one. I want you to build me a database of missing persons. Anyone who disappeared in the last six weeks. Pull reports from around the country and give me a master list with your comments, then we'll start sending coppers door to door to speak to their relatives. Any questions?"

There was silence around the room. Cholmondeley smiled softly at his team and said, "Good. Let's get to work."

* * *

A little later that morning, Leipfold and Maile were sitting down together in the reception area. They'd just finished *The Tribune*'s crossword and moved on to their daily update. Leipfold was most interested in her research into the vocoder, but that was the last thing she wanted to talk about.

"No real progress to report," Maile admitted. "But I'm still working on it. I've shortlisted a number of companies and I've been working through them, but it's a thankless task. Most of them haven't responded to me, and those that did have sent back a standard line about client confidentiality."

"Doesn't surprise me," Leipfold murmured.

"Don't worry," she replied. "I'm starting by taking the official route. If that doesn't work, I've got a back-up plan. I have a lot of friends who love a challenge, like you, and who will give up a couple of hours to help me out. If we can get enough samples from the different devices, we can start to analyse them and try to find some points of comparison. Once we've narrowed down the type of device that the killer used, we'll have a much better chance of getting through to them and being able to recover the original audio."

"Perfect," Leipfold said. "How long will it take to get results?"

Maile shrugged. "A couple of days," she said. "A week at the most."

"Can't you get it done tonight?"

"I'm out tonight," Maile said. "On a second date."

Leipfold looked up at her, sharply. "A second date, huh?" he asked. "Who's the lucky man?"

"Like I'm going to tell you that," Maile scoffed. "Don't worry, I can look after myself. You *know* I can look after myself. And besides, he's a nice guy. It's hard to believe that any of those are still around, but he seems all right."

"Only all right?" Leipfold asked.

"I'm not about to fall in love, if that's what you're suggesting." Maile folded her arms and looked across at Leipfold. "That's not my thing. I'm just looking for something casual. Someone DTF."

"DTF?"

"You don't want to know," Maile replied. She blushed a little and tried to hide her face behind a computer screen. "Google it, if you have to. I'm saying nothing."

Leipfold grunted and a comfortable silence descended upon them. Maile got up to make a cup of coffee.

Suddenly, Leipfold started laughing.

"What's so funny?" she asked.

"I googled DTF," Leipfold said. "Courting has changed since I was a kid."

* * *

Maile left the office at 5PM, and Leipfold shut up shop and followed shortly afterwards. He'd played it cool when she'd talked about her romantic rendezvous, but the truth was that Leipfold was worried about her.

It wasn't that he had romantic feelings of his own. There was no doubt about that. She was like a niece or a daughter, not quite a best friend but a close family member who he was morally bound to protect. Leipfold liked being alone, worrying only about himself, his rent and his reputation. Whenever he got close to someone, it exponentially increased the odds of life serving up a bum deal, like a cancer diagnosis or a tragic accident.

That was why he decided to follow her on foot and in a faded blue duffel coat and a New York Jets baseball cap from the storeroom. He'd never been much of a believer in disguises. In Leipfold's opinion, they tended to attract more attention than they diverted. But he did have a stash of old clothes that he'd used over the years to blend in when he had to. Leipfold knew that Maile would easily recognise him in his leathers, but with the off-blue coat and the cap pulled low over his eyes, he thought he had a reasonable chance of getting away with it.

At first, Leipfold thought she was heading home, but she took a right when she would have normally turned left and made her way a half mile or so in the wrong direction. Leipfold stayed on her tail, sixty paces behind her and strolling along with an air of nonchalance. He followed her to a curry house called Mr. India and took a table for one in a far corner. Maile had been seated on the other side of the restaurant where her date was already waiting. A wooden partition separated the two tables, but Leipfold could just about make them out in the long mirror that lined one wall to create the illusion of a larger restaurant.

Leipfold ordered a chicken vindaloo with pilau rice and a keema naan, then tucked into the complimentary popadoms and mango chutney. A messy eater, he'd spilled lime pickle down his shirt and scattered onion salad across the table before his main arrived, but he was too busy eavesdropping to feel awkward or embarrassed and he'd had enough meals by himself to be comfortable in his own company.

Maile and her date ordered a second bottle of wine, and they both seemed to be laughing as they tucked into the food and struck up idle conversation. Leipfold had learned to lip read in the nineties by watching TV with the subtitles on, knowing it was a useful skill for anyone, whether deaf or not. Their conversation was difficult to follow, partly because it was littered with technological terms and partly because the mirror distorted the shapes of their mouths, but he was happy enough with what he saw.

He asked the waiter for the bill and got ready to pay up and leave the place, satisfied that Maile had chosen wisely. Like an overprotective father, he just wanted to check up on the guy she'd chosen to spend time with, to see whether his asshole detector fired off a warning. He realised that he shouldn't have worried.

A waiter returned with the bill just as Maile and her date got up from their seats and prepared to leave the restaurant. Leipfold tried to hide behind the waiter, but the scene drew their attention and Maile glanced over.

"Boss?" she said. "Is that you?"

Leipfold surrendered and sat back. He nodded glumly and said, "Good food, right?"

Maile ignored him. "Why are you following me?" she asked.

"I wanted to make sure you were okay," he said. "There's a killer on the loose, remember?"

"I told you," Maile growled, "I can look after myself. What I do in my spare time is my business, not yours. I can't believe you followed me."

"I just wanted to—"

"Check up on me, yeah," Maile said. "Go home, boss. Worry about your own life and leave me to worry about mine."

"And what about you?" Leipfold asked.

"Go!" she shouted.

Maile and her date walked out of the restaurant together, and Leipfold was left behind to apologise to the staff for the commotion. They guilted him into tipping them extra, and his wallet was almost empty by the time he got out of there.

* * *

The following day was Wednesday March first, and optimism was in the air across the city of London. Fishmongers were selling their wares in Billingsgate Market, stallholders were shifting legal highs in Camden, rickshaws were trundling up and down along the West End and James Leipfold was alone in his office.

Maile hadn't turned up for work, and that worried him. He guessed she was still mad at him from the night before, and both of them knew she was too valuable to discipline her for missing a day. But she hadn't even been in touch with him, and that was unusual. She usually kept him informed of her every move. On top of that, she wasn't answering her phone when he called her, or replying to his instant messages and emails.

If business had been slow, he might've put in a couple of hours to check up on her, but business was still booming and he was starting to worry about how they were going to manage. He already knew that his finances were in a mess, and he wasn't looking forward to calling his accountant and asking for a little help.

He sighed and picked up the phone.

* * *

Meanwhile, at the police station, Cholmondeley's team was in low spirits. The investigation was progressing, slowly but surely, and there was the constant risk of another murder. Cholmondeley knew that he couldn't afford that. The press already had their eyes on the case. The only thing that sold more papers was paedophilia.

Luckily for morale if nothing else, Jack Cholmondeley had some good news, which he revealed at the daily briefing. They had a full house with over a dozen officers packed into the tiny room. The detective inspector had seen it that busy before, but not for a couple of years.

"Ladies and gentlemen," he said, taking his place at the head of the room. "Please give me your attention for a couple of minutes."

Cholmondeley explained how the case had developed, and how Asif Shaktar, like Marc Allman, had been released without charge.

"Despite the brutality of the murders," he said, "the forensics boys are yet to report any findings."

"How come?" Constable Yates asked. She was sitting near the front with a notebook in her hand.

"This isn't a TV show," Mogford supplied. "It takes time for them to carry out their tests. As soon as they find anything, we'll know. Until then, we've got to do things the old-fashioned way."

"Well said, Sergeant," Cholmondeley said. "I couldn't have put it better myself. Luckily, we decided to run some tests of our own. And now we have some results from the handwriting analysis."

Cholmondeley explained how the analysis worked. The calligraphists could look at different handwriting samples and begin to draw deductions. It wasn't exact, but it was still a science with its own set of rules and laws. With a single, short letter, they could ascertain with reasonable certainty the age, gender and education level of its author, key pieces of information that could make or break an investigation.

"In this case," Cholmondeley continued, "they compared the letter that was delivered to the station with the letter that was sent to *The Tribune*. And guess what. It wasn't a match."

There was an audible gasp in the room as the officers processed the information and realised what it meant.

"Now at this stage," Cholmondeley continued, "there are a number of possibilities. It's possible that the killer has an accomplice, for example, or that the letter that *The Tribune* received was a fraud, sent by someone else who was looking for a little notoriety."

"Are you sure that ours is genuine?" Groves asked.

"Good question," Cholmondeley replied. "Truth is, we can't be sure of the authenticity of either of them, but it seems like the real deal to me. *The Tribune* received theirs with a chunk of the victim, and ours came with a pouch of blood. Both would be tricky to fake."

"Then that seems to suggest the accomplice theory," Mogford said.

"It certainly does," Cholmondeley replied. "And there's more. The handwriting team said that the first note was probably written by a man. They couldn't be certain, but they said it's a pretty good bet. But here's where it gets interesting. You see, they think the second letter, the one that went to our reception, is different. They think it was written by a woman."

* * *

Cholmondeley was back at his desk after the briefing. The task force's daily meeting had been cancelled, which freed up some much-needed time in his schedule. But it also raised a huge question mark when it came to the future of Operation Aftershock. He worried that the case was being transferred because even with a web of information passing between the different teams in the daily meeting, they didn't have much to show for it.

The meeting's cancellation turned out to have an unexpected side effect. He was at his desk when the early blood tests came in, which meant he was able to page the rest of his team with an update. The test they used relied on comparing blood types. While it was a rudimentary test and nowhere near as complicated as the DNA comparisons that the forensics team was responsible for, they had a high probability of success and could be carried out in a matter of hours.

The email with the results contained a bombshell, one that could change the way the entire case was viewed. He gathered the team members who were working from the station and delivered a quick, impromptu update.

"All right," he said. "Listen up because we don't have much time. We have the results back from the blood that was delivered to the station. Now, as you already know, the tests from the package that was sent to *The Tribune* confirmed that our killer had a third victim, because it wasn't a match to either Jayne Lipton or Abu Adewali."

Cholmondeley hushed the murmuring policemen with a look. "Pay attention, please," he continued. "At this point, we're treating the third victim as a John or Jane Doe, but Constable Hyneman here has pulled together a list of missing persons. It's a comprehensive list and will need a little refinement, but it's a start. Groves, Yates and Cohen, I want the three of you to follow up with each of the names. Talk to their friends and family and see if you can find out their blood types. That should help us to make a good guess on our evidence, at least until we hear from forensics."

He paused for a moment to catch his breath, simultaneously refreshing his memory by flicking through his notes.

"Where was I?" he murmured. "Ah, yes. We have the results back on the most recent package, the one that was delivered to Constable Cohen on reception. This is where it gets interesting."

"How's that?" Mogford asked.

"The blood from the police station pouch wasn't a match for any of the others," Cholmondeley said. "As a matter of fact, it was type AB, the rarest type. Could be that the killer is sending us a message. Could just be a coincidence. But one thing's for sure."

"What's that, then?" Constable Cohen asked. He was sitting behind a laptop computer, still taking the minutes of their meetings and briefings even though he'd been promoted to a full member of the team.

"Figure it out, Constable Cohen," Cholmondeley said. "If this new blood doesn't match any of the others, it means there's a fourth victim."

"Holy shit," Mogford said. "But we only have two bodies."

Cholmondeley turned to look at him. "Correct, Sergeant," he said. "Which means the other two could still be alive."

Chapter Twelve:
Chinese Whispers

IT WAS LATER THAT DAY, and Leipfold still hadn't heard from Maile. He checked his records and rang the number she'd listed for her next of kin. It put him through to her housemate, Kat, who seemed confused to be hearing from him.

Leipfold asked her if she'd heard from Maile, and Kat asked if she'd been into the office. The answer was no on both counts.

"I didn't get home until late last night," Kat said. "I thought she was in bed when I got in, but there was still no sign of her this morning."

"She's not answering my calls," Leipfold said.

"She's not answering mine, either."

Leipfold paused for a moment to think it over. "Have you tried anything else?" he asked. "What about through those games she plays?"

"I have no idea how they work," Kat said. "I sent her an IM, but no dice."

"Hmmm," Leipfold murmured. "If she doesn't want us to find her, we're not going to."

"What do you mean?"

"She's a clever girl," Leipfold said. "And she knows what she's doing. She's good at covering her tracks."

Kat laughed. Leipfold could hear voices in the background. They sounded angry, official.

"Listen, Mr. Leipfold," she said. "I've got to go. I'm at work and my boss is giving me the heebie jeebies. Looks like he's just stepped in something unpleasant, and I get the feeling he wants to take it out on me. Just do me a favour, okay?"

"What?"

"Text me when you hear from Maile," Kat said. "I'm sure she'll be fine, but it'd put my mind at ease. She likes to get herself into trouble."

"Will do," Leipfold said.

Kat cut the call, and Leipfold sat back in his chair. He took a deep breath and exhaled slowly. He wondered where Maile was and if she was mad at him. He figured she probably was, but that didn't make it any easier. It took her disappearance to make him realise how much he relied on her, as well as how much he worried about her. Suddenly, her mother's insistence that she carried pepper spray around didn't seem so unreasonable.

Leipfold made himself another coffee and sat back down at his machine, then tried to busy himself with a little paperwork. He had some invoices to send, a couple of contracts to prepare and a report to deliver on a pyramid scheme which had pissed one punter off enough for him to spend a little cash to uncover it. It was boring, tedious work, but it paid the bills.

By lunchtime, there was still no word, although he did take a call from Jack Cholmondeley, who wanted to meet up with him after work to talk shop and drink a lemonade. He promised to meet the old cop in the Rose & Crown, then told him about Maile before Cholmondeley had a chance to put the phone down.

"Don't worry about it," Cholmondeley said. "She's probably nursing a hangover. You know the drill, James. Give her twenty-four hours and then report it if she's still missing. My guess is she'll show up to work tomorrow with her tail between her legs and some cock and bull story about her phone being nicked."

"I guess you're right. But what if she was attacked by another creep like Tom Townsend?"

"Tom Townsend is behind bars, James. I'll see you later. The Rose & Crown, right?"

"Right," Leipfold said. He cut the call and put the phone down on his desk. Then he massaged his temples and tried to think for a moment. He didn't get far.

The phone rang and Leipfold answered it.

* * *

"Where the bloody hell have you been?" Leipfold demanded.

It was a couple of minutes later, and Maile had spent the intervening time rattling off a single, long sentence that Leipfold had struggled to understand. He'd caught several apologies and several more excuses, but nothing concrete.

"I stayed out," Maile said. "Sorry, it won't happen again. I had a few more drinks at a bar and then stayed at my date's place. But before you say anything, I don't—"

"You don't want to talk about it," Leipfold said. "Got it. So what happened?"

Maile started to say something, but Leipfold cut her off.

"I don't mean like that," Leipfold said. "I mean how come you didn't call? I've been worried sick."

"You're not my mother," Maile reminded him. "I'm sorry. My phone died, and I didn't have a charger. I meant to call in, but I was hanging to high hell. So I went back to sleep."

"Great," Leipfold said. "Well, thanks for letting me know. Your housemate was worried, too."

"You talked to Kat?"

"Of course," Leipfold said. "Are you coming in today?"

"No," Maile said. "Sorry, boss. I'll be back in tomorrow. My brain feels like it's pressing against my skull."

"Orange juice, bacon and a shower," Leipfold said, automatically. "It used to work for me."

"Already on it," Maile said. "I'll see you tomorrow."

Leipfold cut the call and put the phone down, then tried yet again to get his head in the game. It had been a disjointed day, one of those anxious, stressful days where he'd worked on a dozen different things and not made progress on any of them.

He filed the invoices and called it a day, then sat in his chair and drummed his fingers lazily on the desk, tapping out a tune by Blue

Öyster Cult. He reached the bridge and sighed, then started pulling his things together. He packed his bag and left the office, hitting the lights along the way.

* * *

Half an hour later, a further thirty pages into *The Brothers Karamazov*, Leipfold looked up from his book and spotted Detective Inspector Jack Cholmondeley, wrapped up in a dark coat with a hat slung low across his brow. He raised a hand to wave at Leipfold, who marked his place and put his book away, then ordered a pint of lager and a half of lemonade and brought them over to the little table.

Leipfold was sitting in a corner, and Cholmondeley smiled as they made eye contact. Their spot in the corner gave both men a strong field of view, although Leipfold had the upper hand because he didn't have to rely on a reflection. Cholmondeley slid the lemonade across to him and sat down to take a sip of his pint.

"I needed that," he said, smacking his lips. "How are you, James?"

"I'm good, old man," Leipfold said. "Yourself?"

"I'm grand. Did your assistant turn up?"

"Maile?" Leipfold said. "Yeah, she's fine. Or at least, she showed up and she seems like her usual self."

"I'm delighted to hear it, old boy."

They chatted idly for half an hour or so, catching up on old friends and retelling stories about when the two men were young and had only just met each other. Leipfold talked about his business, how it was on the rise again and making money for once, and Cholmondeley talked about Mary, snooker and the horses. He explained that he was off duty, which is why he allowed himself a lager, and that he wasn't supposed to be talking at all.

"So why are you here?" Leipfold asked.

"The usual. I need your help."

"Again?"

"Again," Cholmondeley said. "We're still receiving the killer's packages. Only this time, it isn't Asif Shaktar who's delivering them.

The Tribune got one when he was in the cells, and another one came to the station after we released him."

"Who was the courier?" Leipfold asked.

"Good question," Cholmondeley replied. "It was a woman. Ursula something. Ursula Doyle, if memory serves. We held her, of course, but I don't think she had anything to do with it. In fact, she was warned that we might bring her in and paid a little extra for her trouble. And the killer is being more careful. This time, the order was placed online. The courier picked it up from a public location, just off Hyde Park. We're going to run the cameras in the area and put out an alert, but I haven't got my hopes up."

"Surely someone must have seen him," Leipfold said.

"Oh, we'll find something." Cholmondeley paused for a moment and took a deep gulp from his pint glass. He smacked his lips appreciatively and set the glass back down. "Problem is, it looks like we've figured out how he works. He likes to taunt us, to put himself at risk, but at the same time he does everything he can to cover his tracks. When it comes to his little parcels, it's like the six degrees of separation. He pays a guy to pay a guy to pay a guy to pay a guy."

"Like Chinese whispers."

"Exactly," Cholmondeley said. "He's lucky that his little packages are even being delivered."

"No," Leipfold said. "Luck has nothing to do with it."

"What do you mean?" Cholmondeley asked.

But Leipfold simply shook his head and said nothing.

* * *

Cholmondeley was two pints further in, and Leipfold was matching him drink for drink with lemonade. They'd started to gossip about the good old days, and Cholmondeley had twice checked his watch and murmured something vague about getting back home to Mary. But by the time he started his third, he already knew he was going to be in trouble. And as if that wasn't bad enough, he'd driven to the pub in his Beemer, which he was no longer fit to drive. He was facing a taxi home and then another one back in the morning.

Leipfold finished his drink and fetched another round. Most ex-drinkers preferred to stay away from alcohol, but Cholmondeley had known Leipfold long enough to know he was different.

Keep your friends close and your enemies closer, Cholmondeley thought.

Cholmondeley checked his watch as Leipfold steered the conversation artfully back towards the case and to Operation Aftershock.

"You don't know the half of it," Cholmondeley said. "There's still a question that you haven't asked me."

Leipfold paused for a moment and then said, "Tell me about it, Jack. Tell me about the latest package."

"It's funny you should mention it," Cholmondeley replied. He was smiling, but it was the smile of a crocodile when a hunter's pointing the barrel of a rifle at its underbelly. "Genitals."

"Genitals?"

"Genitals," Cholmondeley confirmed. "Another set for the collection. Male genitals, the full cock and balls."

Leipfold laughed. Then he tried to turn it into a cough.

"Sorry," Leipfold said. "I was thinking about something else. That's terrible."

"There's more," Cholmondeley said. "There was a note as well. Written in blood."

"The victim's blood?"

"That's the assumption," Cholmondeley said. "It looks like a match, but I'll need more time to say so for sure."

"What did the note say?"

"It didn't *say* anything," Cholmondeley replied. "It was a map. We followed it to a shallow grave in a plot of land just off the M25. There was a body."

Leipfold paused. He didn't look good, and neither did Jack Cholmondeley.

"Who was it?" Leipfold asked, at last.

"Some slick city type," Cholmondeley said. "A guy called Calvin Myatt. Get used to his name. It'll be all over the papers tomorrow."

Chapter Thirteen:
The Oyster Club

"I LOOK FUCKING RIDICULOUS," Maile said. She was examining herself in the full-length dress mirror in Kat's bedroom and trying not to scowl at her own reflection.

"You look fine," Kat said, suppressing a laugh by taking a sip from the glass of wine she'd been nursing for the last half hour.

"No, I don't," Maile insisted. She examined herself in the mirror again. She was wearing a low-cut, deep scarlet dress that revealed too much and concealed too little. It cut off three inches above the knee and even in leggings, she didn't like the way it showed her legs off. "I look like I was dressed by a randy teenager playing The Sims with a nudity patch. I feel like a piece of meat, Kat. How do you wear this stuff?"

Kat shrugged. "It's what I like," she said. "At least I don't go to bed in a Slipknot hoodie."

"Hey!" Maile protested. "It's comfortable. Not like this stuff."

"Look," Kat said, "I just want you to look your best. You never know. You might meet someone."

"I've already met someone."

"What? That salesman dude? Screw that guy. You can do better."

"Not in this dress," Maile said. She was starting to wonder why she'd agreed to this in the first place. It had seemed like a good idea at the time, an excuse for a couple of drinks and a night out. But then the big night rolled around, and she'd forgotten all about it. She'd been looking forward to spending the night playing Halo and unwinding after work. Instead she'd unlocked the door and almost immediately found herself accepting a glass of wine and being led into Kat's bedroom to start getting ready.

The plan was pretty simple. Kat had spotted an ad in *The Tribune* for The Oyster Club, a speed dating group that met once a week in a swanky cocktail bar just off Covent Garden, and she'd signed them both up on the spot. The bottle of wine was to get them good and drunk before they left home so they could save money on the overpriced drinks that helped those swanky bars to make their rent.

Kat was dressed in her best as she always was when she left the house in the evening. She was wearing a black dress and her favourite pair of heels, accessorising with a little gold handbag and her favourite necklace, which hung down and banged against her skin an inch or so above her cleavage.

"Can't I just wear jeans?" Maile had asked.

"Not on my watch," Kat replied. "Come on, it'll be fun."

And so she'd acquiesced, and before she knew it she was sitting in the back of an Uber as it wound its way through the streets into the inner city.

* * *

The Oyster Club was packed to the rafters, and the air inside had taken on that dry, stilted quality it gets when there's too much aftershave and not enough ventilation. The heat inside the place flushed Maile's cheeks a deep, embarrassing crimson. She already hated the place.

The two girls were welcomed at the door by a woman called Lucy Fforde, who introduced herself as the hostess and took their names and email addresses down for her newsletter. She was a redhead, but not in the same way as James Leipfold. The private investigator's short crop of ginger was a far cry from Lucy Fforde's reddish brown locks, which hung down to her shoulders and lit up beneath the club's lights as though her head was on fire.

"Is this your first time?" Lucy asked. Kat nodded. "Excellent," she said. "Well, thanks for coming. Grab yourself a sticker and write your name on it, then stick it somewhere people can see it. We'll be getting started in a couple of minutes."

"Great," Kat said. Then she turned to her housemate and grabbed her by the arm. "Come on, let's get a drink."

By the time that the event actually started, they were already on their second drinks, and Maile was feeling a little tipsy. It wasn't that she wasn't used to drinking; she just wasn't used to drinking this much, and she'd always preferred her Red Bull without the vodka. The event got underway with each of the women directed to a small table, with two to a table so that they all got a fair chance to meet their suitors, and then the men were rotated from table to table every time Lucy rang a little bell that she held. She had to put some power behind it to make the noise heard above the hubbub of a couple dozen stilted conversations.

Maile and Kat were placed on a table together, and they spent more time talking to each other than to the men they were being introduced to. Maile had been expecting some Christian Grey type mega businessman with a penchant for a little bondage at the weekends, but so far all she'd seen were socially maladjusted mummy's boys and damp-smelling weirdos who were destined to live alone. But she was actually enjoying herself. It wasn't because she thought she might meet the love of her life, though. She'd just learned to love the art of people watching through her work with James Leipfold, and this was the sort of gold mine that could have fed the imagination of a hundred novelists. The Oyster Club was where the weirdos went, where the strange in society met their matches. And she was loving it.

The bell rang again and the potential suitors moved around.

Maile found herself sitting opposite a well-built man in his early thirties. He had brown eyes and short black hair that was swept across his forehead. His facial hair was spilling over from stubble into a full-blown beard, but it suited him and gave him a rugged, manly look. He wasn't unattractive.

So while Kat was pretending to be interested in the guy who surveyed quantities, Maile held out her hand to the rugged man and said, "Hi, my name's Maile O'Hara. Nice to meet you."

He smiled at her, flashing a glimpse of pristine white teeth, and then took her hand. He shook it. "Hi, Maile," he said. "That's a nice name."

"Thanks," she replied. "Shame no one can ever spell it. And you're…" She trailed off into silence as she checked his lapel for a name tag.

"Asif," he said. "Asif Shaktar. No one can ever spell that, either."

Maile laughed, but the laughter didn't reach her eyes or mouth. The expression on her face had been wiped blank and her mind was running at a hundred miles a minute. She'd heard that name before, and she didn't think it had been in a round of Call of Duty. She had a feeling it was important.

If only she could remember why.

* * *

The rest of the event went smoothly. While Maile still couldn't remember where she'd heard Shaktar's name before, she found him charming enough. She just couldn't shake the feeling that he was somehow important. She caught up with him again at the end to exchange a few pleasantries and to bum a drink before heading home.

After that, she wandered over to join Kat, who was three sheets to the wind and talking up a storm with Lucy Fforde, who looked more than happy to chat to a new punter even though the event was over and everyone else had gone home.

"I'm so glad you enjoyed it," Lucy said. "These things take a lot of time and effort, and it's not always easy going. Don't get me wrong, it's lovely to see when people meet at the Oyster Club and go on to spend their lives together, but it's like our good friend Mr. Shakespeare said, 'the course of true love never did run smooth.'"

"Love," Kat slurred. "I don't know if I even believe in it."

Lucy laughed, and Maile noticed that it was a bitter kind of laugh, the laugh of a woman scorned who was still feeling the pain of a doomed affair.

Then Lucy started coughing, great whooping coughs that made her shake in a paroxysm of phlegm and mucus. It was gross, even with her hand over her mouth.

"Are you okay?" Maile asked.

"I'm fine," Lucy insisted once she'd managed to get her breath back. She was doubled up with her hands on her knees, but once the coughing stopped, she straightened up as best as she could and took a couple of deep breaths like a yogi in the middle of a pose. "Don't you worry about it. Where were we?"

"Love," Kat slurred.

"Ah, yes," Fforde said. "I don't believe in love, either. Not anymore. You wouldn't believe what I've seen since launching this thing."

"Try us," Maile said, spotting her chance to join the conversation and inserting herself into it with all the grace of a surgeon embedding a pacemaker. Lucy looked taken aback for a moment, as though she'd been caught off guard and she wasn't sure whether she'd said something she shouldn't have. But Maile smiled nervously at her and the tension broke.

"We get all sorts in here," Lucy said. "A couple of weeks ago we had this little kid come along, must've been fourteen or fifteen. He looked it as well, a little white-haired runt of a thing. We kicked him out of here, of course. Now he's got some sort of vendetta. He started up a blog about us and everything. Keeps saying he's going to kill me. I'd be scared if I hadn't met the kid."

"Bloody ridiculous," Kat murmured.

"Too right," Lucy replied. "Our goal here is to create an environment for consenting adults to meet each other. We want people to fall in love and to spend their lives together. We want them to start families and to live happily ever after. But it doesn't always work out like that."

"What do you mean?" Maile asked.

The expression on Lucy's face changed. Her eyes darkened, her brow furrowed and she took on the look of a woman who's just tasted something unpleasant. She took a big swig out of her mojito.

"Cheaters," Lucy said. "I hate cheaters. Always have. But you've got to have a good nose if you want to sniff them out."

"I don't follow you," Maile replied. Beside her, Kat looked like she was ready for a long lie down, and Maile couldn't blame her. It had been a long day.

"Most people join the Oyster Club because they're looking for love,"

Lucy said. "But some people join because they're trapped in a loveless marriage and they're looking for a little something on the side. Those people don't last long here, but if they take their ring off and cover themselves with a clever backstory, they sometimes last long enough."

"Does that happen often?" Kat asked

"More often than you might think," Fforde replied. She looked suspiciously at the two of them. "You *are* both single, right? I'd hate to think—"

"Lady," Kat interrupted, "you don't know the half of it."

"Ha!" Lucy said. "Yes, well. Excuse me while I get another drink."

"Hold up," Kat said, reaching automatically for the purse in her Louis Vuitton handbag. "We're coming, too. Right, Maile?"

But Maile shook her head. She was tired, confused and convinced that she'd missed something, and there was an Xbox controller on her bedside table with her name on it.

"You've had enough," she said. "Let's go home."

Chapter Fourteen:
The Briefing

IT SEEMED LIKE half the station was there. After almost a month of miscommunication, Cholmondeley's superiors finally had the bright idea of hosting a big briefing that brought all of the different task force teams together for the first time since Operation Aftershock had started.

It was a pointless meeting, like all meetings were. The superiors had insisted on a show of force, so instead of tailing Asif Shaktar or processing the body of Calvin Myatt, the police force's finest were sitting in a board room. There were six different teams with four or five people on each. Cholmondeley's team was there, of course, and so were the forensic team and the morticians. Top brass was there as well, three men and a woman in impeccable black suits and with eyes as dead as a pharaoh's. Then there were the first responders, who'd been drafted in as consultants, and a final team of independent ombudsmen whose job was to make sure no one made a mistake.

Cholmondeley's team was the largest. The boss sat in the middle with Sergeant Mogford to his right and Constable Groves to his left. Constable Hyneman was there as well, and so were Constables Yates and Cohen. Cohen was wearing new aftershave and taking notes in an efficient shorthand which no one else could read.

The meeting was headed by Superintendent Isabelle Richards, a woman whose notoriety preceded her. She'd been in the force for almost as long as Cholmondeley, but her ambition and her empathy had carried her higher up the ranks. Privately, Cholmondeley was glad of it. She was a good superintendent but a lousy cop, and her place at the top of the food chain suited everyone. But it didn't make her any easier to deal with. She wasn't a woman of honour, at least not in the sense that Cholmondeley knew. She'd support her officers, but if they made a mistake then she'd be the first to throw them under the bus. Her loyalty lay with the public, and not with the officers who served under her. That made her dangerous.

And Cholmondeley had another reason to worry. He'd convinced her to let Leipfold sit in on the meeting in the guise of a subject matter specialist. Officially, he was there as one of the world's foremost thinkers on the subject of serial killers. Unofficially, he was just plain old James Leipfold. Superintendent Richards was well aware of who he was, but she'd reluctantly agreed that his input might be useful, as long as he could be trusted. She'd already threatened criminal charges if any information was leaked outside the room.

The meeting started late, but that had always been inevitable when the invitations went out. It was standing room only, and the room was aglow with tablets and laptop computers. Constable Cohen, meanwhile, had opted for a large pad of paper and a couple of Sharpies. He surrounded his notes with sketches to bring them to life, which was one of the reasons why Cholmondeley had made him the investigation's unofficial secretary. There was no telling when one of his sketches might spark an idea or a memory, or hint at a new connection or an underworked area of investigation.

Superintendent Richards stood up and waited for silence. It didn't take long for her to get it.

"Thanks for coming," she said, brusquely. Her voice was sharp and clipped, a well-spoken BBC English, and Leipfold, who was on his best behaviour, wondered whether she'd had elocution lessons. "I know we're all busy, so let's make this one as quick and productive as possible."

"Here here," one of the forensic guys grunted, a big man with a walrus moustache and a scar above his eye. "Let's catch this bastard before he kills someone else."

"Yes, well, that's certainly the plan," Richards said. "Now, as you all know, we're here to talk about Operation Aftershock, the investigation into the Tower Hill Terror. The Terror, as I'm sure you'll already know, is the nickname that the press has given to the serial killer that's currently operating throughout the city."

"No shit," somebody murmured. Superintendent Richards glared around the room like an angry bullock and nobody dared to laugh.

"Gentlemen," she said, aiming her gaze at the forensics boys. "When you're done fannying around, we have a killer to catch."

* * *

The briefing got off to a slow start. Superintendent Richards kicked it off by introducing each of the teams and asking them to summarise their work so far. With so many teams—and so many people, so many egos—in a single room, the process was long and arduous. But Cholmondeley saw the point of it. It would help to facilitate communication between the teams. For Leipfold, it was essential. He only knew Jack Cholmondeley.

After the introductions were out of the way, Richards went over the case to date, delegating occasional explanations to the heads of the teams in question. They started with Jayne Lipton, the first victim, and worked up through Abu Adewali and Calvin Myatt, covering their final movements and the results of their autopsies. Richards also explained that tests on the packages revealed that there was a fourth, as yet undiscovered victim, almost certainly another new female.

Richards talked about public perception and the press, and how there was pressure on them to solve the case without further casualties. As part of that, one of the teams had been tasked with building a scientific profile of the suspect, using statistics and data from other cases and other countries to make educated guesses on who exactly it was that they were looking for.

Sergeant Riggs, the man who'd been in charge of the profiling, took the lead, attempting to condense two weeks of research into a thirty second elevator pitch.

"For a start," Riggs said, "the killer is probably male. Most serial killers are. Since we're operating on the basis that it's a repeat offender, that had to serve as our starting point. Then there's the nature of the attacks."

Riggs paused for a moment to shuffle through the briefing notes. He stifled a cough and said, "If you'll turn to page seventeen, you'll see some photographs of what this man is capable of. We're not just looking for a serial killer. We're looking for a monster, someone who mutilated the bodies of his victims."

"Another reason to believe that the culprit is a man," Superintendent Richards said, gesturing for Riggs to continue.

"Exactly," Riggs said. "But unfortunately, we have no real proof when it comes to the gender. And there's more. Despite the fact that the victims appear to have been alive when they were mutilated, our suspect shows no real sign of medical skill. At a push, they could be a butcher, but it looks like a brute force job with a sharp knife and a hell of a lot of determination. They didn't make it easy on themselves. It would have been simpler to kill but not to mutilate, or to mutilate after the victims were already dead. They seem to have gone to a hell of a lot of effort to make a statement."

"And what statement is that?" Cholmondeley asked. Heads turned to look at him, but he was respected by most and hated by few and so the majority wore expressions of indeterminate goodwill.

"We're still working on it," Riggs said. "We'll keep you posted."

"Yeah," Cholmondeley murmured. "Fine. It's not like there are lives at stake."

* * *

Leipfold was bored, so bored. When Jack Cholmondeley invited him to the briefing, he'd hoped to be inundated with new information. He'd been raised to fear the police and not to respect them, but over the years he'd arrived at the conclusion that policemen weren't *bad*; they were just usually incompetent. So far, the meeting had done nothing to change that perception.

They'd been in the room for an hour and a half with no break. They hadn't even been given a fresh batch of coffee, and his throat was drier than a camel's mouth. He'd resorted to chewing nicotine gum because it was the only gum he had, but it didn't help. If anything, it made his mouth feel drier, sandier, and much, much more mammalian. And there was still no sign of water, coffee or orange juice.

Cholmondeley's team was the last to speak, and the old man had a surprising amount of information when compared to the heads of the other departments. Privately, Leipfold felt sorry for him. He couldn't believe how empty the conversation was and how useless it made him feel. It seemed like the cops were more interested in ticking boxes than getting anything done, and Leipfold knew that Jack Cholmondeley was a man of action. Waiting for something to happen must have been killing him.

But at the end of the meeting, when he was given the floor and allowed to speak about his findings, Leipfold realised that there was life in the old dog yet.

"First off," Cholmondeley said, "I'd like to extend my thanks to Superintendent Richards for arranging this meeting and for inviting my team and I to attend. I'm not sure about everyone else, but I've found it to be extremely useful."

Liar, Leipfold thought.

"Now, I appreciate we're all busy," Cholmondeley continued, "and so I'm going to keep this as short as possible. As you know, the killer has been taking trophies from his victims and sending them with notes to a number of agencies that are close to the case, including both the press office at *The Tribune* and to my own team at the station."

"We're all very aware of that, Detective Inspector," Richards said. "You've done an excellent job so far of keeping the rest of us up-to-date with the latest developments."

"So far," Cholmondeley said. "But there's another one, a new note with a new message and a new chunk of meat for forensics to take a look at."

Cholmondeley paused for a moment. He consulted his notebook and flipped through until he found the relevant pages.

"Let me see," he said. "Ah, yes. Now, as Superintendent Richards explained, it appears from the latest packages that the Terror has a fourth victim within their power. We'll need forensic results to prove that, and the package has already been shipped to the laboratory."

"My team is working on it as we speak," the man with the moustache replied.

"Good," Cholmondeley said. "We'll need results as quickly as possible. We're working on the assumption that the sample is from a fourth victim, but we'll need independent verification."

"If it's unverified, where did the intel come from?"

"Good question," Cholmondeley replied. "The package contained another note in which the Tower Hill Terror asserted that he had a fourth victim in his power. He even gave us a name: Meg Jackson. My team is already following up with missing persons and checking the census to find an ID. If we can find out who Jackson is and where she lives, we can check up on her. If he's telling the truth, and I don't see why he wouldn't be, then we might have a chance to save her before another body is found."

Leipfold sighed and folded visibly, but none of the coppers noticed. Inside, he was wondering: *If there's another victim out there, what the hell are we doing in this room?*

Superintendent Richards, meanwhile, looked like she was choking on a lemon. "Put a rush on it, Jack," she said. "If this woman exists, we need to find her."

"Will do," Cholmondeley said.

"Did the note say anything else?" Richards asked. "Anything that might have a bearing on the case?"

Cholmondeley nodded. "I'm afraid so," he said. "I've never seen anything like it. He said he'll deliver her sexual organs within forty-eight hours."

"What were the demands?" Richards asked.

Cholmondeley shook his head. "That's just it," he replied. "There weren't any."

Chapter Fifteen:
A Needle in a Haystack

THE MEETING LASTED for two more hours, and it was the middle of the afternoon by the time that the room was vacated and each of the teams went their separate ways. Leipfold was asked to stay back so that Superintendent Richards could have a word with him, but Cholmondeley didn't stick around to see what it was all about. That was more than his job was worth.

At the end of their shift, he summoned Yates and asked her to report on the search for Meg Jackson. Most of the cops were heading home, but Cholmondeley, Mogford, Yates and Cohen were working late to follow up with a couple of leads.

"I haven't got much so far," Yates explained apologetically. "It's not an easy job. If I find Meg Jackson, it could lead us to the killer. But I can't."

"Why not?" Mogford asked. His face was red and swollen from the stress, combined with a bad diet, a lack of sleep and too many nights on white wine. His voice was gravelly, grumpy, like it cost him something to speak to them.

"I just can't find a likely suspect," Yates said. "It's like she doesn't exist."

"Maybe she doesn't," Cholmondeley replied, thoughtfully.

"I found a couple of hits on the census," Yates continued. "Constable Cohen helped me to process them, but there's no sign of anything suspicious. We managed to speak to all of them eventually, although a couple of them were hard to track down. We pulled off a report for you guys to take a look at, but I wouldn't get your hopes up."

"I told you it was a waste of time," Mogford said, turning to look at Jack Cholmondeley. But his boss shook his head and disagreed.

"No lead is a waste of time," Cholmondeley replied. "You never know what you might find. This time, I guess we're out of luck. Maybe the killer lied about his victim's identity."

"A lying serial killer?" Mogford scoffed. "Who would have thought of such a thing?"

Constable Yates cleared her throat and leaned on Cohen for a little support. "We're going to work late tonight," she said. "There must be something else we can do. I want to get the tech team to take a look for us. I still think we're missing something."

"I agree," Cohen said. "We can look at different variations of the name. Perhaps Meg is her middle name. Perhaps it's a nickname or a reference to something else. Who knows?"

"Well, you two bloody don't," Mogford grumbled. "That's for sure."

"Take it easy," Cholmondeley warned. "Morale's bad enough at the moment without you making things worse."

Mogford grunted an apology and gestured for Yates to continue. She didn't look bothered by the interruption, but Cohen was an unconfident copper and his usually pallid face took on an embarrassed red hue. Yates glared at Mogford and put a hand on her colleague's shoulder.

"Leave it with us," Yates said. "If there's something out there for us to find, we'll find it."

"May I suggest looking into the missing persons reports?" Cholmondeley asked. "We have a database of the latest cases. Look through the reports and see if you can find any leads that might point us to Meg Jackson's true identity."

Yates laughed and picked up a stack of papers from the desk in front of her. It was well-worn and dog-eared, punctuated by multicoloured Post-it Notes poking out from between the pages. Jack Cholmondeley could see the spidery scrawl of her handwriting, as well as the occasional note in Cohen's cursive.

She held up the papers and said, "Already on it, boss."

* * *

It was the following morning, a Thursday, and Leipfold and Maile were sitting together in the reception area and talking about the day ahead. They'd already finished off the crossword, a particularly fiendish puzzle from Alan Phelps at *The Tribune*. It took them ten minutes, a typical time, but a good result for a tricky puzzle. It filled the two of them with confidence for the day ahead.

"So what's the plan for today, boss?" Maile asked.

Leipfold grinned at her and started flicking through his notebook. "First things first," he said. "I need to bring you up to speed with what happened at the cop shop."

"I thought you said you weren't allowed to talk about it," Maile reminded him.

"I'm not," Leipfold said. He tipped her a conspiratorial wink which made her laugh because it looked clumsy and felt incongruous with his rocky personality. "But since when has that ever stopped me?"

And so Leipfold told Maile what had happened at the police briefing, successfully cutting the mammoth session down into a twenty-minute recap. Even though he offered to give her a photocopy, Maile took notes of her own because she said it helped her to remember things. By the time that he'd finished, they were ready for another coffee, so Maile did the honours while Leipfold started to jot down a couple of tasks for her to spend the day on.

"I want you to listen out on social media," Leipfold explained. "I want to know about anything unusual."

"Have you ever even *been* on the internet?" Maile asked, still clattering away in the kitchen and trying to find a spoon she could wash to stir their drinks with. "*Everything* is unusual. Could you be a little more specific?"

Leipfold grinned and said, "This is your area, not mine."

"Yeah," Maile replied, "but I still need to know what I'm looking for."

Leipfold paused for a moment to check his notes again. Sometimes, he struggled to read his own handwriting.

It's lucky I've got a good memory, he reflected. That was an understatement. Leipfold's memory was better than 99.9 percent of the population. He could remember what he had for breakfast on St. David's Day several years ago, what his best friend at primary school used to sound like and the winning lottery numbers for every draw in the last two years of the twentieth century. He remembered things as easily as other people forgot them. He swallowed up the little details, stored them somewhere in the overworked brain of his and then accessed them with the same confidence with which Maile searched the web.

"I want you to look for Meg Jackson," he said. "At the moment, I've only got a name for you. Your job is to put a face to the name and then to put a person to the name and face. This is a woman that the killer claims is in his power. We need to find out all about her. Where she went to school, who her friends are and where she works, eats and sleeps. All that stuff. The more we know about her, the more likely we are to find out how the killer got hold of her."

"Oh," Maile said. "Is that it? That'll be easy."

"Good."

"I was joking," she said. "You're asking me to look for a needle in a haystack."

"If anyone can do it, you can," Leipfold said. "A needle in a haystack, huh? I guess you'd better start looking for a magnet."

* * *

Maile was working on her research, following every lead she could and dumping the results in a document so Leipfold could read her notes and draw his own conclusions if she missed something.

As far as the internet was concerned, Meg Jackson didn't exist. Maile even hit up a few of her techie friends—Mayhem, ProfSyntax and Krypt0—but none of them were able to help her. Their specialties lay elsewhere, mostly in breaching websites or hacking email accounts.

Leipfold, meanwhile, wandered over to his corkboard, which was leaning against one wall and which was still covered with printouts, handwritten notes and lines of string connecting one lead to another. It was a relic of his last investigation, when he looked into the death of Donna Thompson. He frowned, remembering the depths of depression that he'd sunk into along the way. He'd solved the case, eventually, and he swore to himself that he'd solve this one, too.

He asked Maile to put her research on hold to come and give him a hand, and the two of them carefully removed the old case notes and packed them up into a lever arch folder, which Leipfold added to the collection he kept in the storage cupboard.

When they were done, Maile got back to work and Leipfold began the long, arduous task of pinning a map of central London to the corkboard. It was a big board, but even with the map spread across it, it didn't stretch as far as the city's outer edges. Hammersmith was there, just about, but he'd been forced to sacrifice Hackney, Dulwich and most of the Docklands. It didn't matter to Leipfold. None of the victims had been found there.

Leipfold flicked through his notebook until he found the plan he'd made the night before, when he'd been lying in bed and staring at the low ceiling, trying to will himself to sleep. On a case like this, sleep was a luxury that he could rarely afford.

He was there for the best part of half an hour, consulting his notes and then picking up pins, which he pushed one-by-one into the map. He used red pins for Jayne Lipton, blue pins for Abu Adewali, green pins for Calvin Myatt and yellow pins for the as-yet-unidentified fourth victim, who the killer claimed was called Meg Jackson. He was precise—as precise as he could be with the scale of the map—and he was patient. A pattern was starting to form, but there just wasn't enough data to draw any conclusions.

Maile wandered over from her desk and said, "It's beautiful. What is it?"

"It's the answer to our problems," Leipfold replied.

"Uh-huh," Maile said. She paused while Leipfold continued to stare at the map with a yellow pin in his hand. "Care to elaborate?"

Leipfold sighed. "It's a map of the city," he explained. "With colour-coded pins to show where our victims lived, where they worked and where their bodies were found. I'm looking for a pattern, something that might tell us how the killer chooses them."

"Uh-huh," Maile repeated. She stepped back so she could see the map in its entirety. Leipfold was still holding the pin, trying to figure out where to put it.

"This one's for Meg Jackson," he said, holding the yellow pin up towards the light. "I've got three of them ready to go, I just don't know where to put them."

"I'm working on it," Maile said. "I'm doing my best."

"I know," Leipfold said. "Perhaps I can help you out with it."

The detective grabbed a Sharpie and tied it to a length of string, which he measured against the map and cut to size with a pocket knife. He pinned the string in the centre of the city, right on top of Lambeth North tube station, then extended the string and took the lid off the Sharpie. With the string taut, he pulled the nib of the pen across the map to draw a near-perfect circle around the centre point.

"What are you doing, boss?" Maile asked.

"I'm making deductions," he said. "See, look at this. All of our victims lived and worked within the circle. They were all found there, too."

"So what does it mean?"

"It means that the killer is operating within a ten-kilometre radius of the centre of the city," Leipfold said. "At least for now. I want you to take that supposition and run with it."

Leipfold paused for a moment. Then he reached up and ran his fingers across the map.

"If you're going to find Meg Jackson," Leipfold murmured, "you're going to find her somewhere in here."

* * *

Suddenly, it all came together.

Maile had been thinking about Asif Shaktar ever since she'd met him at the Oyster Club, and not just because she liked his beard or because she wanted to ask him about his dental routine. Something about the man had been bugging her, and she realised what it was the second that his name cropped up.

"That's it!" she shouted.

Leipfold paused and turned to look at her. He'd been jotting notes on a flipchart while running through some sort of monologue, verbalising his train of thought without even realising it. Asif's name came up as he was thinking about FunRunz, the company that had delivered the killer's trophies to *The Tribune*.

"That's what?" Leipfold asked.

"That's where I'd heard his name before," Maile said. "Asif Shaktar. I met him the other night."

"Where?"

Maile blushed and realised that she hadn't thought this through.

Stupid Kat, she thought. *Damn her and her stupid bloody dating sites and damn the fucking Oyster Club.* It wasn't that she was ashamed of spending her evening at the dating event. She just preferred to keep her love life and her professional life strictly separate. She didn't want to be *that girl*. She didn't have time for boys. They were a hindrance. But sometimes at night she thought it would be nice to have someone to hold her.

She looked over at Leipfold. Then she shook her head and bit the bullet.

"I was at a dating event," she admitted, before telling Leipfold what had happened at the Oyster Club and how she'd exchanged numbers with the deliveryman. She even told him about the conversation she'd had with Lucy Fforde after everyone else had left.

"Strange woman," Maile said. "It was like she had split personalities. One moment she was playing the welcoming host and the next moment she was ranting about loverats and cheaters."

"She must have been hurt by someone," Leipfold replied.

"You got that right." Maile paused for a moment and then started to chuckle. "I've just remembered," she said. "She was talking about some kid who tried to pass as an adult and ended up getting kicked out. Said he's been writing about her on his blog. I wonder what he said."

Leipfold grunted and turned back to his flipchart. He was sending her a pretty clear "do not disturb" signal and it was obvious that he'd lost interest. But Maile hadn't, so she put her headphones on and listened to a little music while searching for the blog that Lucy Fforde had mentioned. She'd thought it would be good for a laugh and that she could send it to Kat to put a smile on her housemate's face, but it turned out to be good for much more than that.

She found the blog all right, and she also found out who the white-haired kid was. There was a picture of him right there on the about page.

"Uh, boss," Maile said, pulling her headphones off and letting them rest around her neck, a death metal double bass drum beat echoing out and breaking the sacred silence of the office. "I think you should come and take a look at this."

"What is it?" he asked.

Maile swallowed and took another look at the picture. "I think I've just found a link between Asif Shaktar and Lukas White."

Chapter Sixteen:
Hypocrites

LEIPFOLD AND MAILE hopped on the back of Camilla and made their way to Lukas White's place. They weren't expecting a warm welcome, and so they weren't surprised when they didn't receive one.

"What do you want?"

It was Lukas White's mother, and she didn't look happy to see them. She was clearly in the middle of something in the kitchen. She was wearing an apron and there were telltale trails of flour across the front of it.

"We'd like to speak to your son," Leipfold said. He tried to smile at her, but it came across more like a grimace. Maile was almost tempted to laugh, but this was important and so she forced herself to take control. She was hardly a social butterfly, but she was still better at holding a conversation than James Leipfold.

"He's not in any trouble," Maile said, anticipating the woman's train of thought and seeking to defuse the situation before she was able to tell them to fuck off and to slam the door in their faces. "We just think he might be able to help us."

"What's this about?" Mrs. White asked, glaring at her suspiciously.

"It's about the Tower Hill Terror," Maile replied. "I'm sure you've read about him in the newspapers. I think your son might be able to help us to stop him."

"Lukas? You're kidding."

"We're not, Mrs. White," Leipfold said. "But don't worry. I don't believe he's in any danger. That said, he may be in possession of some information that could help us to bring a murderer to justice."

"Well…" The woman looked them up and down again and then seemed to arrive at a conclusion. "Okay, you can come in. Quickly, now. And take your shoes off and leave them in the hallway, please. I've just done the housework and I'm in no mood to start all over again."

Maile and Leipfold did as they were asked and were shown into the living room, which looked considerably tidier than it had on their last visit. Mrs. White leaned through the doorway and shouted her son's name from the bottom of the stairs and then asked her guests to wait as she went back into the kitchen to check on her baking.

Lukas entered the room shortly afterwards and did a visible double take when he saw who his visitors were. The colour drained from his face except in his cheeks, which flushed a deep crimson.

"What do you want?" he asked. "I already told you everything I know."

"Not quite," Leipfold said. He was sitting comfortably in one of the armchairs and looking for all the world like he owned the place. He made no effort to get up. "You didn't mention the Oyster Club."

Lukas White looked straight back at Leipfold with a dormant expression on his face, as though the lights were on but no one was home. For a second, he looked as though he was going to deny it and to claim that he'd never heard of it. But then his head dropped slightly and he glanced nervously towards the kitchen, where his mother was still clattering around with her pots and pans.

"I think we'd better go to my room," he said.

* * *

Lukas White's bedroom was pretty typical for a boy his age, a little box room with a single bed beneath a small window, a chest of drawers with clothes poking out and a stand with a flatscreen TV and a couple of consoles. A stack of Marvel comics poked out from a cardboard box beneath the bed, and the floor was a minefield of dirty clothes and unwashed crockery. It was pretty clear that he spent most of his time in there.

The room was too small for a desk or a chair, so Lukas White cleared a space on his bed and sat down on it. Leipfold winced as the kid raked his arm across a pile of fresh and folded laundry, placed there by his mother no doubt, and sent it tumbling towards the floor on top of his sweaty gym socks and empty crisp packets. The kid gestured for Maile and Leipfold to sit down beside him, but they declined his invitation and remained standing. It gave them a height advantage and blocked off the exit.

"So why are you here?" Lukas asked.

"We found out about your blog," Leipfold said. "You know, the one about the Oyster Club. What's the matter, kid? It's just a stupid club. Why the whole vendetta?"

Lukas mumbled something that they couldn't hear and Leipfold asked him to repeat it.

"I said, 'I can't stand hypocrites.'"

"Hypocrites?"

"Yeah," Lukas said. "How much do you know about the Oyster Club, anyway?"

Leipfold and Maile just looked at him. It was Leipfold's go-to trick, relying on the inherent human need to plug the awkward silence in a conversation. It rarely let him down.

"I went along to the Oyster Club for a laugh," Lukas said. "I heard about it online and I wanted to see if it was as ridiculous as it sounded. It was."

"What were you even doing at an over-twenty-one club?" Maile asked. "You must have known you'd get caught."

"That was kind of the point," he said. "I thought it'd be fun, something to do for the evening. Just a little distraction, that's all. Don't you ever get bored of life?"

"Kid, you're fourteen years old," Leipfold said. "What have you got to be bored about?"

Lukas White shrugged. "Whatever," he said. "It was something to do. But when I got there and did a little digging, everything changed. The girls that go, they're mostly regulars. They know what's going on behind the scenes, and I started to hear some stuff that I couldn't unhear if you know what I mean."

"I don't follow you," Leipfold said.

Lukas White laughed, but it was a bitter laugh that was full of scorn. "Remember when I said I hate hypocrites?" he said. "Well, that place is full of them. That's why I started my blog, Mr. Leipfold, and that's why I post what I post on there."

"Why are they hypocrites at the Oyster Club?" Maile asked.

"It's the woman who runs it," Lukas said. "That *bitch* Lucy Fforde. She talks a big game about how she hates cheaters and how her shitty little club is all about monogamy, but she's just the same as the rest of them. She was married, you know. When she first started putting the events on."

"So?"

"Don't you get it?" Lukas asked. He grinned. "You should go back to my blog and read all the posts on it. They'll tell you everything you need to know. But here's the long and the short of it. Fforde met a man there and her marriage fell apart. The husband found out and broke things off with her. Then he just sort of…disappeared. She called the cops and they tried to find the guy, but nothing. Nobody's seen him since. A couple of months later, she shacked up with the guy she met at the Oyster Club."

Lukas White looked at them both and smiled sheepishly. "Now can you see why I wanted to expose their hypocrisy?" he asked. "This shit's too good to miss. You couldn't make it up."

Leipfold shook his head. "No, kid," he said. "I don't. Why do you even care? I'm not buying that you're so invested in Lucy Fforde's love life that you wanted to shut her down."

"That's all I've got for you."

Leipfold scowled at the kid and then asked his next question, the question that was the main reason why he'd wanted to see him in the first place.

"Does the name Asif Shaktar mean anything to you?" he asked.

Lukas shook his head. "No," he said. "Should it?"

"It was worth a shot," Leipfold said. He thought of another question, a longer one. "What about a chap called Marc Allman?"

That shot hit home, and the whites of White's eyes were overtaken by darkness as his pupils expanded in recognition.

"Yeah," he said. "I know him. We've just been talking about him. He's the guy from the Oyster Club who hooked up with Lucy Fforde."

* * *

They talked to Lukas White for another half hour or so, but if he had any more information, it was buried somewhere inside his mind where he couldn't access it. He wanted to help, they could see it in his eyes, but he was also holding something back. Leipfold wondered what it was, and the fact that he didn't know left a sour taste in his mouth.

When they left the kid's room, they bumped into his mother on the stairway. She'd taken her apron off and was halfheartedly brushing the eaves with a feather duster, but she wasn't fooling anyone.

"I thought my ears were burning," Leipfold murmured as she escorted them to the door.

Lukas White's mother followed them outside and then closed the door behind her.

"Okay, Mister," she said. "What's all this about?"

"I'm not sure I follow you," Leipfold said, turning around to look at her. He could see the kid leaning out of an upstairs window and listening in on them, but he didn't see much point in telling her. It was poetic justice.

"I won't pretend that I wasn't listening in on your conversation," she said. "I'm a mother, after all, and my son is still a child. Why were you asking him about Lucy?"

"Lucy Fforde?"

"Yes," she said. "Why were you asking about my sister?"

"Your *sister*?"

Mrs. White looked just as surprised as Leipfold was. "You mean you didn't *know*?" she asked.

"I think we'd better go back inside," Leipfold said.

But Mrs. White shook her head. "Let's go for a walk," she said. "I don't want my son to overhear us."

"Very wise," Leipfold said, thinking of the boy in the window above them. He fell into step to her right while Maile moved to her left. They looped the block three abreast as they continued to talk.

"My sister stole some money from us," Mrs. White explained. She didn't look at them while she talked. "A large amount of money, if you must know. This is several years ago now. It came at a bad time for us, and so we had to downsize. Lukas had to change schools, and he's never forgiven her. The kids bully him, you know. I try my best for him, but I can't really blame him for skipping school and getting himself into trouble. That's what this is about, I take it?"

"Something like that," Leipfold said. "At first, I thought your son was connected to the Tower Hill Terror, but I'm starting to doubt it."

"Good. My Lukas would never be involved in something like that. He's a good kid. He's just a little bit…well, rebellious at the moment. You know how it is. You were a boy once."

"Indeed," Leipfold said. When he was Lukas White's age, he'd been rubbing shoulders with petty criminals and sneaking into pubs. He couldn't help thinking that Lukas White had got off easy. "So how does Lucy Fforde fit into it? That's what I want to know."

"I have no idea," Mrs. White said. "All I know is that she stole Luke's future and we've never forgiven her. That money was supposed to go towards his tuition fees. Nine grand a year? They must take us all for fools."

"I wouldn't know," Leipfold said. "I never went to uni. Thanks, Mrs. White. That explains a lot. I see now why your son might have a grudge against her."

"But what did he *do?*"

Leipfold stopped suddenly. Mrs. White turned around to look at him, almost knocking Maile over with her shoulder. They'd finished their loop of the block and were approaching the Whites' front door.

"You should probably ask him that yourself," Leipfold said.

* * *

Leipfold needed to talk to Maile, but they couldn't talk while they were wearing their helmets and she was riding pillion on the back of Camilla. It had to wait until they got back to the office, but they got started as soon as he'd parked up and they continued to talk as Leipfold led the way up the narrow staircase.

"It's the Oyster Club," Leipfold said. "It's related to the case. It has to be. How can it not be? It's the only thing I can think of besides the Tower Hill Terror himself that links Lukas White, Asif Shaktar and Marc Allman."

"But what about the victims?" Maile asked. "What links them?"

"I have no idea," Leipfold replied. "But I'm going to find out."

"I don't get it, boss. If Lucas White and Lucy Fforde are related, what did he hope to gain from going to her dating night? He must have known he'd be recognised."

"I suspect that was the point," Leipfold said. "He wanted to cause a scene. To embarrass the woman in her home turf. Maybe he just wanted to remind her that he existed and that she'd stolen the money his mother had put aside for his education."

"Maybe."

By this point, they were inside the office, and Leipfold had chucked his helmet down beneath the coat rack and headed straight into the kitchen to put the kettle on. Detective work was a thirsty business, and he was dying for a brew.

"You know," he said, grabbing a couple of cups from the mug tree and rinsing them out in the sink in case they had any dust in them, "I was starting to think it was an inside job."

"You were?"

"Of course," Leipfold replied. "Weren't you?"

"I mean, I guess."

"The Tower Hill Terror seemed to know too much," he said. "Whoever he is, he's a master at the game. He's been playing the police force off against itself, and I was starting to think that it had to be someone on the inside. It was the only thing that made sense. But now I'm not so sure, and perhaps this is the lead we need to figure out the truth here."

* * *

Maile spent most of the early evening at her desk in front of the computer screen. As a relatively new employee—and Leipfold's first ever official hire—she was on an hourly contract with time and a half for overtime. Leipfold told her to knock herself out, to work as hard and as long as she needed as long as she came up trumps with some information.

Leipfold's trick with the map had given Maile an idea, and she was able to narrow down her search to specific areas. She pulled data en masse from social networking sites and then worked some magic with the CSV file, filtering through the information to look for common trends in different areas.

She even found accounts that were linked to Abu Adewali and Calvin Myatt, although Jayne Lipton had kept her private life offline. But so far, Maile had been unable to find anything useful. The victims all talked about the usual stuff—the shows they watched, the music they listened to, the books they read and the friends they hung out with. Maile spent the best part of an hour trawling through the data and had nothing to show at the end of it.

Frustrated, she changed tack, filtering posts based on their geographic location. She was looking for anything unusual around the time of the murders, giving herself a couple of days' leeway on either side.

Jayne's murder had sparked a barrage of gossip, largely because she was connected to the previous case and because her name had already been in the papers. Maile browsed through the feed, pausing every now and then to look at a photo or to read the ill-advised sentiments of sixteen-year-old kids with nothing better to do than to troll their time away. But there was nothing there of significance.

Adewali's death had passed by virtually unnoticed, apart from the initial flurry of speculation when the photos of the scene were first released. Maile cursed Lukas White, and the stupidity with which he'd blindly agreed to do a favour for a man on the street. But she was also grateful for the opportunity it created. She was able to filter through every response and to catalogue every share. Perhaps the killer had made a mistake somewhere.

Who are you? Maile thought. *And why are you doing this?*

Calvin Myatt's murder had caused the biggest buzz of all, thanks to the widespread press coverage and the tabloids' bad habit of glamorising the macabre. Myatt's death had been front page news across the country, and it was already all over the news channels. Speculation was rife, and Maile indexed tens of thousands of posts about the atrocity. She'd have her work cut out for her if she wanted to make sense of it, especially because her only option was to filter through it manually, looking for that one post, somewhere, that would give them the lead they were looking for.

She found reports of road work on the day of Lipton's death, a sketchy-looking guy in a car a couple of hours before Adewali was found, and strange noises from a shipping container in Battersea, not far from where Calvin Myatt worked. It was the last report that intrigued her the most. The person who'd posted it had said it reminded them of a wounded animal. They'd said that the sounds were faint and weak, like a dog with a broken leg that had been left to cower alone in a basement.

It wasn't much but it was a lead, and they had precious few of those if Leipfold's wall-mounted map was anything to go by. Maile walked over and took a look at it. She grabbed one of Leipfold's yellow pins and jabbed it into the board where the shipping container was. It was just inside Leipfold's circle.

The boss, meanwhile, was watching her every move from the comfort of his desk, where he was updating the company's finances on a piece of complicated, outdated software.

"What are you doing?" Leipfold asked.

"I think I've got a lead, boss," she explained. "A shipping container in Battersea. I haven't got an exact address, but I can hone in on it within a half-mile radius."

"What's so important about the container?" he asked.

So Maile brought him up to speed with her research, starting with her methodology and finishing with the post she'd read about the noises from inside the container. Leipfold frowned and stared indecisively at the corkboard. Then he jumped up from his seat, pulled on his leather jacket and grabbed the keys to Camilla.

"Where are you going?" Maile asked.

"I guess I'm going to Battersea," Leipfold replied. "We need to find this container and see what's what."

"Could be dangerous."

"It could be," Leipfold agreed. "I'll give Jack Cholmondeley a call and see if he can send over some officers. In the meantime, there's not a moment to lose. A woman's life could be at stake."

He rushed towards the door and opened it, then paused on the threshold. He turned back to look at Maile.

"You coming?" he asked. "You can ride side-saddle."

Maile grinned. "Of course," she replied. "Give me a second. I'll grab my pepper spray. Someone's got to look after you."

Chapter Seventeen:
Armed Response

IT WAS LATER THAT EVENING, and Leipfold and Maile were in an undisclosed location in Battersea, looking through a mesh fence at an industrial unit that housed several dozen corrugated shipping containers. It was like a bizarre game of Tetris or dominos. Each container was a different shape, a different colour, a different brand.

"Jesus," Maile murmured. "It's where shipping crates come to die."

"Yeah," Leipfold said. "Let's hope that's the only thing that dies here."

Leipfold and Maile paused for a moment, standing in silence to listen out for the noises that had been reported in the area. But there was nothing—at least, nothing that they could hear over the thrum of the passing traffic and the noise pollution from the industrial estate. Then they heard the distant sound of sirens, and Leipfold grinned and nodded in their approximate direction.

"Cholmondeley's on his way, then," Leipfold said. "Better make this quick."

Leipfold grabbed hold of the fence and leapt at it. He was in his element, reliving his army days with relish. He scuttled over the fence and dropped down on the other side, rolling as he hit the ground to soften the impact. It was at least a ten-foot drop onto concrete, but Leipfold took it like a pro and, apart from complaining about his knees when he got up again, he seemed unfazed and uninjured.

"Keep watch," he commanded, frowning at Maile from the other side of the mesh. "When Cholmondeley gets here, tell him where I am and what I'm doing."

"And what *are* you doing?" Maile asked. "Be careful, boss. It could be dangerous."

"I should bloody well hope so, too," Leipfold said. "If it's not dangerous, we're in the wrong place. Wait here."

* * *

Maile watched from a distance as her boss raced off into the labyrinthine maze of packing crates, racing from container to container and pausing every now and then to put his ear against the walls to listen. Every time he stopped, he'd shout "hello?" and wait for a response. Meanwhile, the sirens were getting louder and louder.

"Come on, boss," Maile murmured. The stress she felt was like a living organism coursing through her veins in an elaborate attempt to take over her body and to stop her brain from fully functioning.

Then Maile saw the lights, and she flinched as a half-dozen cop cars raced past her towards the entrance of the facility. They were joined there by two riot vans. Maile watched from a distance as their doors opened and two armed response units spilled out of the vans and onto the pavement.

She gestured frantically at Leipfold, pointing in the direction of the entrance. She thought about shouting across at him, but she wasn't sure if her voice would carry. Besides, she didn't want to attract the attention of the police force.

Leipfold, meanwhile, was gesturing frantically back at her. He pointed at the container he was standing beside, then at the lock, then back at the container. He shouted something, but it didn't quite carry to where she was standing. But she knew what he meant, all right. He'd found something.

She hoped it was something worth finding. There was a crash from the lot's entrance, the shrill, steely scream of the gate being bashed in. She could see a flurry of movement, a sure sign of the armed response team. Their dark jackets did the job, helping them to melt into the night and to gain the element of surprise. And they were armed to the teeth. The best way to spot them was to catch the light pollution glinting off their rifles.

Leipfold shouted something again, and the men with guns raced towards him. He held his hands in the air to show he was unarmed. But Maile was worried for him, and her heart was in her mouth as she watched the scene unfolding before her on the other side of the complex's cold mesh fence.

Jesus Christ, she thought. *I hope he knows what he's doing.*

* * *

"What the hell do you think you're doing?"

Jack Cholmondeley was in a bad mood. He'd been hoping for a lazy evening, a night spent rereading the case notes in front of the telly while Mary went to Zumba. She wasn't too happy about taking a taxi, especially because her husband had let her down at the last minute. But when there was a choice between doing his duty and ferrying his wife around in the back of his Beemer, there was only one real option for Jack Cholmondeley.

Now he had to deal with James Leipfold, who'd crashed the party before the response team arrived and put the whole operation in danger.

"Sorry, Jack," Leipfold said. "You know how it is. A woman's life is at stake. You should be glad that I called your boys at all."

"This isn't a joke, James." Cholmondeley sighed. He grabbed Leipfold's arm and dragged him away from the container. At the same time, the armed response team took up positions around the outside of it. "You could have died. This killer is dangerous, brutal."

The leader of the armed response team, a man who Cholmondeley knew by face if not by name, was scanning the container with some sort of electronic device. He checked the readout and nodded, then asked Cholmondeley for instructions.

"You ready?" he asked.

Cholmondeley nodded. "Let's do it," he said.

"All units, on me." The man gestured towards the door, and one of his men raced up to it with a pair of bolt cutters. They sliced through the rusty chain as easily as a military laser cutting through the rubber skin of a balloon. The chain popped with a sound like a gunshot and four men from the response team rushed forward and swung the heavy doors open.

At first, it was too dark to see inside, but the men led with their guns and followed up with flashlights. Ghostly motes of dust drifted down from the ceiling and were caught in the beams, like stars falling from the sky. The soldiers swept their beams around the room and Leipfold and Cholmondeley leaned closer. It was like looking through a window into hell.

The inside of the container looked like the slaughter room of an abattoir. It reeked of shit and piss and the sweet, coppery tang of blood that's been spilled and left to congeal. The walls were damp with mildew, the floors were thick with dust and the unit was packed with heavy metal.

The flashlights lit up a gurney and passed on, then veered back over to focus on it.

"Jesus Christ," Cholmondeley said. "There's someone in there."

The armed response team leapt into action, and Cholmondeley was forced to take a back seat. He no longer called the shots.

Forensics will be pissed, he thought. The armed response team was destroying valuable evidence, but to hell with it. There was a life at stake.

When Cholmondeley had taken the call with Maile's intel and ordered the raid on the container, he'd had the presence of mind to order an EMT. They were hanging back, waiting for the all-clear from the response team. They worked quickly, scouring the scene for booby traps before beckoning the medics into the container once they were satisfied. They didn't bother to look for suspects. Whoever they were, they were long gone.

Leipfold and Cholmondeley watched on in a stunned silence as two medics raced up to the gurney and examined the body that was strapped into it. One of them took a pulse. It was weak, but it was there.

"We've got a live one," he shouted. "Just about. We need to get her out of here, now."

"Holy fucking shit," the taller man said, his voice carrying eerily on the wind like an echo in a graveyard. "Get a load of this."

Leipfold and Cholmondeley leaned closer, as did a couple members of the armed response team. The rest were establishing a perimeter, sweeping the facility for any sign of life. It was hard to see by torchlight, but there was no mistaking the deep, crimson stain on the sheet that covered the injured woman.

The wound was where the woman's legs met, and if there was any doubt about the unit's connection to the killer, it was dispelled in the second they noticed.

"Oh no," Cholmondeley murmured, burying his face in his hands. He was aware of the eyes of his colleagues upon him, torn between the awful scene inside the container and the unusual sight of the seasoned copper with tears in his eyes. "Oh no, no, no. We're too late. The bastard already got to her."

* * *

Jack Cholmondeley, the armed response team and the EMTs had a long, long night ahead of them. With the unit secure, the medics carried the wounded woman out into the back of a waiting ambulance and rushed her to hospital. Cholmondeley explained to Leipfold that she wouldn't be taken to just any old A&E. She was on her way to a military hospital where they'd be able to deal with the damage.

Meanwhile, the armed response team continued their sweep of the area. Leipfold wanted to go with them, but Cholmondeley had rebuked him.

"You're not even supposed to be here," he said. "Where's that assistant of yours, anyway?"

Leipfold blanched. He'd forgotten all about Maile. "She's just outside," he admitted. "On the other side of the fence."

"Better bring her in," Cholmondeley grunted. "She can't wait outside all night, and I suspect we'll be here for a while. Either bring her here or send her home."

And so Leipfold had given Maile the choice. True to form, Maile met

Leipfold and Cholmondeley at the entrance to the facility, where they spent the next ninety minutes waiting for confirmation that the place had been secured.

Midnight was on the horizon by the time that they were given the all-clear, and it was one or two o'clock before the forensic team arrived and began their investigation. Leipfold and Cholmondeley were allowed to watch from a safe distance, although they had to wear protective suits to avoid cross contamination. Maile, meanwhile, had to stay by the entrance with the two men who were keeping a lookout, with their hands on the triggers of their weapons, in case the killer returned to the scene. Leipfold suspected they wouldn't, and Jack Cholmondeley agreed with him. But there was protocol to follow, and it was better to be safe than sorry.

The search for clues continued throughout the night, although hope started to fade at around 3AM, when the dawn was still several hours away and the heavens opened up and started to rain down on the crime scene. Satisfied that the area was secure, most of the response team had returned to base for a debriefing, although four men were left behind on sentry duty with the promise of relief in the morning.

Cholmondeley didn't feel relieved. He felt depressed, upset, like a failure. He just hoped that his team was getting a good night's sleep because there wasn't enough coffee in the world to keep him awake and alert for the morning shift, which he was due to start in just under six hours. He wanted to go home.

And Leipfold was barely present at all. His mind was elsewhere and his cold, numb hands were struggling to drag the nib of a biro across the pages of his notebook. He drew a copy of the map from his office wall, then tore out the page and handed it to Cholmondeley. He explained its significance and asked the cop to carry out an investigation of his own.

"It's a pattern," Leipfold explained. "I'm sure it is. So far, every victim has lived, worked and been discovered within the city. Odds are that our killer lives here as well."

Cholmondeley thanked Leipfold for the information and promised to look into it. He took a photo of it and emailed it, with a brief explanation, to Groves and Mogford. They wouldn't be working, but they'd probably beat him to the office in the morning and he wanted them to start looking into it first thing. He copied in Constable Cohen so he could cross-reference the map with their missing persons database. He wondered, vaguely, whether the latest victim was one of the women that they'd already looked at, or whether this was something different, something new.

Then he shrugged his shoulders and got back to work.

* * *

Nobody else had spotted the cameras, but it was the first thing that Maile thought to look for.

She knew a lot more about psychology than Leipfold thanks to the books she read. She wondered if her boss knew what could be learned from books about Ted Bundy, Peter Sutcliffe and Jack the Ripper. She doubted the thought had ever occurred to him. Leipfold was a man of action. He gleaned his knowledge from the streets, not from books and documentaries. That was just one of the reasons why they made a good team.

No, Maile had a good idea how the mind of a killer worked, and a killer like this, whose crimes had been played out in the pages of *The Tribune*, would want to see the results of their labour. And besides, Maile had a suspicion, like an itch she couldn't scratch. The killer *knew*, somehow, that they were coming. Maybe it was paranoia and maybe it was a lucky guess. Either way, they'd left their victim to die in the lockup, sure she'd bleed out or suffocate when the air ran out. And whether the woman survived or not, the killer had already taken their trophy. She wondered idly whether it would end up at the police station or at the offices of *The Tribune*.

The Tower Hill Terror had kitted the place out with little cameras, which were invisible from the inside of the container. But someone could see them on the outside, if they looked hard enough. They'd drilled little holes in the corrugated metal, attached the cameras and then plastered over them with second-hand shipping labels. The cameras couldn't be seen, but the bulges could. Maile suspected that it was a similar setup to her own, which had come in useful during their last case.

At first, it was just a suspicion, but the suspicion slowly grew when she took a proper look around the facility. She had to bide her time and wait for the men on sentry duty to settle in for the long night and to stop paying her attention. She couldn't get into the unit—not without being spotted—but she didn't need to. Hell, she didn't *want* to. But she *could* take a little look around.

She found the first camera within a couple of minutes, and cameras two and three followed shortly afterwards. They'd been hidden well, but not well enough: one inside the twisted knot of an overhanging tree, one amongst a pile of rubble and one lying flat on top of one of the neighbouring containers inside a discarded cigarette packet.

That's one of my tricks, Maile thought.

She picked up the camera that had been lying in the rubble and held it in a gloved hand. She looked into the lens, then turned it over and around. It was a simple camera, with a single, low-quality lens attached to a router and a battery pack.

Holy shit, she thought. *Whoever this creep is, he's watching us. Like, right now. Streamed live in 240p.*

Maile shivered. Then she twisted the camera around so that it pointed at her face and slowly, calmly, deliberately raised a narrow middle finger. Then she put it back amongst the rubble where she found it.

She wandered over to Leipfold and Cholmondeley to tell the two men what she'd found. They were predictably delighted, and Cholmondeley shouted across to the forensic team to ask them to come over and take a look.

Good job I was wearing gloves, Maile thought. *I've never been this grateful for winter weather.*

Chapter Eighteen:
Jane Doe

THE RAIN GOT STEADILY WORSE throughout the night, and Leipfold and Maile gave in and headed home at 4:15 in the morning. Maile rode pillion while Leipfold meandered through the empty streets, guiding Camilla with a tender hand and a calm sense of mastery. Conditions were poor, and her tyres slipped on the concrete as though she was gliding across snow and ice. He didn't dare take her above thirty, especially not with Maile riding behind him. He didn't mind risking his own life, but he'd never forgive himself if something happened to her.

Leipfold dropped her outside her house and watched her walk to the door, calling after her to tell her to take the morning off. But she didn't, and neither did he. They just drank more coffee than usual and walked a little sluggishly. Every time the phone rang, Leipfold winced and Maile swore. They both had the same tension headache that Leipfold had felt for five years straight when his business was going down the pan and he had no idea how to save it.

Cholmondeley called at 10:45, a half hour after Leipfold and Maile finished *The Tribune*'s crossword. Leipfold left her to man the office and hopped back on to Camilla. She needed refuelling, but she'd have to make do with a couple of litres from the Shell garage because that was as much as Leipfold's empty wallet could stretch to. Then he hit the streets and cruised towards the Old Vic.

Cholmondeley met him at a diner around the corner from the police station. It was a strange place, a converted American schoolbus that served fries, burgers and coffee and invited customers to sit inside. The food was okay, but the coffee was good and both of them needed it after the night before. And it was private, more private than Cholmondeley's office back at the station. As an added bonus, Camilla looked badass, propped up on her kickstand at the front of the vehicle.

Leipfold ordered a coffee and a plate of fries, and Cholmondeley took a quarter-pounder deal with extra pickles. They sat down in one of the booths and looked gloomily out of the windows. It looked like rain again.

"So how are things?" Leipfold asked. "Get much sleep?"

Cholmondeley laughed. "Fat chance," he said. "How can I sleep with the Tower Hill Terror on the loose?"

"You sound just like *The Tribune*," Leipfold murmured.

The two men ate on in a gloomy silence. Then Cholmondeley broke it to give Leipfold an update, but there was little news to report from the police force.

"We still have no suspects," Cholmondeley said. "At least, none we can pin a case on. In the meantime, they're free to kill again."

"We'll keep working on it," Leipfold said. "Maile's back at the office following up on a couple of things, and at least we know where and how they operate. It's only a matter of time, Jack."

"Yeah," Cholmondeley murmured, "but that doesn't help us to make an arrest. We're still no closer to the killer's true identity."

"They'll make a mistake."

"Perhaps," Cholmondeley grunted. He stuffed the last handful of chips into his mouth and swilled them down with a gulp of coffee.

"What about the victim?" Leipfold asked. "How's she holding up?"

Cholmondeley whistled softly. "She's not so hot," he said. "They had to induce a coma. The bleeding's stopped, but her condition's critical."

Leipfold sighed and shook his head. He pushed the rest of his food away from him, no longer in the mood to eat.

"Can I see her?" he asked.

* * *

Cholmondeley pulled a few strings so that Leipfold could visit Jane

Doe—or Meg Jackson, if the killer's notes were to be believed—in the hospital. It was a bitch to organise, and technically in breach of protocol, but he knew people who knew people. Besides, Superintendent Richards had his back. She had to because Leipfold had been allowed to attend one of her briefings. He'd even helped them to find the lockup.

Jackson was in a terrible state. Leipfold guessed she was in her twenties, but the damage to her body made it difficult to tell. He put her height and weight at around five foot four and one hundred and thirty pounds. She was a slight girl, even smaller than Maile, with long, blonde hair that was stained copper from the blood she'd lost. Leipfold's armed escort gave him twenty minutes with the victim, but that was enough for him. He didn't even know why he was there. He just felt a burning desire to see her with his own eyes, to look at what had happened and to boost his resolve to stop it from ever happening again. He'd hoped to find a clue of some sort, something that the police had missed or that they'd failed to recognise the true significance of.

He spent the first two minutes examining the victim as closely as he could under the constraints of the police supervision. He spent the remaining eighteen minutes staring thoughtfully at her while jotting down notes in his Moleskine.

Leipfold nearly wept as he left the hospital, but the tears just wouldn't start coming. He remembered his old man, an often drunk, occasionally violent Jack the Lad type who'd threatened to beat him if he cried because "crying's for girls." And so Leipfold bit back the tears and did the only other thing he could do. He promised himself that he'd catch the Tower Hill Terror before they struck again.

He used his phone to check his bank balance, cursed softly when he realised that a couple of bills had gone out and then set himself a reminder to chase up a couple of invoices. He wasn't broke, but he did have a problem with cash flow. Money could buy a lot of things, and help was one of them.

Leipfold put in a couple of calls and hopped on his bike. Then he started her up and hit the streets again.

* * *

Back at the office, Maile's research had finally started to pay off. After modifying the parameters of her search software and downloading vast swathes of information from a couple of different social networks, she'd built up enough of a database to start searching through it. She aggregated it all, filtered out some of the noise and then created a list of links ranked by how often they'd been posted.

That gave her a list of around 1,800 links to look through. Unfortunately, there was no real way to automate it, so she found herself manually checking every link, bookmarking a couple and discounting most as worse than useless. But she forced herself to keep going. It felt like a waste of time, but there was no way of knowing until she finished the job and took a look at where it led her.

Leipfold returned to the office when she was a hundred links in, and she got up to make a quick coffee when she was halfway to a thousand. Then she sat back down and continued the search.

Twenty minutes later, she had a hit. The link had hardly gone viral. It had been shared a couple dozen times at most by random accounts with no obvious ties to connect them. She realised, relieved at the sudden burst of knowledge, that Lukas White's name was nowhere to be found.

Good, she thought. *I guess he wasn't involved.* In Maile's head, the kid was too young to have played a part in the brutality. He should never have been exposed to it in the first place.

The feed was password protected, but she dropped Mayhem a message and her hacker friend was more than happy to help break into it.

"Shouldn't take long," Mayhem had said, his fingers striking some keyboard somewhere and keeping her updated on his progress. Maile had promised him a beer for his troubles, and he'd been only too happy to help. "Let me get back to you."

He got back to her a half hour later, after he'd run the link through some brute force tools which tried to guess the login by repeatedly keying in credentials until they managed to get inside.

"It's like the guy *wanted* us to crack it," Mayhem said. "The username's 'administrator' and the password is 'Hebrews134.' Dictionary words and a couple of numbers, pathetic. And that's not all."

"Go on," Maile prompted, her own fingers hitting the keys so hard that Leipfold asked her to keep it down.

"Looks like the login is a new thing," Mayhem said. "I did a little digging myself. My guess? The live stream was open to the public, and then it got locked down at the end of the broadcast. You're going to want to take a look at it."

"I sure am," Maile replied. "BRB."

Maile loaded up the link again and keyed in the credentials that Mayhem sent. It took a while for the site to load, but once she was in, she was in.

It was a sparse site, hosted on a Ukrainian server with a Japanese domain name, and it had been created for one purpose only. It was a simple video repository, and it housed a seemingly endless stream of videos, all around nine hours long. Maile clicked through them at random. It was pretty damn obvious what she was looking at.

Each of the files contained the footage from a different camera, including two different angles on the inside of the container. Maile laughed delightedly and shouted for Leipfold to come over.

He was halfway over to her desk when the intercom buzzed, breaking the tranquillity with a harsh, grating sound that always gave the two of them a headache.

Leipfold told Maile he'd be right with her and wandered over to answer the door.

* * *

It was five minutes later, and Maile was bustling around in the kitchen to make a round of drinks for Leipfold and his visitors. There were three of them, three men who looked like they'd fallen out of *EastEnders* and spilled into their messy office.

Leipfold introduced them all to her by name. The first man was a Craig. He stood about five foot eleven and looked like a former addict, with gaunt features, too-thin skin and bandy legs and arms. He was wearing a Burberry jacket and knock-off Levi's, and the ends of his fingers were stained yellow with nicotine.

The second man was introduced as a Thom with a silent "h," a greasy-looking youth of nineteen or so who was wearing a black tracksuit and an expensive pair of Nikes. The third man was Fletch, a flat-faced weasel of a man who looked like he'd rob his own mother for the change in her piggy bank. Maile shook hands with each of them in turn, out of politeness more than anything, then sat back down at her desk. She reached into her second drawer for a small, plastic bottle and then sanitised her hands surreptitiously while watching events unfold.

Leipfold sat the three men down in reception and then hurried over to his desk to pick up a sheaf of papers. Maile recognised the pages as the suspect profiles she'd developed as part of their case notes. Each profile contained a brief bio and description, a summary of their histories to date and a selection of recent photographs that Maile had swiped from search engines and social networking sites. Leipfold separated the piles into three and handed a stack out to each of his visitors.

"Take these," Leipfold instructed, "and familiarise yourself with them. And no trading papers, understand? I've given each of you a different assignment. It's nothing too difficult."

"What's the assignment?" This came from Fletch, who'd spun his chair around and was sitting with his legs spread and the back sticking up between them.

"I want you to follow them," Leipfold said. "I'm not expecting it to be perfect, but I want you to do the best you can."

"And are you going to pay us?"

Leipfold frowned and crossed his arms. "What kind of man do you think I am?" he asked. "You'll get paid when the job's done."

"Okay," Fletch replied. "It's just that last time, you—"

"This time is different," Leipfold interrupted, holding up a hand to call for silence. "And work is work, take it or leave it. Have you boys got a better offer?"

Leipfold paused for a moment, waiting for a reply that never came.

"Good," he said. "Now, you'll find the information I have on each of your marks in the packs that I gave you, including photographs, approximate heights and weights and a list of known haunts. I want you to follow them, as much as possible, and report back to me on their movements."

"What exactly are we looking for?"

"Good question, Thom," Leipfold said. "And I'm afraid it's a tricky one to answer. Just log their movements and send me updates. If something seems suspicious, there's probably a reason for it. Okay?"

The three men nodded their assent.

"Okay," Leipfold said. "Fletch, you'll be following Lukas White. He's just a kid, but he's connected to a case that I'm working on and I want to rule him out as a suspect."

"Got it."

"Thom," Leipfold continued, "I want you to tail Asif Shaktar. He works as a courier and so you're going to have your work cut out for you. Speak to my assistant. She might be able to give you a bug or something to attach to his bike so at least we know where he is when he's out on the job if you can't keep up with him."

"Will do," Thom said.

Leipfold nodded and said, "Craig, I've saved the best for last. You'll be following a man called Marc Allman. I want you to be careful with him. He's already been interviewed by the police and to be blunt, we have no idea what he's capable of. We don't know much about him. That's why I want you to follow him."

"I can do that," Craig said. It was the first time he'd said anything, and Maile noticed that his voice was low and raspy like Tom Waits or Leonard Cohen, born from too many bottles of whiskey. "Is there anything else?"

Leipfold shook his head. "Just that time is of the essence," he said. "I need you to get started as soon as possible."

"And what about the money?"

"Don't worry about the money," Leipfold said. "If you find something, I'll make it worth your while."

* * *

"So what have you got?"

It was ten minutes later and the afternoon was turning slowly into evening. Leipfold's guests had left the office. He was leaning lazily against the wall beside Maile's desk while she scrolled her mouse through the latest news. She pulled up the bookmark she'd saved of the video repository and started flicking through the footage.

"I found the feed for the cameras at the lock-up."

"How?"

"Like Ringo Starr," she said. "With a little help from my friends. I'll send over the link. Log in with 'administrator' and 'Hebrews134.'"

"Got it," Leipfold said. Maile believed him. Her boss had an uncanny ability to remember things, not quite preternatural or eidetic but close enough to pass for it on a foggy day. In another life, she was sure he was counting cards in some backwater casino. "Like the Bible."

"Like the what?"

"Like the Bible," Leipfold repeated. "Look it up."

So she did. Hebrews 13:4. *Marriage should be honoured by all, and the marriage bed kept pure, for God will judge the adulterer and all the sexually immoral.*

"Weird password," Maile said, but she let it go. "It doesn't matter, forget about that. That's not important. This is."

"What?"

Maile grinned and switched tabs, then blew up the footage until it took up the whole of one of her two screens.

"Look closer," she said. She moved her pointer to the bottom left of the screen and spun it around in little circles. Leipfold leaned in. "There. You see it?"

"What is it?"

"It's hard to tell." Maile shrugged and ran her hands across the keyboard again. It honed in on the square of pixels that they were looking at and ran through a couple of enhancements that she'd already worked on. They ran the same piece of footage in a loop, tweaking the brightness, the contrast and the sharpness.

"Looks like a piece of paper," Leipfold said.

"That's what I thought." Maile gestured at the screen, tracing a finger along the contours on the footage. The inside of the lockup was built from corrugated sheets of metal and the camera was tucked against the floor, flattened tight against the curves.

"Wait," Leipfold said, snatching Maile's hand away from the mouse to stop her from cycling through the footage again. "That's not just a piece of paper. It's an envelope."

Maile squinted at the screen again. Whatever it was, it had been overlooked by the armed response team. The video cut out shortly after forensics arrived, but they hadn't found it in the ten minutes or so that they'd been caught on tape.

"I wonder what's in it," Maile murmured.

"I don't know," Leipfold said. "But I bet it's addressed to Jack Cholmondeley. And whatever it is, I don't think it's going to be good news."

Maile shrugged. "Is it ever?" she asked. "This guy's smart, boss. He knew we were coming, but how?"

"I don't know," Leipfold said. "We're going to have to be more careful. Maybe he has someone on the inside. Some connection to the case."

"Is that possible?"

Leipfold sighed and shook his head. "At the moment, Maile," he said, "anything's possible."

Chapter Nineteen:
A Bleak Sun Rises

LATER THAT EVENING, when Leipfold was alone in the office trying to catch up with his financials, he took a phone call. He glanced down at his second phone, the one which only Jack Cholmondeley had the number for, and picked it up.

"Leipfold speaking," he said. "What's up, Jack?"

There was a pause on the other end of the line, and Jack Cholmondeley took a deep breath before saying, "Hi, James. I have bad news, I'm afraid."

"What is it?"

"She's dead," Cholmondeley said. "Jane Doe. Meg Jackson. Whatever the hell she's called."

"You still don't have a hit on who she is?"

"*Was*," Cholmondeley said. He sounded wretched, miserable. "Not yet. We're still working on it. We've had the lab boys run prints but they didn't find a match. Whoever she was, she wasn't in the database. She's either not a criminal, or she's so good at what she does that she's never been caught."

"Anyone reported missing?"

"Nope," Cholmondeley said. "At least, no one that matches her description. But we've had our tech boys crunching some data or whatever the hell they do and they've given us a few possibilities. The most likely suspect is Jennifer Megan Jackson, one of the names on our shortlist from the census. Constable Groves is on her way over as we speak. I'll let you know if we find anything."

"Understood," Leipfold said. He paused, thinking back to Maile's analysis of the footage of the crime scene. He took a gamble and asked, "Did you find the letter?"

There was silence on the other end of the call again. It sounded like Cholmondeley was still at the station. Leipfold could hear the distant, shrill call of a telephone and a background murmur of voices, as well as the telltale sound of Jack Cholmondeley rapping his knuckles thoughtfully against his desk.

"How did you know about the letter?" he asked.

Leipfold laughed. "It's a long story," he said.

"I've got time," Cholmondeley replied. And so Leipfold told him about Maile's suspicions when she saw the cameras and her subsequent discovery of the live stream, the password and the biblical verse that it referred to. Then he told him how Maile had sharpened the feed until they were able to make out the details and how he'd made an educated guess from there.

"So you see," he finished, lamely. "That's how we figured it out. What did the letter say?"

"Nothing useful," Cholmondeley said. "Sounded like the ravings of a madman."

"Interesting," Leipfold murmured.

"It is?"

"Of course, it is," Leipfold replied. "In the other notes, the Tower Hill Terror sounded as sane as you or I. Angry, perhaps, but still sane. So what's changed?"

"Perhaps the pressure is starting to get to him," Cholmondeley said.

"I doubt it," Leipfold replied. "Can I get a look at the letter?"

"It's with forensics. They won't let anyone go near it."

Leipfold paused. "If you haven't got access to it," he asked, "then how do you know what it said?"

"I have a scan of it," Cholmondeley said. "I'll send it over. Strictly confidential, you understand. But you already know far too much about the case for your own good. What harm can one more document do? Besides, who knows? Perhaps you'll be able to make some sense of it."

Leipfold laughed, nervously. "I doubt that," he said. "Not without the original. But send it over and I'll see what I can do."

"It's a deal," Cholmondeley said. "And James?"

"What?"

"Work quickly, okay?" Cholmondeley paused again and a gloomy lack of optimism weighed heavily on the dead air between them. "This guy just doesn't stop. I don't think he *could* stop even if he wanted to."

"Got it."

"I'm serious," Cholmondeley said. "He'll only stop if we make him stop."

Leipfold grimaced, all alone in his dimly-lit office with the remnants of the day's papers scattered before him across his desk. He'd seen plenty of cases throughout his career, but this was the first with such a serious and bloody history. Most of the time, he was hired by jealous spouses or sketchy businessmen who wanted a leg up on the competition. Half of the time, no crime had been committed. This time it was different.

"I wouldn't worry," he said. "We'll make him stop all right. You leave it with me, Jack. Go and get some sleep."

* * *

A bleak sun rose on an indifferent city on the morning of Thursday 4th March, but it wasn't indifferent for long. A special edition of *The Tribune* was out and it was already making its way across the city to be delivered by kids on pushbikes and stocked by little shops and off-licenses.

The entire front cover was dedicated to the murders, illustrated by a rerun of the sketch that Maile had made with Lukas White. It felt like an aeon ago, but Leipfold realised with a start that it had only been a week or two, if that. But a hell of a lot had happened since then.

And now the story was front-page news again, but Leipfold suspected that the police hadn't had a hand in it. This wasn't off the back of some press release from the station, asking for the public's help to track down a criminal before they had a chance to commit a crime. This was full-blown fearmongering.

"Sweet Jesus," Leipfold murmured as he cast his eyes over the story. "Cholmondeley isn't going to be happy about this."

Ironically, Leipfold noticed, the article itself was well-written, well-researched and almost entirely factual. True, *The Tribune* had somehow got its hands on some information that had never been made public, but they hadn't resorted to making things up to sell their papers. Every inch of the article was true, but seeing it down in black and white somehow gave it more gravitas, reflecting exactly how important it was for the killer to be caught.

Unfortunately, Siobhan Dent, the woman whose name was attached to the byline, had used her column inches to criticise the police and to ask for answers. *Why is the killer still on the loose? What's the police force doing to stop him? When will our streets be safe again?*

Leipfold called Cholmondeley to let him know about the article but had to satisfy himself with leaving a message. Then he switched to his main device and put in a call to Alan Phelps, his main contact at the local rag.

Phelps answered quickly and sardonically told Leipfold that he wasn't going to give him the answer to 14 across. "You're going to have to wait for the next issue if you're stuck on the answers, pal," he said. "We've been through this before."

"I'm not calling you about the bloody crossword," Leipfold growled. "As a matter of fact, I haven't had a chance to look at it."

"You'll like it," Phelps said. "It's a real humdinger. Some of my best work. I had to *research* this one. You have no idea how difficult it is to research—"

"Alan," Leipfold interrupted. "Shut up for a second, okay? This is important. I need a favour."

"I know you do," the journalist replied. "You always do. That's the only time you ever call me."

"Touché," Leipfold said. "Well listen, this one's an easy one. I'm not asking you to do anything. I'm asking you *not* to do something."

From the other end of the call, Phelps sighed. Leipfold always pictured the man in a garden shed, compiling his crosswords by hand on A3 paper while leaning on a cutting mat. In reality, the man worked in front of a computer screen in the grey, dead office that *The Tribune* shared with a sister publication. Leipfold knew that—he'd seen it with his own eyes—but that didn't stop him from picturing Phelps as a hermit in a shed on a mountainside.

"What do you want, Mr. Leipfold?" Phelps asked.

"It's easy," Leipfold replied. "Stop talking about the Tower Hill Terror."

"The Tower Hill Terror?"

"Don't play the fool with me, Phelps," Leipfold said. "I know you like to play silly buggers, but this isn't a game you're going to win. I need you to stop talking about the serial killer."

"So it's true," Phelps murmured. "I mean, that's the word on the streets, but there's no word from the police yet. So the cases are connected?"

"It's a serial killer," Leipfold said. "And every time you write about him you give him what he wants. What the hell were you thinking? Why did you let that Dent woman run her mouth about the police on the front page of the biggest bloody paper in the city?"

"*Let* her?" Phelps asked. He laughed into his handset, and the tinny sound was like sandpaper in Leipfold's ear. "Mr. Leipfold, I'll let her do anything she damn well pleases."

Something about the way he said it seemed to strike Leipfold between the eyes like the toothless bite of an elderly rattlesnake. "Why's that?" he asked.

"Siobhan Dent is in charge of the place while Pam's on maternity leave," Phelps said. "I can't stop her. If you want her to stop running stories, you're going to have to talk to her yourself."

* * *

Maile O'Hara was worried. Her housemate had gone out for drinks the night before and she hadn't come home. That in itself wasn't unusual, but she also hadn't heard from her and every time she dialled her phone number, it went straight to voicemail.

It's not like her at all, she thought. *She hates it when her battery dies. It means her plants die on that stupid bloody game she plays.*

At first, she'd tried to push those nagging thoughts out of her head. She'd turned on the TV in the living room and gone to lie on her bed with her laptop so that the sound would leak through the walls and make it seem as though everything was normal. But everything *wasn't* normal, and not even a couple of deathmatches on her Xbox could take her mind off it.

After the second game, she said goodbye to Mayhem and removed her headset, and then she walked back out into the living room and wandered around it, looking for a note that she might have missed or some sort of clue that could tell her where her housemate was. She even had a cursory look around her bedroom, but there was nothing.

Maile walked back into her bedroom and flopped down on her mattress, then grabbed her phone from the bedside table and put in another call to her housemate. It took a while to connect and for a second, she expected it to start ringing. She had a sudden mental image of the phone going off on the other side of the wall in Kat's bedroom, but then the line clicked and Kat's voicemail message started to play, the dull, robotic voice that came as default because she'd never bothered to change it.

"Kat," Maile said, "it's me again. Listen, I'm starting to get worried so give me a call or a text as soon as you can, okay? I don't want to hassle you and if you need some time and space I can dig that, but I need to know you're okay before I go crazy and start calling people up and sending out a search party."

She paused for a moment and thought about what she'd said. Then she laughed sheepishly and added, "Look, come home soon, okay? It's your turn to take the bins out."

Then she put the phone down.

She didn't sleep well that night. She kept having bad dreams about her housemate and awful thoughts about the ongoing investigation into the Tower Hill Terror. She was 99 percent sure that Kat was okay, but that left a little margin for error. She didn't want to take the chance.

At 4:30AM, Maile had given up. She pulled herself back out of bed and made herself a black coffee on the Tassimo machine, then settled down on the living room sofa with her laptop propped on top of her Pokémon pyjamas.

If I haven't heard from her by tomorrow lunchtime, she thought, *I'm going to have to do something about it.*

* * *

Cholmondeley's team was in for a busy day. *The Tribune* story hit the ground running and it was trending across the country by 11AM. By lunchtime, a ragtag group of protestors had gathered outside the station to wave their signs and sing their songs as they demanded action from the police force.

Ever pragmatic, Cholmondeley held another of his impromptu press conferences, meeting with the protestors on the steps of the station to answer their questions. The goal was to change the flow of the demo before all hell broke loose and he found himself so busy dealing with the protestors that he had no time left to investigate the case.

"I'm going to keep this short," Cholmondeley said. "Short and to the point."

At this point, he was interrupted by a tomato which hit him on the shoulder and splattered across his uniform. He looked down at it, reached into his pocket to grab a handkerchief and then did his best to wipe the juice and pips away.

"Please," he said, holding a hand up, "don't do that. I just had this dry cleaned."

The crowd murmured. Cholmondeley wondered whether it was a laugh or a threat.

Probably both, he mused.

"Look," he continued, "I'd love to stay and chat with you all. I really would. But there's a killer on the streets and we intend to catch him."

"What are you going to do about it?" somebody shouted. That was followed by a round of jeering and an echo or two as the question passed from lip to lip and got repeated, like a perverse game of Chinese whispers but with higher stakes.

"I can't comment on an active investigation," Cholmondeley said, stepping smartly to his right to dodge a flying banana. "Stop that. If I find out who's throwing fruit at me, we'll put them in a cell and throw the key away. We're on the same side."

The shouts from the crowd redoubled. To Cholmondeley's right, Gary Mogford unhooked his baton and tapped it in his hands.

"Careful, boss," he murmured. "This could turn nasty. We can get a riot team in here, but not on the double. We'd both be pulped before the shields arrived."

"Don't worry," Cholmondeley replied. "They're not here because they want to hurt someone. They're here because they want answers."

"Point taken," Mogford said. "But the thing is, boss, we don't have any answers to give to them. And I get the feeling that they'll use force if they think it'll help them to catch the Terror. The last thing we want is an angry mob of vigilantes."

"Sir!" The voice belonged to Constable Groves, who'd been ordered to stay inside the precinct. Cholmondeley had surmised that the more officers they sent to deal with the protest, the more likely it would be to turn into a melee. His face flashed red as his eyes rested upon her, but then they lost their colour like the rest of his face when he saw her grim expression.

"What is it?" Cholmondeley asked. "It better be good. I don't know if you've noticed but we've got a situation out here."

"It's good," Groves said. "In fact, it's better than good. Although it's bad, too. Worse than bad."

"What are you talking about?" Mogford growled. "Come on, spit it out."

Groves snapped off a smart salute and looked nervously across at the protestors, who'd quietened down a little to keep an eye on the new development. One guy, a Welshman with a megaphone, started a slow chant of, "The truth, the whole truth and nothing but the truth."

Groves raised her voice a little so she could make herself heard above the hubbub. "You need to come with me, boss," she insisted. "There's been a development in the case."

"What kind of development?"

"The biggest development yet," Groves said. "Come down and see for yourself. We've got a guy in custody."

* * *

Cholmondeley, to his credit, asked Groves to wait for him to talk to the crowd so he could explain the situation. The crowd didn't swallow it, but when he walked back inside they started to disperse until there were only a couple dozen of them left, including the Welshman with the megaphone, who was still trying (and failing) to lead the chant.

Groves led Cholmondeley through the station to the cells, where the suspect had been locked up while they waited for legal representation. The cells always smelled of disinfectant, and Cholmondeley mentally winced at the idea of having to go in there. It was his least-favourite room in the station.

While they walked, Groves explained what had happened. "We took a call from a neighbour who complained about the smell from the flat upstairs. Constable Cohen went out with Yates and called it in. You're not going to believe it."

"Who was the victim?" Cholmondeley asked.

"Carina Merin," Groves said. "Fifty-nine years old. She's about five foot eight, maybe nine stone tops, with long, white hair down to her elbows. Bit of a hippie if you ask me."

"And how did she die?"

"It was the same MO," Groves said, "right down to the mutilation. So much for peace and love. We found her body right there in the living room, surrounded by model unicorns, tie-dyed wall hangings and incense burners. Weird place."

"You said you have a man in custody," Cholmondeley said, urging her on. "Who?"

"It's the husband, sir," Groves said. "He gave his name as Pete Merin. He's a big guy, looks like a pro wrestler."

Cholmondeley shuddered. "And Cohen and Yates took him down?" he asked. "How did they manage that? I can't see them fighting their way out of a paper bag."

"He came of his own accord," Groves said, grinning slightly. She grabbed Cholmondeley by the shoulder and slowed him to a halt outside the door to the cells. "Listen, boss. It's a weird one. He got the details right and he confessed to the crimes, but he couldn't give us any specifics. He says he killed his wife because she wouldn't stop spending his money."

"And why did he kill the others?" Cholmondeley asked.

Groves shrugged. "He didn't say," she said. "Does it matter?"

"Of course," Cholmondeley replied.

"But he confessed to it."

"So what?" Cholmondeley frowned and looked towards the door. "Until we have some evidence that he did something, it's better to hedge our bets."

"Oh, he killed her all right," Groves said. "He was bending over the body when we got there. We've got a knife with the victim's blood on it and what looks like a clear set of prints. It was him. Simple."

"Perhaps," Cholmondeley said. "But that doesn't mean that he killed the others. He could be a copycat."

Groves shrugged and stepped away from Cholmondeley, leading the way towards the door.

"Well," she said, "I guess there's only one way to find out."

* * *

Leipfold and Maile knew nothing of the latest developments, and they were whiling away the last few hours at the office by tying up the loose ends in a couple of cases and recapping his chat with Alan Phelps about the front page of *The Tribune*.

"At least we got a mention in the write-up, boss," Maile said.

Leipfold grunted.

"There's no such thing as bad publicity," she reminded him.

"You're right," Leipfold said. "But there is such a thing as irresponsible journalism. If they're not careful, they'll have another victim's blood on their hands."

"That's not true," Maile said. "Only one person is guilty and that's the Tower Hill Terror."

"But if journalists piss him off then they play a part." Leipfold shook his head. "No matter, it's not our problem. The press has a game of its own to play. I'm more worried about ours. It's nearly full time and we're a goal down."

"What are you talking about?" Maile asked.

"Football, Maile, football." He slammed his fist down on the desk and knocked an empty mug to the floor. It smashed at the handle and rolled off across the room. "And serial killers."

He descended into a gloomy silence, and Maile took the chance to put the kettle on. She refilled both of their drinks and grabbed a packet of pretzels from the snack cupboard. Leipfold hadn't kept food in the office until she joined him. He joked that she spent half of the day with a snack in her hand and wanted to know how she managed to stay so thin. Maile, meanwhile, swore that her boss didn't eat because she rarely saw him do it. James Leipfold appeared to be powered by caffeine alone.

Maile sat back down at her desk and ran a couple of searches, then asked him, "What's going to happen next?"

"I don't know," Leipfold said. "Perhaps *The Tribune* did us a favour. After all, at least people will be on the alert now. We need more witnesses, damn it. We need people to come forward and point a finger at someone. So far, that forensic team hasn't found anything worth looking for. Could be that an eyewitness is what we need to narrow in on a suspect."

Maile thought about it for a moment. "I've got a couple of ideas," she said. "For starters, let me put the word out on the net. I'll draft something for your blog and get you to take a look at it."

"If you think it'll help," Leipfold said, doubtfully. He paused for a moment, deep in thought. "It's no good. We need to catch him in the act. That's the only way we'll know for sure. Problem is, there's still a big question that we haven't been able to answer."

"What's that then?" Maile asked.

Leipfold shrugged and stood up, then wandered over to the board on the wall with his case notes scribbled across it, right next to the map of the city with the pins in it. He sighed again.

"We still don't know how the killer finds his victims," he said.

Chapter Twenty:
Meeting People

MAILE WAS WORRIED. It was quiet at home. Too quiet. It wasn't that Kat was a problem to live with. In fact, Maile knew that she was the noisy, untidy one, and she often reminded herself how lucky she was to have a housemate who put up with her. Kat usually kept to herself, even though her name was on the lease and so the place belonged more to her than to Maile, but it had been a couple of days since they'd last bumped into each other in the kitchen or argued about who'd get to jump in the shower first.

It was a Friday morning and Maile hadn't seen Kat since Wednesday night. It wasn't unusual for her to stay away from home for a day or two, but it *was* strange for her to ignore her housemate's messages. She was usually glued to her phone, just like Maile with her laptop. But Maile had tried to call her a half dozen times in the last twenty-four hours and her phone had gone to voicemail each time.

It's probably nothing, she thought. *It's just like when she and Brad broke up. But still...*

Maile trod carefully around Leipfold that morning because he had a face like a wolf with a sore tooth. He hadn't shaved since the previous weekend and a five-day stubble was poking its way through. His beard had changed from grey to brown to ginger, but Maile only mentioned it once. He didn't take it well.

But she had a favour to ask of him, and she made a fresh cup of coffee before she broached the subject. It helped that they solved the crossword in a little under seven minutes. Not a record, but a big "fuck you" to Mr. Phelps all the same.

She told him as she brewed their second cup of coffee, when her resolve ran out and she had to bring it up before the worry threatened to break her down.

"Kat's missing," she said.

Leipfold grunted and bowed his head towards the computer screen. He pulled up a number on his browser and started to key it into his phone.

"Did you hear me?" Maile asked.

Leipfold grunted again. He sighed and set his phone back down. "Sorry," he said. "Who are you talking about?"

"Kat," Maile said. "My housemate."

Leipfold rubbed his eyes and said, "Start again."

So Maile told him how her housemate had fallen off the face of the earth. Unlike Maile, Kat was punctual and communicative, the kind of person who'd ask a neighbour to keep an eye on their house while they went away.

"I'll be the first to admit that I don't always listen to her," Maile said. "I mean, the woman turns talking about rubbish into an art form. But if she was planning on going away, she would have said something. And if she'd said something, I'd remember it."

"How can you be so sure?"

Maile laughed. "I would have moved my Xbox through and plugged it into the big TV in the living room," she said.

Leipfold nodded and pretended to jot something down in his notebook. Maile knew him too well and recognised it for what it was. He was doodling, probably a cartoon of a bird or a half-arsed sketch of a dog or a wolf.

"What do you want me to do about it?" Leipfold asked.

"Isn't it obvious?" Maile replied, glaring at him across the room. "I want you to find her."

"No can do," Leipfold said. "Sorry. Look for her yourself if you want to. I can give you a little time off if you need it."

"I've already looked," she said, thinking guiltily about the ten minutes she'd spent fruitlessly searching for clues. "Just do me a favour."

"What?"

Maile smiled sweetly at him and said, "Give Jack Cholmondeley a call. Just pass it on."

"He's a busy man, Maile."

"So are you," she said. "Just tell him."

"Why?"

"Kat can look after herself, but it's unusual for her to go this long without messaging me," she said. She shook her head. "Call me crazy, I guess. I'd just feel better if you called Cholmondeley. And besides…"

Leipfold stared at her. "Besides what?"

Maile looked him straight in the eye and said, "It could be connected to the case."

Leipfold shuddered. "I hope not," he said. "For her sake."

Leipfold was still reluctant, but Maile continued to grumble until he eventually caved and made the call. The policeman didn't answer, but Leipfold left him a message and Maile was happy with that.

"You could always go to the police directly," Leipfold said.

Maile shook her head. "It'll take them too long to act on it," she replied. "But Jack Cholmondeley won't let us down."

Cholmondeley called back about half an hour later, apologising half-heartedly and explaining that he'd been in a meeting.

"With the bosses?" Leipfold asked.

Cholmondeley laughed and said, "With a suspect." There was a pause for a moment before he added, "What can I help you with?"

"You know my assistant?"

"I remember her well."

"Her housemate is missing," Leipfold said. "She's called…" Leipfold held a hand over the phone's receiver and mouthed something over at Maile.

"Kat Cotteril," Maile said.

"Kat Cotteril," Leipfold repeated. "She's what, twenty-six, twenty-seven?"

"She's thirty-one," Maile growled. She hopped up from her chair and ran across to him. "Give me that."

Maile took the phone and talked to Jack Cholmondeley directly. She grabbed his email address and sent him a photo while they were talking, and she also did her best to describe Kat. She was even able to give Cholmondeley a list of the clothes that Kat was last seen wearing.

"It was Tuesday night," Maile recalled. "I remember now. She was meeting a guy so she was dressed to kill. And when she wasn't at home in the morning, I figured she spent the night with him."

Cholmondeley repeated the list back to her and then asked Maile how Kat knew the man.

"She used an app," Maile said. "That's how everyone meets these days. I need your help. Please."

Cholmondeley sighed and said he'd do what she asked of him. "I'm not going to head it myself, you understand?" he said. "I'll pass it on to one of my constables. And I'm not promising anything."

"Understood," Maile said, as Leipfold gestured for her to finish up. "I've got to go. My boss wants the phone back."

"Of course," Cholmondeley grumbled. "He always wants to talk to me." He sighed. "Okay," he said. "You'd better hand me over."

* * *

When Leipfold took the phone back, he put Cholmondeley on loudspeaker and gestured for Maile to sit down next to him. She grabbed one of the plastic chairs from the reception area and dragged it over, then sat beside Leipfold to listen.

"How are you doing, Jack?" Leipfold asked.

Cholmondeley grunted and said, "Get to the point."

"All right." Leipfold paused and glanced down at the doodle—*a wolf and a fox*, Maile thought—and made a clicking noise with his teeth. He winked at Maile and stalled a little longer. He did it just to annoy him. Jack Cholmondeley was an easy man to irritate.

"Okay," Leipfold said. "I've got a theory. I need you to do a couple of background checks and see what you can find."

"On who?"

"On the victims," Leipfold said. "Who did you think? See if any of them were using dating apps."

"Like whatsername?"

"Kat," Maile said.

"Precisely," Leipfold said. "See, I've been thinking. The killer must have some way of meeting people. Strangers, of course. If they were connected to each of the victims, we would know by now."

"We've looked into it," Cholmondeley said. "It's possible, but unlikely."

"So how do you meet random people?" Leipfold asked. "I mean, *really* random people?"

"In a bar?" Cholmondeley asked.

Leipfold shook his head vigorously, hit his desk so hard that he finally left a mark on it and said, "You'd know about it. So would I, for that matter. Come on, Jack, we've both done our homework."

"A dating app could work," Maile murmured, thoughtfully.

"What are you basing this on?"

"A hunch," Leipfold said. "Nothing more."

"I'll get someone to take a look at it," Cholmondeley replied. "But there's only so much we can do without something a little more solid than one of your hunches."

A silence descended as the two men thought it over. Maile, meanwhile, stared thoughtfully into the distance. She got up and walked over to Leipfold's corkboard, where his map of the city was laid out with its colour-coded pins and his spidery handwriting on sticky notes. She picked up a pin—a black one, her favourite colour—and pushed it into the map. It marked the house that she and Kat lived in and it fit perfectly into the middle of the map.

"James, are you there?" Cholmondeley was saying.

Leipfold was about to reply when Maile cut in, racing back across the room to pant breathlessly down the line.

"It's the apps," Maile said. "It has to be. And I can tell you exactly why."

"What do you mean?" Leipfold asked.

"It's simple," Maile said. "We should have thought of it before. It's been staring us in the face every time we look at the map on the wall. Sites like that use geolocation. Their users connect with each other based on the distance between them. They're supposed to introduce you to people in the local area so you can get out from behind the screen and meet up with them."

There was silence for a moment as the three of them considered the implications. Then Leipfold sighed and said, "Sounds plausible enough. We're going to have to look into it. Over to you, Jack."

Chapter Twenty-One:
In a Bind

LATER THAT DAY, while Cholmondeley was following up on Leipfold's latest lead, the detective led Maile out of the office, locked the door behind them and then hopped on the back of Camilla. Maile rode behind him as they wound their way through the streets towards Maile's apartment.

For a moment, Maile was elated, riding high on the bike with the wind in her face, although she couldn't feel it through Leipfold's spare helmet. She was on the back of a beautiful bike, enjoying the thrill of the chase, and she was getting a cheeky ride home, too. But then she remembered the trail of the dead from Jayne Lipton to Meg Jackson. And she remembered her missing housemate, too.

Kat hadn't read or responded to any of her messages, nor had she answered any of the missed calls or the voicemails. Maile was half-hoping to find her sitting on the sofa in the living room, but no dice. The apartment was as empty as she'd left it, silent except for the shuffling sounds that Leipfold made as he searched for clues, like a prize pig sniffing out truffles.

"Has she got a computer?" Leipfold asked. Maile nodded. "Can you crack the password?"

"No need," Maile said. "I already know it. But you're not going to find anything. It was the first thing I checked and I, unlike you, know what to look for."

Leipfold laughed and said, "Get me a log of her emails and her internet history. I'll go from there."

"Already on it."

Maile tapped a few buttons on her phone and emailed the files across to him. Leipfold, meanwhile, was sweeping through the apartment, starting with the chaotic living room. He opened drawers and scoured the bookcases, not really sure what he was looking for, and then rooted through the bin in search of receipts, letters, or anything else that might offer a clue. He found nothing.

Maile's eyes burned into the back of his head as he walked out into the corridor and looked towards the other rooms. He checked the bathroom first, which made her smile.

Never thought I'd see James Leipfold poking his nose around my housemate's makeup, she thought.

That thought was swiftly followed by another one, which arrived just in time for her to do something.

"Oi!" she shouted.

Leipfold paused with his fingers stretching out towards the door handle. "What?" he asked.

"That's my room," Maile said. "And I haven't tidied up since the weekend."

* * *

Maile made them both a cup of coffee, and then they tackled Kat's room, although Maile refused to leave him alone in there.

"It's not that I don't trust you," Maile explained. "I just know what Kat's like. She doesn't trust you. She doesn't trust anyone. If this all turns out to be nothing and I let you look through her stuff, she won't be happy."

Leipfold laughed and agreed to her terms, though he reminded her that time was of the essence, and then combed through the room once Maile was ready to escort him. It was an arduous, thankless task. Kat loved clutter like her housemate loved her Xbox, and Leipfold insisted on cataloguing every piece of it. He made his way methodically around the room, peeking into drawers and lifting up ornaments, checking envelopes and opening books and DVD cases. Maile followed closely at his heels, taking photographs for their reference when they headed back to the office.

Leipfold knelt down and looked under her bed before checking behind the headboard and beneath the pillows and mattress. Then he moved towards her dressing table and opened up a jewellery box. He reached in and gently removed a handful of necklaces, then stopped abruptly and took a closer look. The box had a false bottom, so he lifted it out and reached a hand inside.

"What do we have here, then?" he murmured. Maile wandered over and looked a little closer.

"Holy shit," she said. "I forgot about that."

Leipfold held the object up to the light, then brought it to his nose and sniffed it. He frowned and put the baggie back in its rightful place.

"I wouldn't have thought she was the type," he said. And the search continued.

Leipfold turned his attention to the wardrobe. Maile chatted to him while he searched, narrating the history of her housemate's clothing collection. Leipfold found a shoebox with a bunch of old photos, and Maile wandered aimlessly around the room while he worked through them. She opened up the drawers and started to look through them, feeling slightly ashamed to be hunting through her housemate's underwear. Kat owned a disproportionate number of thongs and more than her fair share of trashy lingerie. She was a woman who clearly didn't dress for comfort. Then Maile saw something that made her feel even worse. She picked it up and wordlessly dropped it into her back pocket.

Leipfold finished his search of the wardrobe and made his way over to the chest of drawers, but he only gave them a cursory search.

"Looks like your housemate likes lingerie," Leipfold observed, sliding the last drawer shut and looking around the room for anything he might have missed. He wandered over to the windowsill and checked that, then shifted the furniture forward so he could look beneath it.

"Nothing wrong with that," Maile said.

Leipfold shrugged. "Whatever," he said. "We're done here. I've got nothing."

She sighed and nodded across at him and an awkward silence

descended. They walked back into the kitchen and leaned against the counters. Leipfold finished his coffee and dropped the mug into the sink.

"So where do we go from here?" Maile asked.

Leipfold shrugged. "I have no idea," he said. "I need to take the night to think about it."

"Then take it," Maile replied. "I'll stay here in case Kat comes back."

Leipfold left shortly afterwards. Maile watched from the window as he hopped on to Camilla and rode her away into the night.

Then she walked into Kat's room to put the vibrator back in the drawer.

* * *

The following day was a Saturday. Cholmondeley and Mogford were hosting another of their impromptu press conferences. The crowd was larger now than at their last one, and Cholmondeley's coppers had been forced to arrange for a PA system as well as, ironically, hired security. They had a couple of men in uniform, but only enough for a token presence. The rest of the team was on the beat, keeping the streets clean and following up minor leads for Operation Aftershock.

"I always hated doing these," Cholmondeley murmured to Gary Mogford, although he still smiled benignly for the benefit of the media. "But it came down from above."

"Superintendent Richards?" Mogford guessed.

"You got it," Cholmondeley replied. Then he stepped up to the podium and leaned towards the microphone.

"Ladies and gentlemen," he said. "Thank you, as always, for coming. I'd like to take a little of your time today to tell you about a couple of updates in our investigation into the murders of Jayne Lipton, Abu Adewali, Calvin Myatt, Jennifer 'Meg' Jackson and Carina Merin."

As he spoke, Sergeant Mogford held up photos of each of the victims. Each photograph had the victim's name as a watermark, and Cholmondeley explained that the information was available from the press area of the force's website.

"We're also looking for an individual who may or may not be related to the case," Cholmondeley said. "A young lady called Kat Cotteril has been reported missing. At this stage, we have no reason to believe that foul play is involved. However, we can't rule out the possibility entirely. We'd like to speak to her and we're hopeful that the public will help us to find her."

Cholmondeley paused while Mogford held the photograph up for the journalists to look at. He took a gulp of water from a plastic bottle and glanced down at his notes.

"I'd also like to talk about Carina Merin," Cholmondeley continued. "Most of you are probably unfamiliar with her name, so allow me to elaborate."

He turned to look at Sergeant Mogford and nodded. The copper flipped back through the photos he was holding and switched to one of the ex-hippie.

"Ms. Merin was found dead in similar circumstances to the other victims," Cholmondeley explained. "We were able to detain her husband, Pete Merin, at the scene of the crime. Mr. Merin confessed to the murder of his wife, as well as to the murders of Jayne Lipton, Abu Adewali, Calvin Myatt and Jennifer Jackson."

An audible murmur passed through the milling journalists and one man, styling himself as the group's unelected representative, stood forward and shouted, "So you've got him? You've made an arrest."

The crowd launched into a spontaneous round of applause. Some of the journalists were holding their phones up, live-streaming the whole thing across the web. Cholmondeley swallowed nervously and lowered his voice.

"We made an arrest," he said. "But we don't believe he's the Tower Hill Terror."

* * *

Cholmondeley was in a bind. He was tongue-tied, sweating buckets despite the cold weather, and for a moment he wasn't sure how to continue. The applause had stopped, the journalists were watching silently with their mouths hanging open and Gary Mogford was looking nervously across at him with his eyes shouting, "I told you so."

Cholmondeley fiddled with the microphone and said, "Let me explain. We've arrested a fifty-six-year-old male called Pete Merin, Carina Merin's husband. We believe that he killed his wife and tried to make it look like she'd been murdered by the Tower Hill Terror. Unfortunately, for Mr. Merin at least, the murder was overheard by his neighbours, who called the police."

"But why did he confess to the others?" This came from one of the journalists, who fell silent when Cholmondeley turned his eye on him.

"I'll take questions at the end," Cholmondeley said. "As it goes, the suspect is refusing to answer. He still stands by his original story. But there are too many inconsistencies. He told us about things that didn't happen and didn't mention things that did. We believe that he panicked when our officers arrived and, knowing that we'd caught him red-handed, decided to change his plan. Instead of pretending that the Tower Hill Terror had murdered his wife, he pretended that he *was* the Terror. If you're going to go down, you might as well go down in style."

Cholmondeley paused again and the silence of the crowd was overwhelming. It was the awkward, stilted silence of an exam hall, the special type of silence that can only come from a group of people making an effort to keep quiet.

"Besides," he said. "Mr. Merin appears to have an alibi for two of the murders that he admitted to. Even if he was involved, he wasn't working alone. That's why we'd like to ask the public to continue be on their guard and to contact the police station if they have any relevant information. Despite Mr. Merin's arrest, we're still treating it as an ongoing, active case."

Cholmondeley paused again to consult his notes and then said, "I'm also pleased to reveal that we have some additional information. We believe we now know how the killer selects his victims. We suspect that the man we're looking for has been using dating apps and hook-up websites to find his victims. We believe that he does this using false profiles to meet victims without leaving a trail for us to follow. We're currently working with a number of different service providers to monitor their platforms for any unusual usage patterns. We're hoping we'll be able to identify the profiles that were used and to tie them back to the Tower Hill Terror's true identity."

Several of the reporters raised their hands, but Cholmondeley cut them off with a gesture and Mogford continued to stare stony-faced and silent across at them. He was still holding up the photographs, only he'd switched back through to a shot of Kat Cotteril with the police force's missing persons number emblazed across the bottom in a prominent font.

"As such," Cholmondeley concluded, "we're asking—no, *begging*—the general public to avoid using dating apps and dating websites. This is just a temporary measure, but it's a necessary one. Once we've tracked down the real Terror, we'll be able to reveal more information. This is for your own safety and for the safety of the rest of the community."

Cholmondeley paused again. The crowd started to babble excitedly. He was lit up by flash photography and cursed under his breath, wishing he'd had time for a shave before kissing Mary goodbye and driving his Beemer to the station.

"That's all we've got for you right now," Cholmondeley said. "If you have any further questions, now's the time to ask them."

Chapter Twenty-Two:
No Ordinary Sunday

KAT COTTERIL'S EARS were burning, but the rest of her felt like it had been sprayed with liquid nitrogen. She had a headache, the kind that seemed to split the skull apart, and her memory was like a boat with a hole in it. She tried to remember something, anything.

There was something about a date and a restaurant, which explained why she was wearing what she was wearing. She'd been running late and she was out of breath by the time she arrived at the place, an Italian restaurant with a name like Giovanni's or La Dolce Vita. Her date had been ready and waiting, already sitting at a table and sipping from a glass of wine. She'd hurried across to him, apologised, and they'd settled into the humdrum routine of a first date.

The food was good and so was the company. They'd finished a bottle of wine between them and had made a good dent in a second by the time that they'd finished their desserts and settled the bill. Her date held her hand and walked her towards a nearby taxi rank and then…nothing.

She tried again, but it was like trying to picture the face of someone she'd passed in the street several months ago. There were dim shadows and a fleeting, teasing sense that she was close to a discovery, but the harder she pushed, the flimsier the memories became until she realised the only way to get them back would be to wait until they returned to her.

She tried to look around, but all was in darkness. It was a complete type of darkness. Unlike a regular room, which still let in light from the windows or the cracks beneath the doors, the room she was in was born from a lack of light itself. It was pitch black, the blackest of blacks, and too dark to see anything at all. She couldn't even make out the contour of the walls. Her eyes were open, but all she could see was the darkness.

She tried to move, but her hands and ankles were bound by chains. She realised she was standing upright, hanging from wall-mounted manacles and slumped forward slightly. She struggled, but they held tight and chafed against her skin, gouging red welts into her wrists and legs.

The manacles rattled in the darkness, echoing spookily and leaving Kat with the impression that she was in some sort of cavern or perhaps a medieval dungeon, just waiting for the jailer to interrogate her with a red-hot poker. She struggled again and screamed for help, but there was no response except for the ghostly echoes of her own voice bouncing around and coming back to haunt her.

Kat went silent again and let gravity drag her back into her previous, passed out position. She breathed slowly and deeply, trying to calm herself. She reached out for a memory again, some sort of sign that might explain how she got there. But there was still nothing except for the vague feeling that she'd hit her head. It hurt, but without checking her skull, it was hard to tell what was causing it.

Either way, she needed to pull herself together. The trick was not to panic. She'd learned that from Douglas Adams and the countless crime docudramas she liked to binge on. She tried to bring her breathing back under control.

I need to get out of here, she thought. *Or at the very least, I need to find a way to communicate with the outside world. But how?*

She probed her memories again, but they still came up blank, so her thoughts started to drift to another question, an unpleasant one. One that she wasn't sure if she wanted an answer to.

Where the hell am I? she thought. *And who brought me here?*

* * *

Sundays were usually slow at the station, but this was no ordinary Sunday. Cholmondeley had cancelled his day off, Mogford was on call and Constable Cohen was working overtime to manage the information that was trickling in from the general public.

Most of it was useless, but it always was. The key, Cholmondeley knew, was to filter through the nonsense for the one little clue that would be useful. It was always difficult to find it, but it was the thrill of the chase that kept them going. It was like a drug addiction, and coppers got hooked because they could never beat the high of that first discovery.

Most of all, it was the hunt for the missing woman that was causing all of the trouble. The police had received reports of over a hundred sightings, including one woman who thought she'd seen her working in a Liverpool McDonald's and a man who claimed she'd bought a painting from him at a jumble sale. They'd even received a couple of foreign sightings through their social media team, thanks to a plea for information that went viral and caught the attention of the public far more effectively than any of the coverage from the news channels.

Cholmondeley had plotted the reports against a map of the city on a wall-mounted board that looked almost identical to the one he'd seen in Leipfold's office. He had officers working around the clock to follow up on each of the leads and to report back.

And he was also working with James Leipfold.

Officially, Leipfold had joined a team of civilian volunteers that Mogford had been tasked with assembling. He'd accepted Leipfold into the team in spite of his better judgement.

"We don't need him, boss," Mogford had insisted.

But Cholmondeley just laughed and said, "We'll see about that. I know he's a loose cannon, a dangerous man to have so close to the case. But he has his moments. And besides, he has a motorbike. He can canvass twice as many locations as Groves and Cohen and we don't have to pay him for the privilege."

Between them, the impromptu task force was just about able to keep up with the intelligence that was flowing in, but it meant a lot of overtime and the ever-present threat that someone might actually find something. And, as if that wasn't enough, Cholmondeley's press conference had backfired and created an entirely different type of problem, one that they had no control over. People were downloading dating apps in droves, spurred on by the papers to see what the fuss was about. One of the companies involved had even responded with a marketing campaign, which was especially infuriating for the police force because they pulled it off overnight and took them by surprise.

Cholmondeley had released another statement, this time via a press release on the force's website, but it had been to no avail. It seemed like people were willing to put their lives at risk for the thrill of it, and Cholmondeley just hoped that they were doing their homework before they started sending dick pics or doing whatever the hell people did on dating apps. And he hoped that he hadn't exacerbated the problem by taking the killer's hunting grounds and filling it up with easy game.

The old man sighed and paid a visit to the coffee machine. It was going to be a long, long day.

* * *

Kat was hungry, thirsty and disoriented. She thought that she'd slept, if it could be called sleep. At some point, she'd heard movement from somewhere above her. But nobody had come to feed her and she'd quickly lost track of time. There was still no light, no nothing. She couldn't even hear the sounds of the city.

She thought back to another documentary. This one had been about sensory deprivation tanks and some of the experimental work that was being carried out with them.

This is what that must feel like, she thought. *No light. No noise. No contact with the outside world.*

The panic hit her like a freight train, and she gasped aloud as her pupils contracted and her heartbeat sped up until it felt like a dove trying to break out from her ribcage. She swallowed and willed herself to calm down, but her spit tasted like blood and metal. She bit down on her lip until she broke through the skin.

And then she screamed until she couldn't scream any more, but her voice was muted by the darkness and nobody came. She was all alone.

She twisted against the restraints again and tried to pull herself free.

The wrist manacles were starting to loosen and she had to console herself with slowly testing her wrists against the chain and moving her body as much as possible to keep the circulation going.

After the first eight hours or so—*or was it eighty?*—Kat had an idea. Ideas were in short supply in the darkness and so she latched on to it like a drowning sailor clutching at a floating hunk of his sinking ship.

She reached behind her and touched the wall, then started filing away at the cement between the bricks. It was a long, painful process, but the wall was old and the cement had started to dry out and return to dust. She used her fingernails to begin with, switching between them when the pain was too great, but it didn't take long until they were splintered and ragged, bleeding freely and unable to take any more of a beating. It was a long shot, but if she could weaken the wall then perhaps she could pull her manacled hands free from the brickwork and make a bid for freedom.

But by the time she was forced to switch tack, she'd already made a dent, and the work got a little easier when she switched to using the ends of her fingers. It still hurt, and it was much, much slower, but the soft cement started to come away and the manacles began to feel a little looser. When she strained against them she could almost feel the walls creaking as the brick tried to pull itself free.

Kat was a fighter, and so she kept clawing at the wall between bouts of unconsciousness. After a couple more hours (*days?*), she realised what she'd known all along. She was determined, resolute and unwilling to just roll over and give up. Someone had put her in this predicament and whoever they were, they were likely to return. Even if she couldn't set herself free, she was determined to put up a fight.

She strained at the manacles again, breaking her skin and sending a fresh stream of blood along her arm. She felt the wall crying out in pain and the tension in the metal as it strained against its moorings. It held, but it felt a little looser.

Her right hand was clenched in a fist, the skin showing white as she tensed and strained again. In the darkness, she couldn't see anything out of the ordinary, but she could feel her little secret and she treasured it.

Kat's fist was full of the fine powder that she'd scraped from the gaps between the bricks. While it wasn't exactly her housemate's pepper spray, it'd still hurt if it hit her captor while his eyes were open.

It's not much, Kat thought, *but it's all I've got.*

She tensed up and pulled once again against the manacles.

* * *

Cholmondeley's team was starting to flag, and he'd sent several of his coppers home to get some sleep. It was 10PM and they'd had to stop going door-to-door for two reasons. The first was that it was getting late and Superintendent Richards wouldn't be happy if a disgruntled member of the public filed a complaint. The second was that they were running low on manpower and the public was still coming forward with information.

Meanwhile, the Tower Hill Terror was lying low. There'd been no good lead on Kat Cotteril, but there also hadn't been another body. Cholmondeley saw it as a case of "no news is good news."

Even so, he was itching to leap into action. And, like Leipfold, he'd arranged to have each of their suspects tailed on the off chance that they'd somehow incriminate themselves and that they could make an arrest. And there was also a missing person. If there was a chance that geeky Lukas White, unpredictable Marc Allman or smooth-talking Asif Shaktar was behind the disappearance, it was a chance that Cholmondeley thought was worth taking.

So far, none of the suspects had actually *looked* suspicious, and Cholmondeley wondered if he'd got it wrong. What if Pete Merin, with his dead wife, his big frame and his bushy beard, really *was* the man they were looking for? And worse still, what if he wasn't, and what if neither were the three that his team was tailing?

They were questions that haunted him, and the only way to stop them from circling his brain like a rabid dog was to keep himself busy. Unfortunately, Cholmondeley's job was to keep the machine running and the actual grunt work fell to his ragtag team of constables. The old cop had to settle for wandering between teams and badgering them for updates while simultaneously doing his best to appease Superintendent Richards, who kept calling him and asking for information.

And it didn't help that he was in the middle of two separate but possibly connected investigations. On the one hand, he was trying to find the Tower Hill Terror before he had a chance to strike again and before the media crucified the police force. On the other hand, he had Kat Cotteril to think about.

Their best lead on Kat was the young woman's laptop, so Cholmondeley strolled along the corridors towards the tech labs to ask for an update. Luckily, his old pal James Leipfold had delivered the machine while he was helping the civilian team to go door-to-door, and he'd been good enough to provide the password to go along with it.

"Anything?" he asked, as he strolled into the room and leaned against the wall inside the doorway. The computer room was a musty place, and it reeked of stale clothing and the metallic funk of computer hardware. The tech team was almost a law unto itself, and Cholmondeley was reminded of the story he'd heard about the FBI, who'd been forced to cancel their drug testing programme because too many of the top hackers came pre-installed with a dope habit. His boys didn't touch the stuff, of course. But they also didn't shower much, and they had the second-rate people skills of an automated call centre.

"Nothing yet, sir."

Cholmondeley couldn't tell which of the half-dozen techno-cops that came from, but it didn't matter much. They were all the same to him, and they even *looked* the same with their ponytails and unfashionable jackets. And that was just the men. The women were even worse, and yet Cholmondeley always marvelled at how this relatively underfunded and extensively underappreciated department was sometimes able to blow a case right open.

But not this time. Cholmondeley murmured "as you were" and slouched back out, then wandered along the corridor to the mess room, where he expected to find Constable Cohen. The man was the station's equivalent of a gossip magazine. If there was something worth knowing, Cohen was likely to know it. But Cholmondeley didn't have his hopes up.

In fact, his hopes were the lowest they'd been since they'd discovered Jayne Lipton in one of the rooms of the Grosvenor House Hotel.

* * *

Kat was tired and hungry. She ached all over, and she'd been struggling with the realisation that she might not be able to fight her way out. There had still been no demands, no threats, and worst of all, no food and no relief. It was starting to look like she'd been chained up and left to die, a thought that had never occurred to her.

For the first time in her life, she was confronted with her own mortality. And worse, she realised that the downhill slope to death wasn't necessarily quick and painless. She still had a little fight left, but not much. And as the hours drifted slowly by and she was further deprived of food, sleep and water, that little fight was threatening to leave her.

Since first coming to and discovering her predicament, Kat had been visited only twice. On both occasions, her captor said nothing and refused to react when she twisted in her shackles or tried to fight out against them. They simply waited in the interminable darkness, then approached her once she quietened down.

The first time had taken noticeably longer. Kat, fearing death, had fought like a cornered wildcat, but she'd quietened up when she felt a rough pair of gloved hands on her face. They pinched her cheeks tight and forced her mouth open, and then a bottle of water was poured down her throat. It took her by surprise and she started to choke on it, but she was so desperate for it that she swallowed as much as she could. Once the bottle was empty, it was taken away and Kat was left alone in the darkness again.

When she was given water for a second time, she knew that they wanted her alive. It would have been all too easy to leave her there in the dark until she breathed her last and passed on, but they needed her. She tried not to ask herself why.

The second time, she drank slowly, more carefully. She could sense someone standing there in the darkness, watching as they teased the bottle across their prisoner's parched lips. And then, to Kat's relief, they left her there. It was horrible being alone down there, but at least they hadn't hurt her. Yet.

Her arms were tired, but on the plus side, her manacles were starting to come loose. She could feel that the screws had a little give in them.

Kat grimaced. Her body was going through hell, and she wouldn't be surprised if she'd dislocated one or both of her shoulders. She strained at the manacles again, then slumped down, exhausted, to hang from them. She started to shave away at the brick again, to free up another of the screws that bolted the manacles to the wall. Then she stopped. She thought she'd heard something, some noise, some sign of human life in the distance.

She listened, her ears pricked and primed for anything, anything at all. For a moment, there was nothing. And then she heard it again, and again and again. A footstep, and then another.

Her captor was coming back to see her. And this time, it might not be to give her some water.

It might be the Tower Hill Terror.

Time stood still. Kat Cotteril stayed silent, barely daring to breathe in case it sped itself back up again. All was silent, except…

"Hello."

The noise of the voice after so much silence made Kat jump, and she instinctively tried to cover her ears and lost a little of her precious dust because of it. It fell down her blouse and onto her trousers, where it clung to the moisture. With no other option, she'd been forced to relieve herself where she stood, and she promised herself a long soak in the bath if she ever made it out of there.

Kat opened her mouth and tried to speak, but nothing came out. She tried again and managed to croak, "You're a woman."

"That's right."

Her captor was standing closer now, and Kat could smell the woman's perfume and hear her ragged breathing. This woman was ill, maybe dying. And a little voice in Kat's head told her that she'd die too, unless she played her cards right.

"What do you want?" Kat asked. Her voice wavered a little, but she did her best to keep it as steady as possible. It was still dark, too dark to see, but she'd been in the darkness for so long that it was starting to feel like a second home. The sound of the woman was enough to help her to turn her head in the right direction. After that, it was all guesswork.

"If I told you that, I'd have to kill you," the woman said. Then she cackled, and Kat forced herself to laugh along with her to try to get on the woman's good side.

"Then let me try another question," Kat said. "Why are you doing this?"

The woman laughed again before breaking out into a coughing fit. Kat waited.

"I'm a terrorist," she said. "A rebel without a cause." She coughed again, but her lungs still rattled with phlegm and unpleasantness.

"You're dying," Kat said, realisation beginning to dawn. It wasn't a question. She just knew it, and she selfishly started to think about how she could work the knowledge to her own advantage.

"That's right," the woman said. "I am. And that's why I'm here to begin with. This is it, for me at least. My last chance to finally do something worthwhile."

"Worthwhile?" Kat asked. She managed to laugh, despite herself. She flexed her aching muscles once, then twice, to bring them back to life again.

"Worth remembering," the woman corrected. "And I like to have a little fun while I'm at it. That's why I'm not a true terrorist. I'm not a bomber or a gunman. I want to see people suffer before they die."

"You can see?" Kat said. "In this?"

"Night-vision goggles," the woman said. "And besides, darkness disorientates. People are scared of the dark, especially when they're about to die."

There was another pause.

"Aren't you scared?"

"No," Kat said.

But her heart palpitations told her otherwise, and she was starting to smell the reek of her own sweat as it leaked from her pores and settled in the cotton of her T-shirt.

I wish I had deodorant, she thought. And then she was struck by the bizarreness of it, so normal on the streets and so unexpected and out-of-place in the darkness. She started to laugh, and as she did so she was hit by a rush of endorphins and adrenaline that brought some life back to her aching limbs.

And then the woman took a step closer to her and grabbed her by the hair. She pulled at it roughly so that Kat had to tilt her head as the woman whispered something in her ear.

"I was in your place once," she said. "If you think I'm bad, wait until you see who's running the show."

Chapter Twenty-Three:
Racing Time

LEIPFOLD WAS RIDING Camilla, and Maile was on the seat behind him. The weather was finally starting to lift, and the winter seemed like a lifetime ago. He was sweating through his leathers, and Maile was cursing his spare helmet and asking where she could find one in her own size so she could see out of the thing.

They were following up on Leipfold's informants. The tails he'd set had found nothing of interest so far, and Lukas White in particular had made for a dull report. The kid just went to school and back, breaking the routine once a week to do a paper round on a Saturday morning. Asif Shaktar met with a couple of small-time gangsters, but none of the leads amounted to much. And Marc Allman had continued to buy cocaine and spend hour after hour at his office.

Leipfold was stumped. He had no idea who the killer was, or what they wanted, or even whether they had Kat Cotteril and what their new location was. There was only one thing he could do. He could take a punt and hope that a hunch paid off.

That was why Leipfold and Maile were following Allman. Craig, the third of Leipfold's three semi-professional stalkers, had called something in.

"Nothing *suspicious*," he'd been quick to explain. "Just unusual. This fella is a creature of habit. He does the same thing, day in, day out. Only not tonight, for some reason. He's taken a different route home."

"Where are you now?" Leipfold had asked.

"Richmond Cemetery."

Leipfold had asked him to repeat the location, then plotted it into his phone and hit the road with Maile in tow. Now, as they approached the cemetery, he called Craig back and asked for an update.

"He's still here," Craig said. "But it looks like he's getting ready to leave."

"What's he doing?" Leipfold asked.

"Looks like he's paying his respects." There was a pause on the other end of the line. "Yeah, boss. He's moving. You want me to follow him?"

"Of course!" Leipfold bellowed. The quality of the call was bad and the built-in headset in his helmet was on the fritz, which didn't surprise him. *You get what you pay for,* Leipfold thought, and he'd bought his second-hand from a man he'd never met before or since. "Stay on his tail and don't let him out of your sight. I'm coming."

* * *

Meanwhile, in the darkness, Kat Cotteril lay limp on her manacles, trying to bide her time. The woman was still talking, and Kat had been able to place both the woman and, more importantly, her surroundings, by the sound that she made as she moved around the room. Right then, they were three or four feet apart.

Kat knew better than to bargain with the woman, to try to win her freedom through words and tears if necessary. That hadn't stopped her from trying, but her pleas fell on deaf ears and they seemed to spark a newfound frenzy in the woman. Kat had tried twice, and both attempts had ended with the woman getting up in her face and shouting some nonsense about it being too late to change anything.

"I haven't seen your face," Kat had said. "I couldn't identify you even if I wanted to."

"That's not the point," the woman replied. There was something about her voice that sounded familiar but Kat couldn't place it.

She started coughing again, and Kat could hear her as she made her clumsy way away from her. There was a plastic crackle and the snap of a seal, and then the gulping sound of water running down the woman's oesophagus. The woman smacked her lips together and slammed the bottle down.

Then there was another sound, and it wasn't a good one. It was the sound of metal on metal like a butcher sharpening his knives. It sounded again and then again, as though the woman was practicing some sort of manoeuvre. And then it got louder as she made her way back towards her prisoner.

"It's time," the woman said.

"Time? Time for what?"

"You're about to find out," the woman said. She started coughing again in what felt like something of an anti-climax. Then, as suddenly as she started, she stopped.

Kat felt a flash of cold against her cheek. She shrieked as she knew it for what it was—a knife, a big one, pressed tight to her in the cruellest of taunts, a promise of what was to come.

"That's right," the woman said. "I've got a knife, and I'm not afraid to use it. Let's see the colour of your blood."

"You can't," Kat said. "Not without a little light."

"Goggles, remember?"

Kat could almost hear the creak of the woman's jaw as her mouth curled up into a smile. Or maybe it was just her imagination. It had been playing tricks on her in the darkness.

"Please don't kill me," Kat whispered.

"Oh, you won't die," the woman said. "Not yet, at least. But you'll wish for it. You'll beg for it. You'll scream for it, if we're lucky."

Kat played along, which was easy. She really *was* terrified, and the fear made its way into her voice like an unexpected visitor. But she hadn't given up, not by a long shot. She tensed herself, then shifted her grip and teased the muscles in each of her hands. She listened closely to discern the movements of her captor as she held the knife to her face in the darkness.

* * *

Leipfold was on foot, pounding his heavy boots against the paved path in the graveyard with Maile a couple of steps behind him, puffing away like a smoker in the middle of a marathon. He marvelled at the fact that she'd managed to keep up with him at all. He preferred to exercise his mind over his body, but if he couldn't do one then he liked to do the other and some of his best ideas had arrived in the middle of a workout when his mind had wandered off and found an answer for him. He was in pretty good shape. Maile wasn't, but she *was* determined.

The two of them raced through the graveyard, then out again through a rear exit and along a suburban street, but there was no sign of either Leipfold's henchman or Marc Allman. Leipfold was still wearing his helmet, and he was listening and bellowing instructions through the headset.

"You're close, boss," Craig said. "Hit a left and then the second right. I'm about halfway down the street, fifty, maybe sixty feet behind him. It's like he hasn't got a care in the world."

"I'm on it," Leipfold replied. "Stay with him."

Maile fell a couple steps further behind him as he increased his pace and pushed his body to its limits. He was a short guy, and not as young as he used to be, but he could still hit a decent speed when he needed to.

Maile was a dozen steps behind him, huffing and puffing like the Big Bad Wolf on twenty cigarettes a day.

"Why do computer games make this look so damn easy?" she shouted. "I'm on zero stamina, boss. You got a potion?"

Leipfold ignored her. He hit the left and then the second right, but Craig was nowhere to be seen. He slowed his pace a little and asked for an update.

Craig hesitated for a moment before replying. "Shit," he said. "Boss, you're not going to like this."

"What is it?" he asked.

"It's Allman," Craig said. "He got away."

Leipfold swore. "How the hell did that happen?"

"Search me," Craig said. "I thought I had him. I really did. Son of a bitch must've slipped me and hopped a fence or something."

"Get looking!" Leipfold shouted. By this point, he was thirty feet away, pulling up to a stop in a quiet cul-de-sac that looked as distant from the case as the iceberg must have seemed to the lookouts on the *Titanic*. But he could see a narrow little alleyway, and he could see Craig standing at the entrance to it, waving frantically at Leipfold and glancing behind him towards Maile, who was jogging along the street to keep up with him.

Leipfold followed Craig into the alley, where the henchman gestured to the dozen doors that opened out into it.

"He must have gone through one of these," he said. "But which one?"

"Start knocking," Leipfold said. "We'll find out."

"What if no one answers?"

"We'll deal with that when we get there," Leipfold said. He knocked at one of the doors while Craig hopped over to the other side of the alleyway. Maile arrived on the scene just as the first door was being opened by a man wearing chef's whites and holding a meat cleaver. He didn't look happy to be disturbed.

* * *

While Leipfold and Craig continued to work through the doors, asking everyone who answered whether they'd seen a man who matched Marc Allman's description, Maile leaned against a wall to catch her breath before making her way to the end of the alleyway, searching vaguely through the detritus that littered it. There was a wall at the end of it, and Maile looked up at the top of it.

"Boss?" she said. Leipfold didn't hear her, so she repeated herself and managed to attract his attention before he knocked at the fourth of seven doors on his side of the alleyway.

"What?" he snapped. "I'm kind of busy here."

"You might be busy wasting your time," Maile said. She looked at the wall again. "What if he climbed over it?"

Leipfold paused and thought about it. "What's on the other side?" he asked.

"Train tracks," Craig said. "Stinging nettles and electricity cables. That sort of thing."

"Woah," Maile said. "I'm impressed. What, did you memorise a map of the city?"

"No," Craig said, shrugging his shoulders. "I boosted myself up and took a look over it when I got here. No sign of Allman."

"Then he must have gone through one of the doors," Leipfold said. "Keep knocking."

"Yes, boss," Craig said.

Maile watched as the two men worked their way towards her. Even if they got a lead on him, Allman could be half a mile away by now, maybe more if he had some sort of transport. He'd just need to enter by the rear and leave by the front, like some guy in a trench coat from an old spy movie.

She looked down again and scanned the bin bags, the flattened cardboard boxes and the other junk that had been left out for the rats in the alleyway. She swept it aside with her foot, wincing as the sludge and muck transferred itself onto her new Nikes. Then she hit metal and bent down to take a closer look.

"Hmm," she murmured. "If he didn't go over the wall then perhaps he went under it instead."

* * *

"I don't understand," Kat said. "Why are you doing this?"

The silence was almost deafening.

"I'm asking you woman to woman," Kat said. "Please, don't do this."

"It's too late."

"Too late for what?"

"It's too late for you," the woman said. She sighed, and Kat flinched as the knife traced a path across her cheek. "You know, I was in your place once."

"My place?"

"I was down here in the darkness," she said. "Captured by the Tower Hill Terror."

Kat moaned, a low, guttural sound like an injured animal. For the first time since she'd found herself in the darkness, she started to realise just how much danger she was in.

"I was down here for weeks," the woman said. "But I talked to him."

"Him?"

"I've said too much."

But Kat wouldn't take no for an answer. She realised that her only chance was if she kept the woman talking for long enough for help to arrive. If help was indeed on its way.

"You mentioned the Tower Hill Terror."

"Yes," the woman said. "I suppose there's no harm in you knowing. The Terror isn't just one person. There are two of us. I'm just one half of it."

"But I thought you said you were down here in the darkness."

"I was," she said. "But then I told a story. But just as I was about to reach the end, I stopped. He had to keep me alive if he wanted to hear the ending. I did that again and again and again and eventually, he realised he needed me. And I needed him."

"Like the Arabian Knights."

"Huh?"

"Nothing," Kat said. "You said you needed him. Why?"

"He completes me," the woman said. "And I complete him. I was his first victim, you know. He didn't have the heart to go through with it. But together, we're unstoppable."

"Stockholm Syndrome."

"No," the woman said. "We're partners. He needed a new way to find his victims. He met me at my dating night. I was the one who suggested using the apps."

"Holy shit," Kat said as the pieces started to fall into place. She *knew* she recognised the woman's voice. And now she knew why. "You're Lucy Fforde."

The woman sighed again. In the darkness, it sounded like a slashed tyre leaking air at pressure.

"Oh dear," the woman said. "Now you're really in trouble."

Chapter Twenty-Four:
The Tables Turned

SOMEWHRE IN THE DARKNESS, Kat Cotteril was doing her best to live, to survive.

"I can't let you live," Fforde said. "Not now you know who I am."

"Please," Kat said. "I won't tell a soul."

"I know you won't," Fforde replied. "I'll make sure of it."

Kat felt a soft rush of air as the woman moved towards her. She countered by throwing all of her weight to the side and letting gravity do her dirty work. Behind her, the manacles loosened slightly but still held, and the shock of the sudden stop sent pain flaring up both of her arms. She felt movement again, or perhaps she sensed it, and some primal instinct told her to readjust and to throw all of her weight the other way. There was a dull thud as she collided with Lucy Fforde. Then the grinding of metal and mortar as the manacles finally came free. The two women hit the floor at the same time, but Kat was the first to react even with the pain in her arms and shoulders.

It was still too dark to see, and Kat was fighting for her life with her hands free but still manacled together. She struck out at random and hit nothing but air, then felt movement to her right and lucked out. Something clattered to the floor and Kat followed the sound, praying that she'd disarmed the woman and not just made her drop a phone. If the knife was still in Fforde's hand, Kat knew she was a goner.

Kat struck out again at nothing, and then she tried again and made contact. Fforde was in front and to her right, and Kat went for the eyes with her fingers and came up against some sort of headgear.

The goggles, she thought. She tore at them with her hands until the strap snapped and the goggles came away. That left them both in the darkness, both fighting tooth and nail as though their entire lives had led up to that moment. In a way, they had.

Fforde went down on the floor and Kat tripped over her, hitting the floor with a crunch that she hoped didn't signify a broken bone. But if something was broken then the pain was delayed, maybe by the adrenaline. As she scrabbled backwards across the floor, her left hand hit the blade. She winced as it cut into her palm, but she swallowed the cry of pain that was fighting to make its way out of her oesophogus so that Fforde couldn't tell where she was. She picked up the knife with her left hand and transferred it to her right with shaking fingers.

Then she started to stand up again. When she got to her knees, she was hit with a flying tackle that sent both women to the ground again. Kat landed on the bottom and tried to roll over, but the woman was too heavy and she had her hands on her face with her manicured fingernails digging into the flesh beneath Kat's eye.

Then Kat screamed, a sort of wordless battle cry, and cuffed the woman in the side of the head. She struck again and then again, fierce little blows to the face that hit like drops of rain against a windowpane. They were tactical blows, left-handed jabs inflicted with the aid of a weapon. The manacles were wrapped around her fist like a knuckleduster.

Fforde loosened her grip, and that was all Kat needed. She brought her right hand up and around just as the woman was reaching for her throat again. There was a sound, a horrible, disturbing *schlop* sound that Kat knew she'd remember for the rest of her life, however long that might be. Then there was a watery gurgle and the rattling, wheezing sound of the woman's lungs, her laboured breathing made worse by the blade that was now sticking through them.

Kat shrieked and crawled away from her, backing up on her hands like a crab on a sandy beach. She paused for a moment to catch her breath and shuddered at the sound that the woman was making. She was whimpering pathetically, and it made Kat's clammy skin break out in goosebumps. She was trying to say something, and Kat crawled closer to hear what it was.

"He's coming," she was saying, slurring her words like a drunk at closing time. "He's coming to get you."

"Who?" Kat growled.

But the woman just laughed herself into a coughing fit. Kat got a little closer, close enough to wrap her hand around the handle of the knife and to wiggle it around in the wound. The woman screamed for mercy, but her pleas fell on deaf ears.

"Who?" Kat repeated.

But the woman couldn't talk. She could barely breathe, and she started coughing again as Kat backed away from her.

Kat scrabbled across the floor looking for the fallen goggles. After what felt like half a lifetime, she found them. She muttered a quick prayer to a god she didn't believe in and then slipped them over her head.

Kat could immediately see the room around her, cast in a sort of greenish hue but still visible enough to make out the walls and the floors and the woman who was slumped on the floor. Even through the goggles, she could tell it was her.

Lucy Fforde.

Kat thought about going to the woman's aid and then decided against it.

Fuck her, she thought. *I've already wasted enough time looking for answers when I could've been finding a way out of this hellhole.*

She grabbed the handle of the knife and pulled it out, wincing at the sound it made and the effect it had on the woman, whose tortured breaths had started to rattle. Removing the knife, Kat knew, could have caused more damage than the initial blow, but it sounded like the woman was already on the way out and besides, it was self-defence.

Kat reached into Fforde's pockets and came up with nothing. Then she reached down again and found something on a chain around the woman's neck. It was a weak, flimsy thing meant for decoration and not for utility, and it snapped easily as she yanked it from Fforde's neck.

There was a little key on the end of it. Her heart leapt as she tried to manoeuvre it into position. But her hands were shaking too much, and the key dropped to the floor. She cursed and ran her hands across the cold and dusty surface until she found the chain, then she scooped it up and tried again. This time, the key twisted in the lock and it popped open. The manacles fell to the floor and she started to rub her hands together to restore the circulation.

Kat struck out into the darkness, picking a direction at random. She reached a wall and started to make her way along it, feeling for a door or an exit. But there was nothing.

Nothing but the woman's ragged breathing and the distant clip-clop of two heavy pairs of shoes as they made their way towards her.

Chapter Twenty-Five:
In the Sewers

THERE WAS A LIGHT. At first, it was just the simple glint of a distant candle, but it started to grow and grow until it was a sun in the sky and Kat was blinded by the glare. Her eyes weren't ready for it.

"What's going on here, then?"

The voice belonged to a man, and Kat could see the rough outline of his shape behind the lamplight when she could hold her eyes open for long enough to see him. He was fairly well-built and struck an imposing figure in the half-light. Kat had been expecting a monster, but it was just a man, any man, a man you could walk past on the street without noticing him.

She could also see the dim outline of the room around her. There was only the one exit, and that was where the man had come from. He caught sight of Kat at about the same time that he saw his partner with blood pouring out of her chest and pooling around her as she twitched and groaned on the floor.

"Please," Kat said. "Please don't hurt me."

"How did you get free?" the man growled.

"She let me go," Kat lied. She needed to keep him talking, at least until her eyes adjusted. She still held the knife in her hand. "But then there was a struggle."

"A struggle?" The man waved the lantern angrily and stepped further into the room, bending down to take a cursory look at his partner without taking his eyes off his prisoner. The strobing light hit Kat hard and blinded her momentarily while he took stock of the woman's wound. It didn't look good. "Jesus Christ, you stabbed her!"

"It was an accident," Kat lied. "Is she alive?"

"Barely," the man said. "She needs medical attention."

"So take her to a hospital."

"It's not as easy as that," the man said. He left the injured woman where she was and put his lantern down beside her. Now that Kat could see, she could get her bearings. The two of them were underground somewhere in some sort of steampunk paradise. It looked like the room had once been a brewery, or perhaps a workshop room for the plumber's guild. The place had clearly been gutted at some point, but it still retained a vibe of its former glory thanks to the curiously shaped recesses in the walls and the odd sections of copper pipe. The walls were built from brick—old bricks, by the look of them—and the floor was of rough earth that had been flatted down and ironed out.

Kat looked around for the exit, but she couldn't see it at first. Then she saw a narrow band of light on one of the walls. It looked almost angelic, like some sort of divine halo, and it reminded her of the portals she'd seen in one of Maile's computer games. Kat saw her chance and she took it, springing into as much action as her aching body would allow. With one shoulder still hanging uncomfortably from its socket, she put in a burst of speed and moved towards the light. Her legs, unused to taking her weight, felt like wobbling stilts beneath her, and she veered from side to side like a drunk driver.

"Calm down," the man said. He intercepted her with ease, barely breaking a sweat. When she tried to bring the knife down, he deflected it with a blow to her wrist which sent it clattering down to the floor again. "You're not going anywhere."

Kat dropped to the floor, exhausted. She just lay there, too tired to move, too crushed and too broken to fight.

"What do you want from me?" Kat asked.

The man looked down at her. He held something in his hand and it sparkled in the half-light. Kat shuddered as she saw it for what it was, another knife, a bigger one, sharper and shinier. The man smiled, and the light hit his teeth and made him stand out of the darkness like the Cheshire Cat.

"You don't want to know," he said.

***

Leipfold, Maile and Craig decided to split up.

"Divide and conquer," Leipfold said. "That's the way to do it. Just be careful, okay? We don't know what we might be getting into. Could be that Mr. Allman is innocent."

"Could be," Craig agreed.

"Yeah," Maile said. "Or maybe he's the creepiest creep in Creep Town. There's something not right about the guy."

"Let's find him and find out," Leipfold said.

Leipfold took one of the doors on the right-hand side of the alleyway and Craig took one on the left. Maile, meanwhile, took a different route in another direction entirely.

Craig's door led to the storage hall of a small supermarket, and he was let inside by one of the employees after claiming to be an off-duty cop who was in pursuit of a suspect. Leipfold, meanwhile, had resorted to jimmying his door with a tool on his penknife, reasoning that if nobody answered, it might be because they had something to hide. It was dark inside, so he summoned up a flashlight on his smartphone and used it to lead the way.

Maile, for her part, had found a manhole, and it wasn't lying flush with the surface. She'd spotted it poking out amongst a pile of rubbish. It caught her eye because it looked oddly untouched, a little out of place in its surroundings. She thought back to what she'd said to Leipfold. "If he didn't go over the wall…"

She lifted up the cover and climbed down the ladder, then looked around at her less-than-salubrious surroundings. She found herself below street level, standing ankle-deep in brackish water in the middle of the city's old Victorian sewer system. Maile had no idea how much of it was still in use, and she didn't care. She was more preoccupied with the stench that assaulted her nostrils and her newfound thankfulness for her big black boots.

If I'd been wearing flats, she thought, *my feet would be wet through with cholera juice.*

The walls were built with thick bricks, many of which had started to crumble and to fade away. In other places, mould and mildew had started to colonise and create new lifeforms, and a dangerous-looking set of electric cabling ran along the opposite wall, presumably bringing life to some sort of sewage machine. She pinched her nose and explored, first to the left and then to the right. She could hear the distant echo of a couple of voices, a man and a woman, but it was hard to tell which direction it was coming from. Maile was afraid to wander too far away from the ladder in case she couldn't find her way back out.

It wouldn't be much fun to die down here, she thought.

A dreadful scream echoed out. Maile spun on the spot and tried to head towards it. She poked her head through what appeared to be a small service hatch, lighting her way, like her boss was, with an app on her phone. In her other hand, she held her can of pepper spray.

There was a movement on the other side of the hatch, and Maile raised the nozzle and placed a finger on the trigger. A head came into view, a ginger one, and the colour of the hair was all that stopped her from firing.

"Boss?" she exclaimed. "How did you get down here?"

"I have my ways," he said. He gestured for her to climb through the hatch and to meet him on the other side. "I found myself in a warehouse. Some sort of aerospace factory by the looks of it, although it's long gone now. They gutted the place when they moved out, but get this. There were footsteps in the dust, and that's exactly what I'm following."

"Yeah," Maile grunted, shuffling through the hatch like some sort of sewer worm. "Great. Help me out here."

Leipfold took her hand and pulled her through, then offered her some support while she struggled upright again.

"This place wasn't built like this," he said. "It's been through some modifications. I wonder who did it."

"Yeah," Maile said. "And I wonder why."

* * *

The man was kneeling beside his partner and checking her wound in the half-light. Kat watched him warily, but she made no attempt to escape him. She just watched him as he applied some pressure to stop the bleeding. He'd taken off a coat or a jumper and was using it to try to staunch the flow of the woman's blood, but it wasn't looking good.

Kat glanced down at her knife and saw that the blade had been dulled by the blood she'd spilled and that the lamplight didn't bounce off the stainless steel. She looked back up, and the man was leaning in closer as Lucy Fforde wheezed and struggled to breath on the floor.

"Help me," Fforde whimpered.

"I'm trying," the man said. "Jesus Christ, she got you good."

"It hurts…"

"I know, baby, I know."

The man glared across at Kat as he absentmindedly stroked his fingers along the knife's handle.

"I've got to finish the job," he said. "Besides, you picked the last one. This one was always mine."

"Woah now," Kat said, backing away from the man and waving her palms in front of her as though she was trying to swat a fly instead of defending herself from a murderer. "You don't have to do that."

"Oh, I do," the man said. "I'm the Tower Hill Terror."

"That's what your lady friend down there said before I stabbed her," Kat replied, stalling desperately for time. "But how do I know you're telling the truth?"

"You'll have to take my word for it," he said, but Kat could tell that something she'd said had got to him.

He wants recognition, she thought. *Sickos like him always do. I might not know his name, but I know him all right.*

Out loud, she said, "Tell me something only the Tower Hill Terror could know."

The man paused, just a couple of feet from her. He was frowning at her, but the knife was still in his hand and she had no doubt that he'd use it if he needed to.

"Like what?" he asked.

Gotcha.

"How did you know the victims?"

"I didn't," the man said. "I found them all on dating apps. Lucy was the first. But instead of killing her, I started to admire her. To *like* her, even."

From somewhere on the floor behind him, Lucy Fforde was still struggling to breathe, pushing the makeshift dressing to her chest with as much force as she could muster. She tried to say something, but neither of them heard her.

"Lucy and I took it in turns to pick the victim," the man continued. "She had a thing for cheaters. She'd been hurt by them before. She liked to do her research. As for me…well, anything goes. I'm a connoisseur of pain. I don't know what I look for exactly. You just seemed like an interesting case."

"You *chose* me?"

The man nodded.

"Why?"

"Enough talk," he said. "It's time to end this."

He took a step towards her, and Kat could smell the stale sweat from beneath his armpits. He had the knife in his right hand, and he took a swing for her. Kat dropped at the last minute and the blade just nicked her, catching her hair and sending a lock of the stuff tumbling to the floor beside her. She was on her hands and feet, crawling backwards across the floor as the man loomed over her, a silhouette that cut out the light from the lantern.

He brought the knife around again, and this time it connected and scored a long, thin defensive wound on Kat's forearm. And then the man was standing right on top of her, reaching out a hand like a zombie in some old horror movie and then—

BANG.

Chapter Twenty-Six:
Friends Reunited

ALL HELL BROKE LOOSE beneath the streets of London, and the air hung thick with sulphur. Kat was exhausted, half-conscious and struggling to breathe, pinned down with a body slumped on top of her. She could feel something moist, something spreading slowly across her, but she couldn't tell whether it was her captor's blood, her own urine or a messed-up mixture of the two of them.

She looked up, as best as she could, straining her eyes to see her saviour through the darkness. He was a man, about five foot six or maybe five foot seven, with a chiselled face and ginger hair and eyes that looked steely grey until the light flickered across them. Kat recognised him immediately.

"Mr. Leipfold," she said. "James Leipfold, right?"

"My fame precedes me," he said. "And you're Kat Cotteril."

Leipfold grabbed the body that lay on top of her and hauled it a couple of feet across the floor. While he was checking the man's pulse, he was joined by another figure that Kat recognised.

"Maile," she said, her voice croaking with emotion. The full enormity of her situation had hit her during the long hours attached to the manacles, but it wasn't until she saw her housemate's face that she realised she was truly, finally free. It was too much for her, and Kat began to cry.

"Shh," Maile said in the same way that Kat shushed her when they were sitting in front of the TV and she wouldn't stop chatting. "I've got you. You're safe now."

Maile gave her housemate a quick once over to check for injuries and then wrapped her up in a hug once she was sure she was going to survive.

"What the hell's going on?" Kat asked.

"I don't know," Maile said.

"Okay. Then let me try another one. Who's that man?"

"I think I can help you with that," Leipfold said. He was standing over her captor, shining the light from his phone on the man's face. "Marc Allman, old buddy. Fancy seeing you here."

Leipfold slapped Allman in the face a couple of times, but nothing. "He's unconscious," Leipfold said. "But I think he'll live. I didn't shoot to kill."

"There was another one," Kat said. "A woman."

"Where?" Leipfold broke the shadows with the light from his phone and lit up another figure on the floor, the body of a woman in a pool of blood. "Good God."

Leipfold ran across to her and investigated the wound. Then he knelt to take her pulse and ended up switching to CPR. He hummed "Stayin' Alive" as he worked her, using the Bee Gees to keep time with the compressions.

"Maile," he said. "I need you to call Jack Cholmondeley."

"We're underground, boss," she replied. "I haven't got a signal."

"Then get yourself the hell above ground," he demanded. "And take Kat with you if she's ready to walk."

"I'm ready for anything," Kat replied. "Just get me out of here."

"Then let's do it," Maile said. Still holding tight to her housemate, she took her weight and helped to hoist her to her feet. "And what about you? What are you going to do?"

Leipfold stopped pumping at the woman's chest and tilted her head back. "I'm going to try to save a life," he said. He forced her jaws open and bent down to put his mouth to hers.

* * *

The paramedics arrived first, within a matter of minutes, and one of them stayed with Kat while Maile led two others back down beneath the streets, explaining what had happened while she struggled through the sewer and along the old Victorian walkway towards the hidden room that the killers had used. At first, the medics had said they'd wait until the cops arrived, but when Maile said she was going back in with or without them, they took a gamble and decided to follow her.

Cholmondeley and his rapid response team arrived shortly afterwards, and with the medic's permission, they followed Kat as she led them back down into the hellhole.

"Are you sure you're okay to do this?" Cholmondeley asked. "You've been through a lot."

"I'm fine," Kat insisted. "And the faster you boys get down there, the faster you can have them in handcuffs. It's them, you know. The Tower Hill Terror."

"*Them?*" Cholmondeley's brows arched so high they would have brushed against his hair, if he had any. "There's more than one of them?"

"There are two," Kat said. "At least, there are two that I know of."

"And they're the Tower Hill Terror?"

Kat shrugged. "It's what she told me," she said. "Come on. You should see for yourself."

The response team checked their weapons and led the way with Kat and Cholmondeley guiding them from behind. Kat was exhausted, sore, dehydrated and drastically undernourished, but she still held her own against Jack Cholmondeley, whose arthritis was playing up. It was only made worse by the moisture in the air.

"It's just through there," Kat said, and the assault team fanned out into an attack position.

"Watch out," Cholmondeley said. "There are friendlies in there. Hold your fire unless you're taking defensive action."

"Yes, sir." It was hard to tell which one of them spoke, because the group acted as a unit and, as they moved into formation with their padded outfits and their helmets, they looked more machine than man. Kat and Cholmondeley held back while the gunmen stormed the room, sweeping the darkness with their mounted flashlights. Lit up, the room looked small, almost insignificant. It was maybe 15"x20", a former pump room designed to clean the brackish sewers of Victorian London. It was empty now, but it still held an eerie atmosphere as though it had secrets that it wanted to tell.

The response team leader gave the all-clear and Cholmondeley led Kat back inside her former prison.

Cholmondeley wasn't surprised to see that Leipfold was there. He also wasn't surprised to see Marc Allman, although he wished things could have turned out differently.

Damn it, he thought. *We had the man in custody. We just didn't have enough to make it stick.* But if Allman survived, and it looked like he might, they'd have all the evidence they needed to put him away for a long, long time. Whether he turned out to be the Tower Hill Terror or not.

He was surprised to see the paramedics on the floor beside the body of a woman. "Another victim?" he asked.

"Hell no," Kat said. "She was in on it. They must have been working together."

"Is she dead?" Cholmondeley asked.

"I'm not sure."

"Not yet," one of the paramedics said, raising his head without looking up at them. "But it's not looking good. She's lost a lot of blood."

"Good," Kat said.

"What happened to her?"

"I stabbed her," Kat said. "But it was self-defence. I managed to get loose and there was a struggle. It was her or me."

"Well, I'm sure we'll be able to prove that," Cholmondeley said. "But I'll need you to make a quick statement to that effect at the station. Once you've been checked by the EMTs, of course."

"Can I go home first?"

"No," Cholmondeley said. "Sorry. I need you to make the statement while everything's still fresh in your mind. Do you have any idea who she is?"

"Yeah," Kat said. She shivered. "She's a woman called Lucy Fforde from The Oyster Club. Are we done here?"

"For now," Cholmondeley said, and so Maile and Kat made their way back to the surface to leave Leipfold and the policemen to it. He walked over to Leipfold and slapped him on the back.

"You too, I'm afraid, James," he said. "I'll need a statement."

"No problem."

"Any idea what happened to Allman?"

"Someone shot him," Leipfold said.

Cholmondeley looked shrewdly across at him. "Any idea who?" he asked.

"Search me," Leipfold replied.

Cholmondeley didn't fancy dealing with the paperwork.

* * *

A second ambulance arrived, and then a third. The EMTs took the woman out first, following Leipfold through the empty warehouse and out the door that he'd jimmied. Marc Allman came next, conscious again and screaming in pain from his gunshot wound. The paramedics said he'd live, though they'd need to operate to remove the bullet, and the police team sent two men to keep watch over him.

Cholmondeley, meanwhile, paged Sergeant Mogford and Constable Groves, who were both officially off-duty but who'd been told to be ready to report if the case developed. It had developed, all right. It had developed big time. He ordered them to meet him at the station, then asked Leipfold and Maile to get in the back of his big, black Beemer.

"What about Camilla?" Leipfold asked.

"You can come back and get her when we're done," Cholmondeley said. "If she gets a ticket, I'll pay for it."

"You'd better," Leipfold said. He leaned over and whispered something to Maile, who nodded at him. Cholmondeley was watching them in his rear-view mirror.

"You know," he said, "strictly speaking, you two shouldn't be talking. Not until we've processed you back at the station."

"I'm not a can of fucking peas," Maile said. Leipfold glanced across at her. Cholmondeley's face turned red, and then the two men burst out laughing at the same time.

"Fair point," Cholmondeley said. "And hey, thanks for your help. You too, James."

"Looks like you needed it," Leipfold said.

Cholmondeley winced. "Perhaps we did," he conceded. He twisted his key in the ignition. "I still don't know who the woman is," he said.

"Is Allman alive?" Leipfold asked.

"So far." Cholmondeley put his Beemer into gear and reversed out of his parking space, then pulled a speedy U-turn and steered the vehicle towards the station.

"Then you can ask him."

"Perhaps," Cholmondeley said. "But we can't ask his partner, the woman."

"Lucy Fforde," Maile supplied.

"Right," Cholmondeley said. "She didn't make it to the hospital. I've got Constable Cohen at the scene to keep me updated."

"So what's next?" Leipfold asked.

Cholmondeley drummed his hands on the steering wheel and thought for a moment. "Looks like we've got a mystery on our hands. I intend to solve it."

Leipfold shrugged and looked blankly out of the window. Maile looked up front and met Jack Cholmondeley's eyes in the rear-view mirror.

"Need any help?" she asked.

Chapter Twenty-Seven:
Visual Confirmation

IT WAS THE FOLLOWING DAY, and to Jack Cholmondeley it felt like half the force had assembled for the meeting. Superintendent Richards was leading it, and she stood at the front of the busy room with a Sharpie in her hand and an A3 pad on an easel in front of her. She was wearing a plain white blouse and a stylish pair of blue jeans, clothes designed for comfort and for action in equal measures. Her grey-white hair was unkempt and unruly, and the bags under her eyes were even saggier than usual, suggesting that she'd stayed up all night and skipped a shower.

Cholmondeley couldn't imagine what sort of stress the woman was under. It was bad enough for him, with the pressure trickling down from Richards and into his department. The woman was like a filter for responsibility, taking the strain from the public and the politicians and diluting it into something more palatable for the officers that served beneath her.

His team was there, too. Ambitious Constable Yates, loose-jawed Constable Cohen and dependable Constable Groves were beside him, and Sergeant Mogford was standing in front with Constable Hyneman. Meanwhile, Sergeant Joe Riggs from the forensic team had made his way to the centre of the room, with two of his officers beside him. They were joined by two of the armed cops and the head of the response team, as well as by an independent commissioner, a secretary to take notes on the proceedings, and three men that Cholmondeley didn't recognise but who looked from their bearing like they were important men indeed.

Leipfold was there too, although Richards had drawn the line at that and told Cholmondeley that Kat and Maile weren't welcome. Strictly speaking, Leipfold shouldn't have been there either, but there were a couple of loopholes that could be exploited to bring him in as a private consultant. Kat and Maile, though, were civilians. Their place was at home, not at the station. It was probably for the best. There was standing room only in the briefing room, and precious little even of that.

Richards kicked off the meeting by clearing her throat and taking a roll call, writing down the names and departments of all attendees on the pad in front of her. Then she cleared her throat again and called the meeting to order.

"Ladies and gentlemen," she said, "I'd like to thank you all for coming. I appreciate that this meeting was arranged on short notice and that many of you are technically off-duty."

A couple of the officers grumbled, including Gary Mogford, who'd had to bail on a round of golf and a couple of pints with the boys, but they were careful not to grumble too loudly. The result was a gentle susurrus of discontent, a sound that Superintendent Richards heard but couldn't act upon. She scowled around the room and shook her head.

"The purpose of this meeting," Richards said, "is to look back over Operation Aftershock and to identify any final areas of investigation. As you all know, we have one suspect in custody and another in the morgue, and we have reason to believe that the two of them worked together. That said, I'd like to be able to tell the public that they're at no further risk from the Tower Hill Terror, and I'd like it to be a guarantee. To do that, we need to understand more. Why did Marc Allman and Lucy Fforde act the way they did?"

It was a rhetorical question, but Richards's delivery had each and every copper in the room trying to rack their brains for an answer.

Then Leipfold raised a hand, struggling to be seen amongst the tall beat cops and the massive men from the armed response team.

"I'll take questions at the end," Richards snapped. Cholmondeley buried his face in his hands, well aware of the woman's thoughts on briefing etiquette. Leipfold, unfortunately, was unused to her way of working. She played it by the book, and Leipfold threw the book out a window and wrote his own.

"Please," Leipfold insisted. "Just give me a couple of minutes. I think I have some information that might be relevant."

Richards sighed and waved her hand. "Oh, very well," she said. "What is it, Mr. Leipfold?"

All eyes were on Leipfold, and he shifted uncomfortably at the front of the room as he took the Sharpie from the superintendent and flipped a page on the easel.

"This won't take long," Leipfold said. "Now, I'm not sure whether you've got official confirmation or not, but we can be pretty sure that the two perpetrators were Lucy Fforde and Marc Allman. My assistant, Maile O'Hara, will be able to confirm that. She was already familiar with Allman through our own investigations, and she met Lucy Fforde at her dating night at the Oyster Club. That's where Lucy met Marc Allman, too. Have you interviewed Kat Cotteril yet?"

"Of course."

"Then she'll have confirmed this too," Leipfold said. "Allman was behind the Tower Hill Terror, at least at first. Fforde was his first victim, but instead of killing her, he made her a partner. They had some sort of connection, some sort of energy that spurred them both on. They were a dozen times worse together than they ever could have been apart. They took it in turns to pick their victims, Fforde finding a cheater and Allman finding whoever the hell took his fancy. Either way, though, they found them through the dating apps. That's how they lulled people into a false sense of security so they could get them under control and strung up in that dungeon of theirs beneath the city. They were a match made in hell."

"But why?" Richards asked. She was glaring at Leipfold like a hawk eyeing up a rabbit as it ran across the fields. "Why did they do it?"

"I think they both had their reasons," Leipfold said. "For Fforde, it was revenge. A crusade against the unfaithful, a war against people who cheat on their partners through dating apps. For Allman, it was hatred, pure and simple. He's just your basic domestic terrorist. They wanted to go out with a bang, to shout one last big 'fuck you' to the world before their bones turned to dust. Nobody wants to be forgotten."

"We won't be forgetting The Tower Hill Terror in a hurry," Cholmondeley murmured. "But how did they choose specific victims? If someone was cheating on their partner, they'd be smart enough to cover their tracks."

Leipfold snorted. "You'd be surprised," he said. "But if it helps, I got Maile to run a little test for me. I gave her a couple of hours and she came back with a list of cheaters for me. You have to use a photo on those sites, and even with a fake name there are ways to figure it out. All you need to do is run a reverse image search and hey presto. You'll know whether they're legit or not."

Superintendent Richards looked pleased, but she didn't look impressed. Leipfold had more work to do if he wanted them to believe his theory, but he didn't really *care* whether they believed him. He just wanted to put the final piece of the jigsaw into place.

"Proving the case is your job, not mine," Leipfold said. "But now that Fforde's dead and Allman's in prison, the attacks should stop. That'll give you enough time to look into it. And besides, Allman wants to be remembered. I think you'll find he's willing to talk."

"We'll need to play this one carefully," Richards said. She looked around the room and settled her gaze on Jack Cholmondeley, just an old, tired cop who'd somehow become a minor celebrity thanks to his impromptu press conferences. "Is that it, Mr. Leipfold? Do you have anything else to add?"

"No, ma'am," he said.

"Good," she replied. "Then please sit down and shut up. This is my briefing, not yours. I'd like you to remain quiet for the rest of the meeting. If you think of something else then please hold it in until the end."

Leipfold nodded to show that he'd understood her, zipped his lips theatrically and pushed his way through the policemen and back to Jack Cholmondeley.

* * *

Superintendent Richards took control of the agenda again, which meant she also took over the oversized notepad. She flipped the pages containing Leipfold's notes and started out fresh, talking her team through the practicalities, what to charge Allman with, what to investigate next and what to say to the media.

"This hasn't been our moment of glory," Richards admitted. "There's going to be an enquiry. A lot of people want to know why we didn't catch this creep."

"But we did," one of the armed response cops protested.

Richards shook her head. "Not at all. Mr. Leipfold caught him, and then he called us in."

"Just happy to help," Leipfold quipped.

Richards fixed her steely eyes upon him. "One more word from you and you're out of here," she growled. "I mean it."

She smiled sarcastically and then turned her attention back to the rest of the room.

"Detective Inspector Cholmondeley," she said, "would you care to say a few words about your investigation into the Merin murder?"

"Of course," Cholmondeley said. He elbowed his way to the front of the room and stood beside the superintendent. Leipfold winked at him from the back of the room. Cholmondeley ignored it and fixed his gaze on an empty stretch of the wall.

"Now," Cholmondeley began. "As you all should know, we've also looked into the death of Carina Merin at the hands of her husband, Pete Merin. Mr. Merin confessed to being the Tower Hill Terror, but subsequent enquiries have ruled that out. We know that Mr. Merin killed his wife, but it looks like the other murders—those of Jayne Lipton, Abu Adewali, Calvin Myatt and Jennifer Jackson—are on the hands of Allman and Fforde."

"Yes, yes," Richards snapped. "What else can you tell me?"

"Only that I think we have a motive for Mr. Allman," Cholmondeley said. "But you'll have to bear with me here. First off, the man is a mystery. There are many sides to Marc Allman, and at least one of them seems to have lost the plot. Some of you may recall the letters we discovered inside the shipping container."

Cholmondeley looked around the room. A couple of cops nodded their heads, but most of them looked blankly back at him. The content of the letters had been dismissed and not widely shared, mostly for fear that they would somehow leak to the media and put people on edge. They were currently in the forensics lab, undergoing rigorous testing and analysis. Cholmondeley was one of the few policemen who thought that there might be something valuable contained within the rambling, half-incomprehensible letters.

"Let me give you an example," Cholmondeley said, flipping through a sheaf of papers to find the document he wanted. He fished it out and frowned down at it as he started to read. "Dear Lotty, I'm beginning to feel like Rudolf Hess. Hess left Hitler, stole a plane and flew to Scotland to try to broker peace and was written off by history as nothing more or less than a joke. I refuse to be a joke, Lotty. I love you and miss you and I'll be with you soon."

"Who's Lotty?"

"A sister," Cholmondeley said. "Charlotte Allman, now deceased."

"By his hand?"

Cholmondeley shook his head. "She was killed in a collision when she was five years old. Allman was eight at the time. My guess is that this is why he's lashing out at society in the first place."

Cholmondeley paused and looked around the room. Everyone's eyes were upon him, and he frowned again as he considered his next move.

"Those letters show us the type of man that we're dealing with," Cholmondeley said, speaking slowly but surely so he wouldn't stumble over syllables. "He's capable of sheer insanity on the one hand and sparkling charm on the other. Truth is, he's nothing but a rage-filled man who hates the world and is striking back at it however he can. He's the arrogant sort, the type of guy who doesn't think he'll ever get caught."

Superintendent Richards glared at him. "Doesn't matter what he thinks," she said. "We've got him."

* * *

There were plenty of unanswered questions, and the rest of the meeting was dedicated to the search for answers. Superintendent Richards wasn't happy with Leipfold and Cholmondeley's explanations, but it was all they had to go on. She arranged for two teams to be formed to work on alternate hypotheses, while Cholmondeley himself would be responsible for finding evidence to support the existing theory. Leipfold, meanwhile, was asked in no uncertain terms to stay away from the case.

"That's fine by me," he said. "The case is solved, over. And once *The Tribune* runs its articles, business is going to go through the roof."

The meeting broke up in the early afternoon with each of the teams briefed on what they needed to do. Richards said she'd deal with the press herself. She told Cholmondeley that she'd debrief him after holding a conference to announce that they had the Tower Hill Terror in custody. "I'll hold back on telling them about Lucy Fforde," she added. "At least for now."

Leipfold and Cholmondeley had a debriefing of their own, held over a clandestine pint of lemonade in the Rose & Crown. Cedric, the landlord, wasn't exactly an old friend, but he'd known both men for the best part of twenty years and had nothing against them going in there. They were bad for business, because they scared other punters away and didn't try to drink the bar dry, but he didn't have the heart to turn them away.

They perched themselves in one of the corner booths so they could keep their eyes on the rest of the premises. They sat in silence for a while, sipping on their drinks and eyeing up the patrons. Then Cholmondeley put his drink down and opened his mouth.

"I've got a proposition for you, James," he said.

Leipfold looked shrewdly across at him. "You have, huh?"

Cholmondeley took a deep breath and said, "I want you to reconsider joining us. You'd make a good cop if you learned to follow the rules."

"I'm allergic to rules," Leipfold said. "I make my own."

"I've noticed."

"Besides," he added, "I'm too old."

"So am I," Cholmondeley said. "That's why I need a little help. Police work has changed since I was a kid. We need new thinkers, new ideas.

Maybe we need someone to break a few rules so we can shake things up, so to speak."

Leipfold laughed. "We've had this conversation before, Jack," he said. "Several times, if I recall. The outcome is always the same."

"This time it's different," Cholmondeley said. "We got lucky. But you could have died when you followed Marc Allman, and then we would all have been in trouble."

Leipfold said nothing.

"Please, James," Cholmondeley said. "We could use your help."

"I'll think about it," Leipfold said. He drained his glass and set it back down on the table. He slid a handful of change across to cover the cost of his drink and then set off, on foot, to collect Camilla.

Chapter Twenty-Eight:
Terminal

MARC ALLMAN WAS ARRESTED and formally charged that evening, and Jack Cholmondeley and Gary Mogford paid him a visit in the cells the following morning to see what the man had to say for himself.

His clothes had been changed at the hospital, and with no next of kin, it looked like he'd be wearing his gown for a few more days until they transferred him to a more secure facility. He'd been shot in the shoulder, but the man had gone down like he'd been punched in the gut. Cholmondeley knew he'd have to find an answer for that, and he'd also have to summon up an explanation as to who fired the shots. Questions were already being asked.

Cholmondeley knew it had been Leipfold, of course, although Maile's presence alone was enough to provide reasonable doubt. In the heat of the moment, and with all of the attention on Allman and his accomplice, nobody had taken the time to swab their hands for gunshot residue. With no weapon found either at the scene or in their possession when they were checked into the station, Cholmondeley was left with a mystery that he didn't want to solve. But he knew that he'd have to give it a good go, in spite of his loyalties.

But right then, it could wait. Allman had been left to calm down during the first few days of his confinement, but they'd heard him calling from his cell, asking to talk to someone and to tell his side of the story. Mogford and Cholmondeley were more than happy to oblige.

Allman was cuffed and led through to an interrogation room. The cops left him to stew in there for half an hour or so, and then they rolled into the room to sit down opposite him. Cholmondeley introduced himself and added the date and time for the benefit of the recording. Then he leaned forward and said, "You wanted to speak to us, Mr. Allman."

"I did indeed," he said.

"Why?"

"Why not?" He leaned back in his chair, looking more like he was visiting a grandparent than like he was under arrest and in cuffs at a police station. "There's no one to talk to around here."

"Allman, make this good," Mogford growled. "I don't have time to waste on little shitstains like you."

"Fair enough," he said. He tried to spread his hands defensively, but the cuffs were tight and they stopped him. He looked down at them and smiled.

"What do you want?" Cholmondeley asked.

"I want to talk to the press."

"Not going to happen."

Allman sighed and leaned forward in his chair. "Listen," he said. "There are a few different ways we can play this. Either way, I'm going to be heard. If you let me talk to the press, I'll tell them everything. I'll also extend the same favour to you. If you don't let me talk to them… well, I can always have my day in court. If I plead not guilty, it'll be the trial of the decade. You can bet that anything I say will be repeated in the papers either way."

"I can't do that," Cholmondeley said.

"You *can't* do that?" Allman asked. "Or you *won't*."

* * *

It was later that day, and Jack Cholmondeley and Marc Allman had been joined in the interview room by Alan Phelps of *The Tribune*. Phelps and Cholmondeley started their recordings at exactly the same time. They both wanted to make sure that they had a record.

"Interview started at 2:17PM," Cholmondeley said for the benefit of the tape. "Present are the suspect, Marc Allman, myself, Detective

Inspector Jack Cholmondeley, and journalist Alan Phelps from *The Tribune*. Mr. Allman, you said you wanted to make a statement. Let's hear it."

"I want to make a confession," Allman said. "I did it. I killed those people, and I'd do it again."

"Did you do it alone?"

"No," Allman said. "I worked with a partner. Lucy. Lucy Fforde."

"Why did you do it?" This came from Phelps, and Cholmondeley didn't look too happy about it.

"Lucy wanted to kill because she was a woman scorned. I wanted to kill because I wanted to be remembered. We were a match made in heaven."

Allman's face was flushed and the veins in his arms were swollen and pushing at the surface of his skin. The wound in his shoulder had reopened slightly and blood was trickling down to his armpit. Cholmondeley and Phelps exchanged a nervous glance.

Cholmondeley found Marc Allman fascinating. He talked like a raconteur, but he also had a habit of going off on tangents or starting sentences with "the interesting thing about that is" before telling a story that could have bored paint.

At one point, about halfway through the interview when it was already too late either way, Cholmondeley held up a hand to interrupt him. "You do realise," he said, "that we're not going to offer you a deal. Don't get me wrong, we appreciate your cooperation, but I'm still duty-bound to let you know how the law stands."

Allman shrugged. "I'm not doing this for you," he said. "This is for the benefit of Mr. Phelps over there. I'm not telling you this because I'm hoping for leniency or for time off my sentence. And I'm not doing it for the good of my soul, either. I don't want deliverance. I have no remorse. All I want is to be remembered. That's all any of us ever wants. It's all we *have*. We'll all die one day."

"But why wait?" Cholmondeley asked. "Why start killing people now?"

"The first one is always the hardest," Allman replied. "For the last twenty-something years, I've been honing my craft, biding my time. I killed birds at first, then cats and foxes. A few dogs and badgers here and there. I worked my way up until I was ready to chase the biggest game of all. People, eurgh. They're all vermin. Except for Lucy, of course."

Cholmondeley exchanged another look with the journalist and made a mental note to ask for a psych evaluation, just in case.

"Lucy was quite the woman," Allman said. "I want you to make sure that you mention that in your article. She was supposed to be a victim, you know. She was supposed to be my first. But we started talking, and I decided to let her live, just for one more night, but then it turned into another and another and before I knew it, we were partners. I released her, convinced that she'd turn on me and I'd have to kill her after all, but instead we started hunting together."

"What about the breasts and the genitals?" Cholmondeley asked. "What's the deal with that?"

"Lucy hated sex," Allman explained. "She never said what, but *something* happened. Something bad that hurt her, *scarred* her, even. The world hurt her, just like it hurt me."

"But why take it out on other people? That hardly seems fair."

"Life isn't fair," Allman said. "If it was, the rich wouldn't be rich and the poor wouldn't be poor. We wouldn't be killing the planet for future generations or electing crooked politicians and dodgy businessmen to lead our countries into the brave new world. I kill people because I can. I want to. It's fun. You should try it sometime."

"I don't think so," Cholmondeley said. "Why did Lucy Fforde join you?"

"She didn't," Allman said. "Not at first. But she came around to my way of thinking, and she's full of hatred too. She's a liar and a thief, a murderess. But she has her own moral code, you know? Lucy wanted to only kill the unworthy, the people who cheat on other people as though they're nothing. So we teamed up and started trawling the dating sites."

"Kat Cotteril wasn't unfaithful."

Allman nodded. "She wasn't Lucy's choice. She was mine. We had different ideas about who to target and how we wanted them to die. She wanted them to suffer. I didn't care how we did it, as long as I could get up close and personal. I liked to see it happen. So we took it in turns."

"And why are you talking to me?" Phelps asked.

"Don't you see?" Allman asked. "I want to be heard. I want to be remembered. I want my name to be passed from mouth to mouth. I want to go down in history."

He turned slightly to look at Cholmondeley. "You can lock me up and throw away the key," he said. "Do what you want. It'll all work out the same in the end. Death is death, whether I die free or in jail. The only way to stay alive forever is to make sure that you're remembered."

"You speak like a dying man," Cholmondeley said.

"I'm not dying, Detective Inspector," Allman replied. "But I will die one day. And so will you. I wonder which of us will be remembered."

* * *

The interview was over and Superintendent Jack Cholmondeley was treating himself to a bland cup of coffee from the machine. He was sitting opposite Alan Phelps in a private room with a Do Not Disturb sign on the door.

"You say we'll be even?" he said.

"Of course," Phelps replied. "Although I'll have to pull a few strings at the office."

"What will you tell them?"

"I'll tell them the file got corrupted." ·

"And that'll work?"

Phelps shrugged. "It's worked before," he said. "Trust me, it won't be a problem."

"What makes you think that?" Cholmondeley asked.

Phelps shrugged again. "You scratch my back and I scratch yours," he said. "Besides, I'm BIB."

"BIB?"

"You've never heard of the Boys in Blue?"

"Obviously not."

Phelps chuckled and got up to leave.

"You might want to look into that," Phelps said. "Maybe even apply for membership."

"But what *is* it?"

"I can't tell you that," Phelps said. He grinned at Cholmondeley, and the detective inspector had a sinking feeling in the pit of his stomach. He knew that when a journalist grinned at a policeman it was never good news. It was like a shark grinning at a surfer.

"Give me something to go on," Cholmondeley said. "Please."

"Just speak to some of your officers," Phelps replied. "The privately educated ones. The ones in charge."

"What have the officers got to do with it?"

Phelps smirked and tipped Cholmondeley a wink that made his blood boil. "Who do you think leaked the tape?" he said. "Goodbye, Detective Inspector. And good luck with your investigations."

* * *

Meanwhile, at Leipfold's office, the detective and his assistant were attacking *The Tribune*'s daily crossword while munching their way through a packet of ginger biscuits. They were making good time, but they disagreed on the correct spelling of 14 down and Maile wasn't convinced it was even the right answer.

Leipfold pulled rank, reminding her that he was the one who paid the bills, and they went with his answer. A couple of minutes later, when they solved 11 across, Maile was vindicated, and they crossed out Leipfold's answer and wrote her solution in its place. They finished in just over seven minutes.

Leipfold flipped the kettle on, and Maile wandered over to perch on the counter beside him. She grinned at him until he looked up at her and offered to make her a coffee. Then she took him up on it and used the subsequent silence to ask him a question that was bothering her.

"So where did you get the gun from, boss?"

"Why do you want to know?"

Maile shrugged. "Just curious," she said. "I've never known a man who owns a gun before."

"*Owned*," Leipfold said. "Past tense. That was the only one I had. And this was the first time I ever had to use it."

"But how did you get it?"

"I have my ways," Leipfold said. "I'm ex-army."

"Is it legal?"

"Hell no," Leipfold said. "Which is why I want you to forget that I ever had it. Did you get rid of it?"

"Yeah," Maile said.

"How?"

"I have my ways." She smirked at him and gratefully accepted the cup of coffee that he'd made. She blew on it and took a small sip. "I'm not going to tell you what I did with it."

"In case I go back for it?" Leipfold asked.

Maile shook her head. "Not at all," she said. "You're not that stupid. But it's better if you never know."

"You didn't take it, did you?" Leipfold asked. He wore the kind of expression that a father might wear on his daughter's prom night.

"Of course not!" she protested. "What would I need a gun for?"

"You carry pepper spray in your purse," Leipfold reminded her.

"That's different," Maile said. "I carry that around for the creeps and the weirdos. I'm not about to shoot someone in the head because they tried to grab my arse as I walked past."

"But pepper spray is fine?"

"Precisely," Maile said. "Don't worry about it. The gun is gone and the cops won't find it. And even if they do, I wiped it clean. There's nothing to link it back to you."

"I just wish you'd tell me what you did with it."

But Maile shook her head. "Can't," she said. "If I tell you, you might let it slip to Jack Cholmondeley."

Leipfold chuckled and gestured for her to get back to work. Then he sat down at his desk.

She's probably got a point, he thought.

* * *

Later that night, Leipfold let his ginger hair down and celebrated like only a reformed alcoholic knows how to. He bought a six-pack of non-alcoholic beers and shot-gunned them all in an hour, then watched repeats of *Countdown* with the volume on low while flicking through the pages of an old paperback.

He had a lot of questions about the case, but he was going to have to wait a while if he wanted answers. With the suspects stopped in their tracks, Kat Cotteril safely back above ground, and no new reports of missing people, he felt that his work was done. It was in the hands of the police force.

And he had work to do.

Chapter Twenty-Nine:
A Different Temptation

MAILE HAD PLANS for the evening.

She was alone in the flat again. Kat's boss had given her a couple of weeks of compassionate leave, an offer that she'd almost rejected. On the outside, she seemed unaffected by her ordeal, but Maile knew her better than that. She always wanted to play the strong woman, the busy executive type that you can always rely on, but sometimes that worked against her.

"That's not what this is about," Maile had told her. "Kat, you don't need to be strong all the time. You've been through a lot. Take the offer and get away for a while."

"I can handle it," Kat replied.

"It doesn't matter," Maile said. "You've got nothing to prove. You survived a situation I wouldn't wish on anyone and now you've earned yourself a break from it all. Besides, the media is going to be all over this. We'll have Siobhan Dent and Alan Phelps from *The Tribune* trying to knock our door down so they can talk to you. You don't need that shit. Trust me, Kat. I know what it's like."

"You do?"

"Yeah," Maile said. "Remember Tom Townsend? You're not the only one who's been held somewhere against your will. I'm not saying it's going to go away, but it gets better. Slowly but surely, day by day, it gets a little better. Here. I have something for you."

Maile held out a hand and Kat took the object she was holding. She held it up to her eyes and took a closer look at it.

"Your pepper spray," Kat said.

"Yeah," Maile replied. "You never know when you might need it."

"What about you?"

Maile shrugged. "I'll get another," she said.

Something about Kat's posture had changed, and Maile knew that her point had hit home. She pressed her further.

"Look, take a laptop and work from home if you have to," Maile said. "Just find yourself somewhere that no one can find you and take it easy until the shitstorm blows over. Then you can get back to work and move on with your life."

Kat nodded and relented, and the two of them spent the next couple of hours making plans. Maile had insisted on not being told where she was going so that the information could never be somehow tricked out of her. Shortly after that, Kat had hopped on the train and headed off to parts unknown and Maile had been left alone in their living room.

Maile had always liked being alone, but something had started to change over the last few weeks as the Tower Hill Terror had taken over the streets. The Terror was no more, but that didn't mean that she could sleep easily. The city had a deep, dark underbelly that she didn't like to think about. But not thinking about something was almost impossible, especially without a housemate around to shoot the shit with.

She checked her bag and pulled out her pepper spray, smiling grimly as she hefted its familiar weight. Then she thought about Leipfold's gun, and she wondered whether she'd done the right thing by disposing of it. Sure, it was an illegal firearm, but Kat's pot stash was illegal and so was Maile's habit of pirating American TV shows so she didn't need to wait for them to air in the UK. And if Allman and Fforde could get away with multiple murders before being apprehended, she was pretty sure she could get away with keeping a gun that she'd never use.

But never is a powerful word, and Maile was forced to admit that if she had a gun in her house, she'd be tempted to use it. Maybe not maliciously, but in an act of random violence after an argument or in self-defence when some asshole tried to chat her up in a bar. God knows, she was trigger-happy enough with her pepper spray.

The gun, and its hiding place in the sewers beneath the city, was still on Maile's mind as she hopped into the back of a cab and told the driver where to go. She scanned his face as she opened the door, satisfied that this was a new man, a man she'd never seen before, and not some sicko serial killer. But he looked fine, almost friendly. Just the average cabbie in a city that blended ethnicities in a metropolitan mixing bowl. He had a warm, inviting voice with a curious accent, which he told her was a conglomeration from three different continents. He didn't try to attack her, which was probably a good thing. Maile still carried a canister, even if she wasn't packing heat.

The cabbie dropped her off at the Grosvenor House Hotel, a place that she still saw in her dreams from time to time. It had featured prominently in her last two major investigations, and every time she thought she'd forgotten about it, it would resurface in her head like a cheap piece of imagery in an indie novel.

But the horror had happened in one of the hotel's guest rooms, and not in the adjoining restaurant. Way back when she'd first started working with Leipfold, she'd followed the footsteps of a man called Tom Townsend, who'd listed a meal at the restaurant as his alibi. Maile had visited it on more than one occasion since then, but she'd never had a chance to eat.

But this night was different. She was there to meet a man about a date. A man she'd met on a social networking site.

It's okay, though, Maile thought, as she was shown to the table at which he was already waiting. *Nolite te bastardes carborundorum. If we change the way we behave, the bad guys win. And besides. He's picking up the bill.*

* * *

Leipfold had tried to write a letter to Jack Cholmondeley three separate times, and each one had ended up crunched into a ball and tossed half-heartedly at the wastebasket. And then he remembered something. An old, handwritten letter in a dusty box file, in storage somewhere but still good. He dug it out, placed a strip of blank paper over the date and the address (which both needed updating), and then ran it through the copier at the corner shop.

It's funny how life is like a circle, Leipfold thought.

Cholmondeley had been encouraging him to become a cop ever since they first met, joining forces momentarily to track down a group of crooks who were stealing wallets from the general public. Leipfold had helped him to track down the culprits—despite being a schoolkid at the time—and Cholmondeley had been in his debt to some extent ever since.

Police work had its advantages. Reasonably regular hours, a guaranteed workload, a regular pay cheque and a sense of structure that was conspicuously missing in his life. But they were outweighed by the disadvantages, most notably the need to work for a boss and to take on investigations that just didn't catch his interest.

If the police are pigs, Leipfold thought, *then perhaps I'm a wolf. Wolves don't take orders. And they work better alone.*

Cholmondeley met him at the food truck by the station, and the two sat and talked for a time about the good old days. The old cop was unusually circumspective, and with his tired eyes cast back over the years, the conversation turned to his early triumphs in the late seventies and early eighties. Leipfold had watched his career with interest, especially after his accident and the subsequent stint in Reading Jail. Cholmondeley had written to him once a week, delivering news from the outside world, new faces on the street, new crimes he needed help with. He'd sent clippings of *The Tribune*'s crossword, which Leipfold had eagerly filled out, usually blitzing through a week's worth of puzzles in an hour or so. And he'd given Leipfold a reason to live, a reason to stay clean.

And just like that, the conversation turned to Cholmondeley's offer.

"Thing is," Leipfold explained, "this time I don't need saving, Jack. I'm doing well, and so is the business. Okay, I might not have much of a pension, but there's plenty of time for that. And Maile's doing a good job, too. I think things might be taking off."

"I'm happy for you, James," Cholmondeley said. "Does this mean what I think it means?"

"Afraid so," Leipfold said. "I can't be a cop, Jack. I mean, look at me. Name a cop that looks like me."

"Taggart?"

"Cheeky swine." Leipfold reached for his drink, a vanilla milkshake, and the two men chuckled.

"Here," Leipfold said. "I almost forgot."

He reached into his bag and grabbed the letter he'd copied, then slid it across the narrow table to Jack Cholmondeley. While the old cop read it, Leipfold stared out of the window at the city, watching life go by from inside the converted school bus.

"The letter just confirms what I told you, Jack," Leipfold said. "I'm sorry."

"That doesn't surprise me," he replied, shaking his head. "But you can't blame a man for trying. Give me a call if you change your mind."

* * *

At home that night, Leipfold gave in to a different temptation entirely. He'd stopped to grab a bite to eat at a chicken shack on the way home, then parked Camilla and headed up to his tiny apartment. It was as he'd left it, cluttered, untidy and far too small for a fully grown man to comfortably live in. Exactly how he liked it.

When he got in, he left the overhead light off and flicked the switch on his bedside lamp, then kicked his shoes off and lay back to relax on the unmade bed. He tried to read his book for a while, but he couldn't focus on the small print and his mind was racing with a thousand and one new possibilities, for himself, for his business and for the future. He put the book back down again, using a scrap of paper from his notebook as a bookmark. Then he pulled out his smartphone and used his fingerprint to unlock it.

Leipfold browsed to the app store and looked through it, then hit the download button and waited for the file to install itself. He wasn't at home much, so he didn't have his own Wi-Fi, but he got a decent signal and he had plenty of data left because he hardly ever used it. The app downloaded quickly and it only took a minute or two to sign himself up to it. Under occupation, he entered "sleuth."

The app prompted him to upload a photo, and the only one he had was an old headshot from several years ago, when his hair was a little thicker and his face fuller. These days, he was looking positively gaunt, mainly because he didn't eat much and because without the booze, the weight had dropped off of its own accord.

With the sign-up complete, Leipfold sighed and followed the instructions. It told him to swipe right if he was interested and left if he wasn't. He checked out the first picture and read the brief bio that she'd provided. *Louise, 33, likes gin, gym and running.* Leipfold swiped left and moved on to the next one.

He swiped for a couple more minutes, overwhelmingly favouring the left. The experience unnerved him and made him feel self-conscious. He was uncomfortably aware of the artificial awkwardness and the way he was being forced to judge on looks alone. He looked back over his relationships—the last of which had run its course almost half a decade earlier—and looked for a common denominator. It was as he'd thought. He'd been attracted not by their looks but by their intelligence. He wanted a woman who kept him on his toes, a woman who challenged him and inspired him to follow his dream to the nth degree. He wanted a woman who was strong in her own right, who'd have her own career to deal with while he worked late shifts in the office or followed beautiful young women along the street so he could report back to their boyfriends about their fidelity or lack thereof. He didn't want *these* women, these *depressing* women, and he was pretty sure that they wouldn't want him either.

Leipfold sighed and thought about his non-existent love-life. *Who am I kidding?* he thought. *I'm too old, too set in my ways. No one would ever put up with me.*

But that didn't stop him from scrolling through the photos. He saw Maile, and a little later he saw Kat. He saw a couple of other faces that he recognised but couldn't put names to, as well as a couple of women he'd gone to school with thirty years earlier. He left-swiped the lot of them.

He swiped left a dozen more times, then swiped right, right, and left in quick succession. Then he stopped, moving his fingers away from the screen with a sharp intake of breath. He was looking at the face of another woman that he recognised.

He was looking at the face of Mary Cholmondeley.

Chapter Thirty:
Gardening Leave

IT WAS FRIDAY MORNING, and all across the city people were sleepy-eyed and tired and looking forward to getting the day out of the way so they could go out and get lashed at trendy cocktail bars. Leipfold got up early and went for a jog before heading back home to grab a shower and a change of clothes. Then he hopped on Camilla and headed out for the day.

At first, he followed the route towards the office, but it wasn't his final destination. No, he had a meeting at the station with Jack Cholmondeley, who said he had something important he needed to tell him.

I've got something I need to tell him, too, Leipfold thought. But he wasn't looking forward to it.

The roads were clear and the conditions were good, and the ride to the station was a rare pleasure, the kind of ride that he just had to enjoy. It reminded him why he'd fallen in love with Camilla in the first place. He reflected that perhaps Camilla was the only woman he'd ever love.

If that's the case, so be it. At least I can rely on her.

Leipfold parked up at the station and padlocked the bike to one of the bike stands, a couple of spots up from a sparkling Harley which must have belonged to one of Cholmondeley's officers. Then he walked inside the station and made his way up to Constable Cohen, who was working the desk. The man looked exhausted and Leipfold felt a momentary twinge of sympathy. Then he decided that it was more likely that he'd been out clubbing than that he'd worn himself thin on too much overtime.

"Oh, it's you," Cohen said. He flashed Leipfold a worn smile and gestured towards the waiting area. "The boss told me to page him when you arrived. Go ahead and make yourself comfortable. He'll come down to get you."

Leipfold nodded and took a seat, then grabbed a paperback from his jacket pocket and sat down to read and wait. Time seemed to slow down, and he was pretty sure he'd heard the same song twice through the tinny speakers that the top brass had installed in an effort to refresh the force's image in the eyes of the general public. If anything, it had the opposite effect. They had it tuned to Magic FM and it was inflicting a subtle form of torture on the unsuspecting ears of their visitors. Leipfold felt another twinge of sympathy for Constable Cohen when he realised that the man had to put up with it every day when he worked on reception.

After an hour or so, Leipfold got up and asked Cohen for directions to the coffee machine. Half an hour after that, he finished his book and slid it back into his pocket. He walked up to Cohen, waited for a young woman with a baby strapped to her stomach to finish asking about a parking fine, then told the man to go and find out what had happened to Jack Cholmondeley.

Cohen nodded mutely and disappeared, leaving the reception desk in the care of another man that Leipfold had never met before. He tried to engage him in light conversation, but then the telephone rang and the man excused himself to answer it. Feeling awkward and conspicuous, Leipfold settled back down on his plastic chair to wait.

The constable returned a couple of minutes later, red-faced and sweaty and with his face torn up with worry. "I'm sorry, Mr. Leipfold," he said. "I'm going to have to ask you to leave."

"Why?" Leipfold asked. "What have I done?"

"It's out of my hands," Cohen said. "Orders from above. If you've got a problem, you'll have to talk to Superintendent Richards."

"What about Cholmondeley? Where is he?"

Cohen's cheeks flushed and he looked down at the floor. "He's at home," he said. "On gardening leave."

* * *

It was raining by the time that Leipfold left the station, but he took good care of Camilla and her tyres were the best in the game. Even though the roads were damp and he broke the speed limit a couple of times without noticing, she handled the weather well and he pulled up outside the Cholmondeley house without a problem. He parked up and went to knock at the imposing Georgian-style doors.

The door was answered by Mary Cholmondeley, who looked somehow regal and resplendent despite the fact that she was wearing a dressing gown. She'd had her hair styled and her nails still bore the paint from a recent mani-pedi. She was wearing a touch of lipstick, and her face had been plastered with enough makeup to hide the crow's eyes that had plagued her since her early forties.

"Oh," she said, as though she'd opened the door to a sack of shit. Her nose wrinkled without her realising, her face contorting into the disdainful expression that only the upper class is able to replicate. "It's you."

"It's me," Leipfold replied. "I was hoping to see your husband."

"I see," Mary said. She paused for a moment. "Wait here. Let me see if I can find him."

Mary Cholmondeley closed the door in Leipfold's face and left him waiting on the pavement while she bustled around inside the house in search of her husband. Leipfold waited patiently, examining the collection of pink flamingos in the garden with an ironic sort of interest, slowly soaking through as the rain continued to hammer down. Cholmondeley came to the door a couple of minutes later and invited him inside, glaring at his wife and barking at her to make the two of them a cup of tea.

"James!" Cholmondeley exclaimed. "Good to see you. How can I help?"

"What happened, Jack?" Leipfold asked. "I went to the station and you weren't there. What's up with that?"

Cholmondeley sighed and led Leipfold through to the living room. He offered him a seat on the low leather sofa, which Leipfold took. Cholmondeley sat across from him on the matching armchair.

"It's a long story," he said.

"I've got time."

Mary walked in and laid a tray on the coffee table before straightening up and walking back out without so much as a glance or a word. Cholmondeley poured them both a cup of tea and went to sit back down again.

"I'm being pensioned off the force, James," Cholmondeley said. "Richards says I'm too old, too slow."

"She has a point," Leipfold murmured.

"What?"

"Nothing," he said. "Continue."

"It's because of the Tower Hill Terror," Cholmondeley explained, staring gloomily into his cup. "We took too long to catch him. I'll be damned if I know why I'm to blame when she had four different teams on the case, but she needs a lamb to sacrifice and I'm the closest one to retirement. So she put me on gardening leave and asked me to tender my resignation on Monday morning."

"I hate that woman," Leipfold said.

"It's not her fault," Cholmondeley replied. "It's politics. She's a smart woman and she's good at her job. It's the right decision for everyone."

Leipfold shook his head in response, more vigorously than the old man had. "Bullshit," he said. "You *are* the police force. How are they going to function without you?"

"They'll manage," Cholmondeley said. "Truth is, the game's changed. Maybe I'm not the best man for the job anymore."

Cholmondeley's demeanour changed. He grinned, suddenly, and looked Leipfold dead in the eye. "I'm on gardening leave," he said. "So I guess I'm going to finally do the bloody garden. But what about you, old friend? How are you going to solve those cases of yours without a man on the inside?"

Leipfold grinned. "Easy, Jack," he said. "I'll stick to my clients and stop helping your boys to catch killers."

Cholmondeley chuckled and murmured something under his breath. To Leipfold, it sounded like, "I'll believe it when I see it."

Acknowledgements

Like all of my books, *The Tower Hill Terror* couldn't exist in its current form without my publishing team. Kudos as always to Pam Elise Harris (my editor and partner-in-crime) and Larch Gallagher (my kick-ass cover designer).

Thanks as always are due to my friends and family, and to Donna Woodings, Carl Woodings, Heather and Dave Clarke and Alan and Olga Woodings in particular for their constant support.

Shoutouts are also in order for my BookTube friends. You know who you are. Special thanks to Todd the Librarian, Mindy's Book Journey, The Mae Cave, Time for Books, KitKatsCanRead, Binge Reader, Charles Heathcote, Anthony Andrews and The Book Lady for their kind words about my books. I hope they enjoy this one, too!

Finally, thanks to all of my readers, from the regular ones who read every book to the newbies who are reading my work for the first time. While I write for myself, to keep myself sane and to scratch my metaphorical itch, it's the readers and their feedback that make it all worthwhile. You guys rock.

About the Author

Dane Cobain is a published author, freelance writer, book blogger, poet and (occasional) musician with a passion for language and learning. When he's not working on his next release, he can be found reading and reviewing books for his award-winning book blog, SocialBookshelves.com.

Join the Conversation

THANKS FOR JOINING JAMES, Jack, Maile and me for the second installment of the Leipfold series. Whether you loved the book or you hated it, I want to know what you think. Join the conversation by tweeting @DaneCobain or visiting me on Facebook, and be sure to keep your eyes peeled for more books in the series.

Reviews are important, and they really do help authors to sell more books. Other than buying another copy and giving it to your friend (which you should do if you've got some money to burn), there's nothing more helpful than posting a review.

And be sure to join me on your social networking site of choice to keep up-to-date with the rest of my adventures. I'll see you in another book soon.

http://www.danecobain.com
http://www.twitter.com/danecobain
http://www.facebook.com/danecobainmusic
http://www.instagram.com/danecobain
http://www.youtube.com/danecobain

MORE GREAT READS FROM DANE COBAIN

No Rest for the Wicked (Supernatural Thriller) When the Angels attack, there's *No Rest for the Wicked*. Cobain's debut novella follows the story of the elderly Father Montgomery as he tries to save the world—or at least, his parishioners—from mysterious, spectral assailants.

Former.ly: The Rise and Fall of a Social Network (Literary Fiction) When Dan Roberts starts his new job at Former.ly, he has no idea what he's getting into. The site deals in death. Its users share their innermost thoughts, which are stored privately until they die. Then, their posts are shared with the world, often with unexpected consequences.

Come On Up to the House (Horror) This horror novella and accompanying screenplay tells the story of Darran Jersey, a troubled teenager who moves into a house that's inhabited by the malevolent spirit of his predecessor.

Driven (Detective) A car strikes in the middle of the night and a young actress lies dead in the road. The police force thinks it's an accident, but Maile and Leipfold aren't so sure. Putting their differences aside and brought together by a shared love of crosswords and busting bad guys, Maile and Leipfold investigate. But not all is as it seems, as they soon find out to their peril...